Praise for *On a City Street*

"Wahler provides a heart-warming roller coaster of emotions and sparks...and who doesn't love puppies?"
—Jeanne Felfe, author of *Bridge to Us*

"I found it really hard to put the book down and loved the twist ending." —Trudi LoPreto for *Readers' Favorite*

"A delightful read for fans of contemporary romance with a touch of real-life angst."
—Louanne Piccolo for *Readers' Favorite*

Praise for *I am Mrs. Jesse James*

"*I am Mrs. Jesse James* tackles the Jesse James story from a new and heartbreaking perspective." —*Missouri Life*

"This is a fantastically researched historical piece that many readers will enjoy, even if the historical genre is not their first choice." —*InD'tale Magazine*

"A vivid, moving tale of the woman behind the man of myth and legend. This is a book not to be missed!"
—Nicole Evelina, author of Chanticleer Book of the Year, *Daughter of Destiny*

Praise for *Let Your Heart Be Light: A Celebration of Christmas*

"The stories are short and engaging...A fun and enjoyable read, especially around Christmas time."

—Gisela Dixon for Readers' Favorite

"*Let Your Heart Be Light* is rich and sweet and will warm your heart."

—Donna Duly Volkenannt, winner of the 2012 Erma Bombeck Global Humor Award

On a City Street

A Becker Family Novel

Pat Wahler

Evergreen Tree Press

Cottleville, MO

This is a work of fiction. Names, characters, places, and incidents either are the product of the author's imagination or are used fictitiously, and any resemblance to actual persons, living or dead, business establishments, events, or locales is entirely coincidental.

Book Layout © 2017 BookDesignTemplates.com
Book Formatting by Jeanne Felfe
Editing by Joy Editing
Cover design by Jenny Quinlan, Historical Editorial

Publisher's Cataloging-in-Publication Data
provided by Five Rainbows Cataloging Services

Names: Wahler, Pat, author.
Title: On a city street : a Becker family novel / Pat Wahler.
Description: Saint Peters, MO : Evergreen Tree Press, 2019. | Series: A Becker family novel.
Identifiers: LCCN 2019939046 | ISBN 978-1-7323876-2-1 (paperback) | ISBN 978-1-7323876-3-8 (ebook)
Subjects: LCSH: Veterinarians--Fiction. | Women--Fiction. | Man-woman relationships--Fiction. | Saint Louis (Mo.)--Fiction. | Life change events--Fiction. | BISAC: FICTION / Romance / Clean & Wholesome. | FICTION / Romance / Contemporary. | FICTION / Romance / Romantic Comedy. | FICTION / Women. | GSAFD: Love stories.
Classification: LCC PS3623.A35646 O53 2019 (print) | LCC PS3623.A35646 (ebook) | DDC 813/.6--dc23.

First edition: May 2019
Printed in the United States of America

To my kids, grandkids, and pets galore—you fill my heart with love, my life with fun, and my head with stories.

Chapter One

As Carolyn lifted a stack of folded clothes from her suitcase, a photo slipped away from them, drifting like a faded autumn leaf to the floor. She bent to retrieve it and couldn't help staring at the image of a young couple sitting atop a weathered wooden bench framed by pine branches. A shock of chestnut hair had flopped over the man's forehead, and the slim blonde woman beside him reached toward it, a joyful laugh lighting her face. Both wore the dreamy expressions of people who teetered on the edge of a feeling so new, they hadn't recognized it yet themselves. Anyone who didn't know better would swear the couple was destined for a happily-ever-after. Her mother's favorite expression bounced into Carolyn's mind:

Appearances can be deceiving.

She shoved the snapshot and—she hoped—the past into a dresser drawer and covered it with a stack of rumpled T-shirts. A touch of regret kept her staring down at the shirts until a man's cigarette-roughened voice called out,

"Dr. Becker, where do you want this last load of boxes to go?"

"In the kitchen, please," she replied.

Thank goodness Bob Last-Name-Unknown-Moving-Man had interrupted the maudlin turn of her thoughts. She slammed the drawer shut and turned away to concentrate on her next target—an overstuffed garment bag. It took three yanks on the zipper pull before the bag burst open and clothes fell out to scatter across the floor. Among them were two pairs of unfamiliar dress slacks with a price tag still dangling from each waistband. No wonder her mother had offered to help pack the bags. First a sneaky photographic reminder she didn't need, and now this—gifts to soften the blow.

She gritted her teeth and loaded her arms with clothes which had to fit in a closet near the size of an old-fashioned phone booth. Even half as many things as she'd brought would be tight, but she pushed and shoved and wrestled in miffed determination. Sweat dampened her hairline before she finally muscled all the items in, despite a smacked funny bone and a nail broken deep enough to make her yelp with pain. She sucked on the injured finger and stepped back to view her handiwork. Calm shades of black, beige, cream, and khaki put her in a slightly more Zen frame of mind.

Despite its dollhouse dimensions, her recently rehabbed apartment enchanted her. Pale gray walls the same color as her mother's beloved French porcelain china, brought the promising scent of fresh paint and new beginnings. A grin lifted the corners of her mouth when she visualized how easily the entire place would fit into her former bedroom suite at her parents' home—with room to spare. Not an issue for her. How much space did one person need anyway?

"Dr. Becker, here's another one you didn't mark." Bob's look let her know he wasn't forgiving of sloppy packing jobs.

She studied the carton he balanced on his shoulder. "I think it goes to the bathroom."

Bob nodded and plunked his burden near the bathroom door with a grunt. He swiped a sleeve across his forehead. "This is a nice place you got here, tucked in neat like it is."

The comment confirmed her newfound affection for tiny-space living. "Thanks. It's close to everything I need, and the realtor said there's a park right around the corner. When the weather's good, it'll be a great place for a walk."

She'd jumped online to fill out an application as soon as she saw the pictures her realtor sent. The open-concept kitchen and living room area along with one medium-sized bedroom and bath were adorable. Oak hardwood planks lined the floor, gleaming like they'd just been varnished. The hefty security deposit she transferred along with a signed lease agreement guaranteed her ducks were in a row before she had said anything to her parents. Ah, the magic of doing business in cyberspace. It provided a swift and seamless transition for anyone in a hurry to get out of town.

Carolyn scrubbed her hands down her jeans and followed Bob to the kitchen where his helper, a young man with deep acne scars marring both his cheeks, had just thumped a large box on the floor. Under bright pendant lights, his catawampus reflection gleamed from the stainless-steel refrigerator like it would from a carnival fun mirror.

"How's it going?" she asked him.

Bob's assistant only mumbled something she couldn't understand and stepped out the door. Okay, so he wasn't the sociable type.

Carolyn tucked wisps of blonde hair straying from her ponytail behind her ears and took a moment to glance out the spacious living room window, in her opinion one of the apartment's best features. Far in the distance stood the landmark Gateway Arch presiding over a staggered assortment of tall buildings. A flood of nostalgic affection washed over her. She hadn't spent any significant time in St. Louis for many years but had grown up hearing stories from her dad about his beloved hometown.

He'd even taken Carolyn and her younger sister, Kathryn, to a Cardinals baseball game at Busch Stadium when the girls were teenagers, buying them all the hot dogs and popcorn they could eat. He'd touted St. Louis as a true baseball lover's city—much more so, he claimed, than Kansas City, where devotion remained more predictable than weather, based solely on the Royals' position in the standings.

"Girls," he pontificated in true courtroom style, "St. Louis is the kind of place that's built on great things. Especially baseball. You know, I once got to see Stan the Man play."

Though he told the story many times, she'd often wondered whether it was true. Stan Musial hadn't played baseball in many years, and her father wasn't all that old.

But everyone knew Tom Becker never minded exaggeration when it improved a story.

It still astonished her he'd decided to move his family away from St. Louis, but ambition trumped sentimentality. As soon as he and his best friend, Jackson Harper, had heard about a law practice for sale in Kansas City, the men pounced. They knew opportunity when they found it, and quickly nurtured their newly acquired firm to superstar prominence, even making a somewhat cheesy commercial—much to her mother's distress—to promote it. The whole town knew them—and their families. The Beckers and the Harpers. For heaven's sake, even their last names practically rhymed! She'd lay odds there wasn't a restaurant in Kansas City that would ever let a Becker or Harper wait to be seated.

But those days were behind her now. She blinked away her thoughts and returned to the bedroom, ready to tackle unpacking the boxes stacked against the wall. A small chest of drawers she'd wrangled from her mother's vast attic should work fine for the folded items—or so she thought until she tried to fit all her things into it. Cramming an elephant into a measuring cup would be easier. What possessed her to bring so much stuff? Even though she'd pared down to a precious few items, she apparently hadn't been ruthless enough. Carolyn smashed the garments and gave the drawer a shove with her hip, knowing the items would require an iron—which she hadn't brought along— before any of them would look decent enough to wear.

Bob poked his head into the bedroom. "It's all unloaded. Anything else we can do before we go?"

"Nothing, thanks." She pulled her checkbook from her purse. "Can I have the bill?"

Carolyn scanned the invoice he gave her and then handed him a check. Bob grinned at her and waved before he and his tight-lipped partner clomped away. She turned to face the boxes on the floor. *Ugh*. After a long drive from Kansas City, anything sounded better than unpacking. A distracting ray of sunlight blazed through the window, catching her attention. It practically called her name. She stepped around the boxes to peer through the glass again.

Two floors below, several people strolled the walkway outside her apartment while cars zoomed up and down the street. The scene looked pleasant and exceptionally inviting. She chewed her lip, glanced around the room, and then wrinkled her nose. Her windbreaker sat on the kitchen counter next to Fred, a plush brown dog with blue self-adhesive vet wrap around his front leg. The stuffed animal had been a sweet gift from her sister when Carolyn started vet school, and her constant companion while she worked and worried her way through years of classes. Now Fred had earned a new place. He'd soon sit on a shelf in her office—lending the support of a silent and quite comfortable old friend. She grabbed her jacket and opened the door. Hours behind the wheel entitled a person to some exercise, didn't it? "See you later, Fred," she called. Dereliction of duties justified, she trotted down a short flight of stairs and went outdoors.

Early October in the Midwest. A gorgeous time of year when the temperature could either blaze like fire or bluster with winds able to zap right through a coat. Today sat perfectly between those extremes with sun gleaming like a radiant ball of buttery gold in a cloudless blue sky. This wasn't a day to stay trapped within four walls, doing something as boring as unpacking.

A stoplight at the corner turned green, and the tires of the first car squealed as it lurched forward. She breathed in the smells of the city: damp asphalt, car fumes, and an odd mixture of cologne and aftershave from passersby. With hands stuck in her pockets, she fell into the same brisk clip as the others.

No gym workouts for her. A walk had always been Carolyn's exercise of choice, and her new home near Lafayette Square stood within blocks of everything she needed. There were restaurants and a wide assortment of specialty shops—she couldn't wait to try the cute chocolate bar—plus an organic market. Even her new job site stood only a half-dozen or so blocks away. Not much need to use the gift her parents had given her when she graduated from Mizzou's veterinary school. The sleek, navy-blue Volvo would likely spend most of its time sitting in a parking lot.

Curiosity nudged her along a path straight toward the clinic. This would be a good test to see how long it took to walk there. She might even get a sneak preview through the window to see for herself what remodeling improvements had taken place since her job interview. They didn't officially open until Tuesday—four days away—but surely someone would be around. So far, she'd only met two people from the Almost Home Humane Society, but running into either one of them sounded better than stacking dishes on shelves. With a purpose in mind, Carolyn picked up her pace.

The closer she got, the more walkers surrounded her. With noon approaching, it must be lunchtime. Most of the women she passed had on skirts and smart jackets but wore tennis shoes in every color of the rainbow. She surmised the high heels required of a corporate job had been left behind at the office. Men sported suits and ties except for the random guys in skin-tight workout gear loping along the sidewalk with glazed eyes and studied determination. Everyone either stared down, looked at a cell phone, or chatted with a companion. The chatters were the ones who smiled in acknowledgment when they caught her looking at them. Carolyn labeled the two women in front of her Chatters. They were obviously pals, and snatches of their animated conversation drifted back to her.

"I've been craving Mexican food. Let's meet at La Hacienda before the party."

"Sounds good if you promise to keep me away from those chips. I can barely zip my new dress as it is."

A small twig of loneliness poked Carolyn's soul. How long would it take to make new friends? She had a feeling the Humane Society director, Jeanne Nevins, and the assistant she'd met—what was her name...oh, yes, Teena Jacobs—who'd be helping at the clinic weren't likely to become future dinner companions. Jeanne had been pleasant enough but brusque and all business as she outlined goals for the clinic. Carolyn's knee had bobbed with agitated anticipation while Jeanne described the project.

"It took years for us to convince the city to let us use this building. Now we need to prove that low-cost spay and neuter surgeries will save money in the long run by reducing the number of strays and bite cases. No one objected to the idea of affordable vet care because poverty's a big problem here, but after the city finally came on board, the mayor caught a tremendous amount of grief over it. The Board of Aldermen will keep a sharp eye out to see if they made a good investment. You know how politics are."

Afterward, Carolyn had shaken Jeanne's hand with what she hoped was a confident grip. The unspoken fallout of failure sounded grim. Yet a challenge had never deterred her before, and she had no intention of it stopping her now. Teena—the woman who would be Carolyn's assistant—had also offered her hand, though her face had a pasted-on smile, and her eyes remained wary. Not a warm greeting to be sure, but since they'd be together for hours each day, it would be nice if they worked together well, even if they weren't fated to become friends. Less than two weeks after her nerve-racking interview, Carolyn accepted the job Jeanne offered.

The two women who'd been walking in front of her giggled, and she listened to them banter with a deep pang of regret. Of all the events that had recently turned her world from fairy-tale-princess happy to an episode of *The Walking Dead*, she realized the deepest cut of all came when she lost the two people she had counted on and cared about most.

Chapter Two

It took her thirty minutes to find the clinic, walking from sidewalks to curbs and then back to sidewalks again. She noticed someone had tacked a vinyl banner lopsided over the entrance of the faded red-brick edifice, and she stopped to admire the sign. Almost Home Animal Clinic. It made her heart skip with pride.

Like other structures near it, the decades-old building sat on a block described by Jeanne Nevins as the "warehouse district." Carolyn wasn't quite sure what Jeanne meant by the term because she hadn't noticed a single warehouse on the street, but she didn't want to ask. At least the clinic, with its new tuck-pointing, looked in decidedly better condition than the other buildings did. Clearly, a bundle of money had been spent on much-needed improvements. By stark contrast, only two blocks farther down, crumbling brick and cracked windows looked like a welcome mat for trouble. She hoped the construction equipment, piles of lumber, and yellow tape roped around orange cones suggested plans were advancing to fix them as well. The untidy scene couldn't have been more ironic. Rebuilding a street appeared to be darn near as messy as rebuilding a life.

A truck backfired loud enough to make her jump, the siren from a police car wailed, and a bus emitted clouds of exhaust as it rattled by. She reached for the coppery knob on the thick wood door and it turned. Not locked—thank goodness—but the bottom panel scraped across the floor when she pushed, as though swollen from dampness. With two hard shoulder bumps, the door creaked open.

Hip-hop music blared inside the clinic—so loud it reminded her of first row seats at a concert. A sniff brought the aroma of bleach, a scent she'd grown to appreciate ever since entering vet school. Bleach water annihilated germs the way penicillin did infection, and from where she stood every bit of the floor, counter, and walls sparkled. Last time she'd been here, she had to step over a ton of boards and rubble cluttered on the floor. Now, the curved counter had been cleared, shelves installed on the back wall, and the old-fashioned black and white tile looked nearly new. To see so many improvements, even when no one knew she planned to stop by, hitched up her enthusiasm by at least two notches. Then, from behind a laminate-topped partition, someone sang out loud, albeit slightly off-key. Carolyn peered over the counter.

A woman dressed in light denim jeans and a royal blue T-shirt knelt on the floor with a stack of folders next to her. One at a time, she pushed each folder into place on the second shelf of several that took up the wall while singing with as much gusto as the sole occupant of a car. Carolyn coughed as loud as she could, and the woman looked up, her jaws hard at work on a wad of gum.

She recognized Teena Jacobs at once. Teena's face, the color of polished deep amber, registered surprise and a shadowed hint of disapproval, which swiftly disappeared when she lowered the volume of music rocking from her cell phone. "Dr. Becker. I'm surprised to see you. Isn't this your moving day?"

"It is, but you can only deal with boxes for so long before going stir-crazy. Besides, it's too nice out. How's everything coming along, Teena?"

"The files are almost in order. We're still missing equipment, but we should have it before opening day. By the way, you'll be glad to know the Humane Society got another grant to replace our crappy old printer with a new one."

"That's terrific. Another item on our wish list taken care of. This will certainly be an interesting project, won't it?"

"If you call trying to do big things on a little budget interesting, I guess so." Teena stood to place the remaining files on the counter. At only five feet five inches, Carolyn wasn't tall, but the top of Teena's head barely reached her chin. Teena's generously round shape made her appear even shorter than her actual height.

"We'll make the clinic a success though, I'm sure of it. It's exciting to think about the possibilities." Carolyn hoped she didn't sound too much like a high-school cheerleader.

"You sure came a long way to take a big chance on things working out." Teena kept her gaze on the files as she shuffled through them.

Taken aback by the remark, Carolyn said, "There are some who might think so, but I did spend a lot of time researching St. Louis. Like a lot of cities, it has problems with strays and overcrowding at the pound. Many of those animals end up being euthanized, don't they? But it doesn't need to be that way. Spay and neuter is the answer, and I'm sure we can make it happen."

Teena grabbed her lower back and stretched before sitting in the swivel chair behind the counter. "I hope you're right. Jeanne sure made it clear if we can't come up with the number of surgeries the city expects, we'll lose their support. I grew up here, and I know it won't be easy to change the way people think about their animals." She smoothed her hand across the desk, whisking invisible dust to the floor.

"No one says it will be easy, but we'll figure out how to make them understand."

An ambulance raced down the street with lights flashing, and Teena lifted a speculative gaze to Carolyn. "Do you mind if I ask you a personal question?"

Right to the point. It didn't surprise Carolyn much. Everything about Teena suggested she tackled things in the most direct way possible. "Why not? We might as well get to know each other. Ask away."

"Jeanne told me about your background after she hired you, and I've been wondering about something ever since." Her dark eyes perused Carolyn curiously. "What made you quit a big successful practice in the best part of Kansas City to come here of all places?"

Carolyn thought about the state-of-the-art facility she'd left behind and closed her eyes for a moment. A fair question. If she'd been Teena, knowing the shoestring budget on which they'd be operating, she'd probably wonder the same thing. "I wanted to get involved in something more worthwhile than what I was doing. The Humane Society's ad showed up in one of my veterinary journals. I read about what they planned to do, and it seemed like exactly the challenge I'd been looking for. Plus, I've always been fascinated by St. Louis. My dad grew up here. He adores the area."

"But I guess not enough to live here—oops. I'm sorry, Dr. Becker." Teena turned her eyes away, and the lovely color of her skin deepened.

Carolyn leaned her elbows on the counter. "Look, Teena. As a two-person practice, we're going to spend a lot of time together, so the first thing I want you to do is call me Carolyn, unless we're with clients, okay?"

"Okay." Teena's posture eased a little.

"As for your question, my family moved to Kansas City not long after my younger sister was born. Daddy started a law practice and his firm got bigger than anything he dreamed possible. It's demanding enough to consume nearly all his time. If he has any spare moments at all they belong to only one person—my mother. She's a force of nature in a crystal-white Cadillac and has him sewn tight into all her favorite charity causes. He doesn't have time left for anything else. Not even a visit to a baseball game in

St. Louis." She leaned against the counter and reminded herself turnabout was fair play. "What about you? Tell me something about Teena."

"Me? Not much to tell. I'm single—but on the lookout for the right guy. I like to work with animals, which is why I became a vet tech." She crossed her arms over her ample bosom. "And I might as well tell you right now, things roll off my tongue that maybe I shouldn't say. It's how I've always been. Ask my brothers. A lot of folks don't like that about me."

"Teena, what you say doesn't bother me a bit. In fact, I wouldn't like it if you didn't tell me what you really thought."

Chomp. Chomp. Teena's gum snapped. "Well, in that case, have you got a boyfriend?"

Carolyn suppressed an unladylike smirk. Teena sure didn't waste time showing the truth of her self-assessment. "No, I don't have a boyfriend."

"What? I can't believe it. A beautiful lady like you? And a doctor to boot? Seems men would line up and you could have your pick." Teena's voice sounded wistful.

"Here's the truth of it. Getting into a relationship has never been a priority for me. As long as I can remember, I've only had one goal. To be a veterinarian. Even as a kid I annoyed the heck out of my parents by bringing home strays. Then the minute I wasn't looking, Mother and Daddy would whisk them away."

Carolyn left the counter for the files on the wall and thumbed through them, knowing she hadn't fully answered Teena's question. Perhaps skirting the issue wasn't the best way for them to start off. She turned to look at her assistant. "I'm sure you must know how hard it is to get into vet school. To make it happen, I had to spend every minute studying. In my spare time, I volunteered at our local shelter, doing what I could to get accepted into the right program. It consumed practically every waking moment and left no time for a social life."

Teena's eyes bulged with surprise. "You mean to say you didn't date anybody when you were in school?"

"Oh, I went places occasionally, but my friends and I would go together as a group. There wasn't anyone special until I started vet school."

Teena tapped the stack of files with her finger. "Aha! You met somebody there, didn't you?"

"I got involved with someone, but it didn't work out very well." Carolyn wasn't ready to say more. Events remained too raw for analysis, and she didn't want to do anything to further batter her own heart. Thickness gathered in her throat, and she cleared it away. "Let's take a look at the supply inventory. I want to make sure we're ready to go on Tuesday." She noticed how quickly Teena's face drooped with disappointment, but to the woman's credit, she didn't ask any more questions.

Carolyn examined the old wooden desk in her office. She loved the heft and substance of it, but the drawers stuck. WD-40? She moved on to check what had been stocked in cabinets and on shelves against a mental list she'd prepared, while Teena finished putting away files. They worked on for a while without speaking to the lowered volume of Teena's music until Carolyn finally dusted off her hands and checked her watch. More than three hours had passed.

"Wow. That's it for me. I need to go home and get something done there. I'll see you on Monday, Teena. We can do a final check and work out procedures to make sure we're ready to go."

"Okay. Hey, thanks for coming in to help, and good luck. Man, how I hate putting stuff away." Teena cranked up the sound on her phone, grabbed a few manila envelopes, and disappeared behind the counter.

Carolyn had lost time she could have used to get her apartment in order, but the afternoon hadn't been wasted. Her stomach had fewer butterflies than before, and she'd learned something about her assistant. Teena was brash but a hard worker, with a background that could prove invaluable in gaining the trust of clients. Carolyn felt sure they'd make a good team—eventually. Maybe, she decided, they could even someday become friends.

Shadows on the ground had started to lengthen, and she fell into step with people walking away from buildings they'd entered earlier in the day. Everyone moved at a faster pace than before, as though to outrun what remained of the daylight. With dozens of walkers around her, no one in particular stood out until she noticed a man. Not by what he did, but by what he didn't do.

The tall man didn't move at all, leaning with an insolent grace against a building at the corner, his arms crossed over a dark leather jacket and collar turned up against the breeze. His solitary vigil made Carolyn's skin prickle, and her mind replayed her mother's many graphic lectures titled Men

Who Launch Attacks at Unsuspecting Females. She kept a suspicious eye on him as she walked. Holy Shih Tzu, he could easily be a predator scanning the area for easy pickings. Her imagination jumped into the spirit of things by conjuring scenes fit for a low-budget horror movie, which brought her to an abrupt halt. A woman behind Carolyn ran into her. Carolyn mumbled, "Oops. Excuse me," and continued to stare at the man, until his wandering gaze caught hers. Their eyes met for a split-second before he shifted away from the building and disappeared around the corner.

Don't be ridiculous, Carolyn. She shook the scary visions from her head and set off again, which quickly eased her concerns. How silly to let the approach of evening turn logical thinking into imaginary worries. She longed to reach home where a hot bath would dissolve her groundless jitters as easily as it did the dust of the city.

Home. She liked the sound of it. First thing, she'd open the box her mother had packed with kitchen supplies, where she knew there would be a bottle of wine—it had been forever since she'd savored a glass—along with something to nibble on while the bath water ran. The joy of unpacking could wait until tomorrow. A musky aroma from worn damp brick filled her lungs as she hurried along, adrenalin pumping her heart into high gear. A new city. A brand-new job. And a new life.

Time to tuck away lessons from the past and concentrate on the future.

Chapter Three

Tuesday morning came, and Carolyn arrived at work early, flushed and breathless after practically speed-walking her way to the clinic's first official day of operation. She shouldered open the front door to find clients already sitting in the waiting area with a variety of pets. A man held the leash of a beefy Rottweiler wearing a wide nail-studded collar. The dog's ears were pricked forward as he eyed a pillowcase on the lap of a lady sitting across from him. The pillowcase undulated like an earthquake to the sound of indignant meows.

Teena stood behind the counter, face pleated in concentration as she stared at a client with a bedraggled-looking black-and-tan dog in her arms.

"I'm sorry, ma'am. I don't know Spanish. Can. You. Call. Someone. To. Translate?" Teena put her thumb and little finger near her ear and mouth to mimic a phone.

The woman shrugged her shoulders helplessly. "*Qué?*"

Teena spied Carolyn, and her face brightened. "I hope you can speak Spanish, Dr. Becker."

"I'm afraid two years of high school Spanish doesn't even remotely make me fluent."

"Then how am I supposed to tell her she needs an appointment for her dog?" Frustration weighted each word like stones.

Carolyn reached out to stroke the animal's fur. He looked like a beagle mix with his dark mournful eyes, a characteristic of the breed. "We can't turn her away. Anyway, there isn't exactly a line out the door." Carolyn kept her hand on the dog. "May I weigh him please?"

Wide-eyed, the woman backed up, keeping a firm grip on her animal. They could hardly play tug-of-war with the poor creature, so Carolyn dropped her hands and thought back to her interview. Jeanne hadn't mentioned a non-English speaking population.

She tried again, speaking softly as she would to a fearful patient and pointed to the scale. "May I take him over there?"

In a cadence that echoed Carolyn's, the woman replied, "*Mi perro está enfermo.*"

The phrase convinced Carolyn beyond any doubt that she'd long ago replaced foreign language phrases for chemical formulas, internal organ structure, and symptom analysis. She caught her lower lip between her teeth, unsure of how to proceed, when a baritone voice with the slightest hint of an accent spoke up from behind her. "She says her dog is sick."

Carolyn turned around toward the source. A broad-shouldered man stood near the door, making the clinic waiting room suddenly shrink. A Spanish-speaking stranger? He must have been sent by some divine stroke of opening-day luck. "Can you ask her what's wrong with him?"

The man directed what sounded like a question to the woman. "*Que está mal?*"

"*Vomitó*," the woman replied.

"She says—"

Carolyn held up her hand. "Never mind. I think I understand. Look, would you be willing to come into the exam room with us while I look at her dog? I have a few more questions and it would be really helpful if you'd translate."

He hesitated a moment, then nodded. Carolyn pointed toward an exam table, and the woman put her dog on it. The man exchanged a few short sentences with the dog's owner and then introduced her as Señora Sanchez. Her dog, Pedro, had been lethargic and vomiting since the previous day. Carolyn put her stethoscope on the dog's belly and poked and prodded while listening to Pedro's other symptoms, courtesy of her unnamed translator. After a cursory exam, she decided the pup had gastroenteritis and prescribed medication to settle Pedro's stomach along with instructions on what to feed him until he recovered. She rubbed the dog's silky ears while the man explained what she'd said to Señora Sanchez. Whatever he told her smoothed the worry lines from the woman's face. She said *gracias* several times to her translator, and he lightly touched her forearm as though to reassure her.

His kind gesture nearly made Carolyn forget to address the clinic's purpose. She pushed a wisp of hair from her face and smiled. "Would you mind asking her to schedule Pedro for surgery so he can be neutered? The clinic's fee is very reasonable."

The man didn't even bother to look at her when he answered. "Not now. She's worried enough as it is. Why don't we call it a day?"

The high-handed remark didn't match his polite nod to Señora Sanchez. He opened the door, and before Carolyn had time to persuade him, the woman picked up Pedro and scurried through the opening with the dog cradled in her arms.

She sighed and for the first time, took a good look at the man who'd helped her. He stood tall, perhaps over six feet, with black hair and skin darkened by sunshine and an obvious Latino heritage. He might have been described as handsome were it not for a slight bend to his nose and the complete lack of warmth in his features. His nose must have been broken some years back and never properly set, Carolyn decided. His stony expression, however, she couldn't explain.

He caught Carolyn's stare, and her mouth dropped open. The man's eyes were a completely unexpected shade of ice blue. The contrast against his swarthy skin and ebony-colored hair made them gleam as though he'd materialized from a science-fiction movie. She dropped her gaze to his shoulders covered by a leather jacket. A tug of attraction kindled, and she quickly looked away. But something drew her back to his face—something nibbling at the edge of her awareness. Manners came first. "Thanks for your help. I'm Dr. Carolyn Becker. And you're…?"

"Rio Medina. There aren't many non-English speaking Hispanics here, but the señora is among them. I'm glad I could help."

He didn't look glad. She stared at him again until it hit her, and she blurted the memory she'd been struggling to recover. "Were you standing across the street from the clinic just before dark on Friday?"

"Possibly." He shrugged. "I spend a lot of time in the neighborhood. When I heard about the clinic opening, I decided to take a look at it before I got started on a new project. Quite a few of my amigos have animals, and they can't afford to go uptown for vet care." He looked around the room. "Actually, this location should be quite convenient for them."

"We do provide basic veterinary care, but our focus is to neuter animals. It's our mission, according to the Humane Society and the city. We've been given grants to do the surgery at a very low cost."

Rio grinned, which transformed his face into an extraordinarily handsome one, crooked nose or not. "You're going to have an uphill battle selling that idea. Men aren't interested in castrating their dogs. It's almost like they'd be castrating themselves."

She drew up her chin. "What a strange conclusion. Don't you know neutering makes a dog healthier and less aggressive?"

"My point exactly. No man wants a dog who isn't game."

"Game?"

"Strong, powerful—substitute whatever word you want."

"Why would anyone want their dog to be aggressive? Surely you don't go along with an archaic idea like that."

He shrugged again. "It doesn't really matter what I think, does it? It's the people out there you'll need to convince."

She smarted at his nonchalant attitude and prepared to argue her point further when Teena interrupted, her voice ticked up at least half an octave higher than normal. "Dr. Becker, your appointments are waiting. Here are the files."

Carolyn took the stack from Teena and turned back toward Rio, her tone snowflake-cool. "Thank you again, Mr. Medina. I do appreciate your help."

He gave her a hard look that converted him back to the formidable-looking man she'd first noticed on the street. "Let me offer you a few words of advice. I know the people here. If your plan is to lecture them or try to guilt anyone into doing what you want, I guarantee they won't listen, and it's likely they won't come back. Pushing doesn't work. You ought to rethink your tactics."

His unsolicited remarks surprised her so much, she had no words. She realized her mouth had dropped open and she sealed her lips tight. *How rude can one person be?*

With a dismissive lift of his hand, he left her standing in the exam room, his shoes silent on the tile floor. Annoyance sent heat rushing into her face. She'd never heard such nonsense before. Men didn't want to castrate their dogs? Didn't he realize they were no longer living in a Neanderthal world?

Yet with a full schedule of appointments, Rio's comments faded away. Minutes multiplied into hours. After she'd treated her ninth patient of the day, a German shepherd with an injured paw, it pained her to realize not one of the animals she'd seen had been altered. Worse, only one owner had any interest in even discussing it. By the time her final appointment left, she felt more frustrated than exhausted. Not even a glance at Fred—now ensconced on a shelf in her office, his button eyes as sympathetic as they'd been throughout all her years of vet school—could cheer her up.

She and Teena completed their closing routine silently, gathered their jackets and bags, and headed to the door. Carolyn turned off the lights and she couldn't contain her exasperation one second longer. "I just don't understand it. Everyone is willing to get a rabies shot for their pet. Or get help if their animal is sick or hurt. But nobody wants to talk about neutering them. Why?"

Teena wrapped a purple plaid scarf around her neck. "That's a question I can answer for you. The city has an ordinance. They charge big fat fines for animals with no rabies shot."

"Oh, I see. Well, it's too bad they don't do the same thing with spays and neuters. It would make our job a whole lot easier." She stopped to consider the idea. "Actually, I've heard of other cities doing something along those lines."

"Don't count on it happening here anytime soon. Nobody seems to give a flip about prevention. Most folks think it's easier and cheaper to let the pound snatch up strays than it is to pass a law that keeps too many animals from being born in the first place." Teena spoke as matter-of-factly as if she were discussing the latest weather forecast.

The comment returned Rio's remarks to Carolyn's mind, and her face warmed anew. "At least the city is giving us a chance to try. Tell me the truth, Teena. How do you think our first day went?"

"About as good as can be expected, I guess," Teena said.

"After today, I admit to feeling a little uneasy about everything, especially surgeries. We need to alter at least fifteen animals a month. Do you have any idea how we'll convince people to do it?"

Teena examined her fingernails. "Remember, things are different here than they are in the fancy suburbs you're used to. A lot of people think it's cool to let their dog or cat have a litter or two. They figure they can sell the babies or even give them away. It'll take time for anyone to accept why it's important not to do that."

"And evidently, it will take a lot of patience. From me, mostly."

Carolyn had already noticed the dogs here were different. She'd seen a Rottweiler, three Staffordshire terriers, and a Doberman. Each one looked as tough as their owner, unlike the teacup poodles and Yorkshire terriers her mother and many of her mother's friends had as pets.

A gust of cool breeze tousled Carolyn's hair, and she shivered. "I'm starving. How about joining me for some dinner to celebrate our first day? My treat."

"Let me check my social calendar." Teena pulled a small appointment book from her purse and flipped through it pretentiously. "Yep. I think I'm free."

"Good. There's a restaurant near my apartment I'd like to try. Soup, sandwiches, and salads. The menu sounds good to me. Do you mind walking?"

"How do you think I get where I need to go? It's my feet or the bus."

Sunset painted the clouds pink and orange, an end to another lovely October day. Carolyn inhaled the cool air and felt her shoulders begin to relax. Huffing only a little, Teena had no problem keeping the same pace. For all her short legs and round body, she moved just as swiftly as Carolyn did.

A few deep breaths and the glorious sky soon had Carolyn voicing her thoughts—a habit she'd started in college after learning Einstein used to do the same. "I keep turning this around and around in my head. How can we encourage our clients to be more cooperative?" She really didn't expect an answer, though it didn't stop Teena.

"First off, you need to chill. One thing at a time. Remember, this is only our first day, and the appointment book is filled for the week. We're doing fine so far."

"That's true, but I still can't help worrying. Jeanne and the city have such high expectations."

"You know what? My mama always told me worrying ain't gonna get you anything but a big fat headache."

Carolyn laughed. "Your mama sounds like a very smart lady."

Two blocks ahead, the neon-bright green-and-red color scheme of Maggie's Grill appeared. The place was so flashy it reminded Carolyn of Christmas gone wild. At first, she wondered whether choosing Maggie's was a mistake. Stepping into the lobby eased her mind. A pungent combination of garlic and smoked beef made her mouth water. The two women slid into an empty bright-red booth, and an all-smiles uniformed waitress promptly arrived to scribble their orders on a thick pad of paper.

After the waitress left, Teena rested her chin on her palm. "Dr. Becker—I mean, Carolyn," she said, amending herself at Carolyn's reproving look. "There's something I should probably tell you, and I'm pretty sure you're not going to like it."

Carolyn tilted her head. "Oh?"

Teena traced her finger in little circles on the table. "I've been doing some snooping. You told me a few things about yourself, but I still couldn't figure out why anybody would run hundreds of miles to work in a bare-bones clinic smack in the middle of downtown. So"—she shifted her body—"I started checking around."

Teena's confession amused her. "What kind of checking around?"

"On the Internet. You can find anything on the Internet."

"Not everything on the Internet is true, you know. I assume you Googled me? By the look on your face this must be a doozy. What in the world did you uncover?"

"Your parents are Tom and Elise Becker. Big shots, from what I saw." Teena's eyes grew wide and bright. "I even found a magazine story on their house with lots of pictures. It's smack in the middle of some fancy golf course in Kansas City. Am I right?"

Carolyn nodded. "Mother and Daddy have lived in the same place for quite a while."

A server brought their food, and Teena paused. Then she picked up her fork and speared a French fry. "I read one really bizarre story. It said you were supposed to get married last summer, but all of a sudden, right before the wedding, the whole thing got called off."

Carolyn's smile turned brittle. The newspaper. She'd chosen to forget all the articles and gossip. The *Times'* Society section had trumpeted the breakup of her engagement as loudly as they'd proclaimed her betrothal. The son of Jackson Harper and the daughter of Tom Becker, among Kansas City's most prominent families, were to be wed. When the storybook romance crashed in flames, the curious public couldn't wait to discover what had happened. Carolyn pushed her lettuce around her plate, feeling prickly and uncomfortable, as Teena rushed on.

"The rest is only guesswork, but since you're the one who ran, he must have done something really bad. A little argument is no big deal. You hash things out and move on. But you left everything and everybody. I watch enough Dr.

Phil to know it means your heart got broken into a million little pieces."

Carolyn put down her fork. This subject was the last thing she felt like discussing. The impulse to get up and leave hit, but another thought stopped her. Connections were built on trust. Without it, there couldn't be a relationship at all. Maybe the time had come to examine the whole thing head-on, rather than banning any mention of the topic as she'd done whenever her mother patted her hand and clucked sympathetically. Or when her father clenched his fist as though he'd like to punch someone.

"Okay, Teena. I'll tell you what happened." She swallowed and let the memories return. "My fiancé, Clayton, and I practically grew up together. How could we help it? Our parents are best friends, and he planned to be a vet just like I did. We got into the same school, shared lab time, and even studied for exams together. Before long, Clay and I started spending all our free time with each other too."

"You fell in love," Teena said with a satisfied look.

"I'm not sure if it was love or more like putting on a comfortable pair of shoes. When our parents found out, they were thrilled. They claimed it was exactly what they'd been hoping would happen. Mother got on the phone right away to call Clay's parents and start planning the wedding. I really think she meant to outdo the whole Princess Diana and Prince Charles thing, complete with a horse-drawn carriage for the bride. I guess she forgot how their marriage turned out. But my mother has always been fond of beautiful events, especially when they're accented with pearls and a touch of diamond."

Teena waved her fork. "Excuse me for saying it, but that sounds pretty wonderful. I wish I had a mama who wanted to show me off to the world. I didn't figure you to be one of those snooty women who turn up their nose because nothing's good enough for them."

The remark brought out her father's talent for countering an argument. "The point is, Teena, I didn't want a big wedding at all. There are lots of better ways to spend money. From the beginning, the whole thing seemed to belong more to Mother and Daddy than Clay and me."

Teena's eyes didn't leave Carolyn. "Well, don't keep me waiting. What the heck happened between you and your man?"

Carolyn resumed pushing the food around her plate. "We just saw things differently. We weren't compatible."

"You couldn't tell that about each other before you got engaged?"

"Maybe I wasn't looking hard enough, until things happened to open my eyes. At any rate, it became impossible for me to consider marrying him, even when Mother reminded me how much our big fat non-wedding would cost. Vendors still expect to be paid whether the bride walks down the aisle or not." She'd never forget some of the things her parents had said. Pointing out they were unhappy would be grossly understating the truth, so she ended her dissertation. "Anyway, that's pretty much all there was to it."

Teena waited expectantly, but Carolyn only took a bite of her salad.

"I see why you might want to break things off if they didn't—you know—feel right. But why the heck would you throw away a good job?"

"Well, there's one other detail I didn't mention yet. Clay and I were hired to work at the same veterinary office."

"Mm-hmm. It's beginning to make a little more sense now."

"It was very uncomfortable to see each other every day. Not good for either of us. When I found the Humane Society's ad, I sent in my résumé and drove to St. Louis for the interview. The minute Jeanne offered me the job, I hired a real estate agent to find a rental, signed the lease, and found a moving company."

Teena had the same wide-eyed look as someone enthralled by a blockbuster movie. "What did your folks say about all this?"

"I won't kid you. It was a day filled with drama. Mother cried buckets, and Daddy laid out his points the same way he argues a case in court. Once they saw nothing would change my mind, they accepted it—more or less. What else could they do? I wanted to leave and I was ready to go. The only thing I felt bad about was leaving my younger sister. I'm not a psychologist like Dr. Phil, but even I know who the target of all Mother's attention will be now."

A gleam of respect dawned on Teena's face as Carolyn forked another bite of salad into her mouth. No wonder people said confession was good for the soul. She felt so much better, she almost offered Teena the rest of the story, but her coworker seemed satisfied enough. At least she didn't ask any more questions.

"Well…" Teena peered at Carolyn and picked up her sandwich. "I knew you came from money, but I didn't figure you had nerve too."

Chapter Four

On the day of her first meeting with Jeanne Nevins, Carolyn carried a notebook filled with charts she'd created to track the clinic's progress. She paced outside Jeanne's office while waiting and tapped her fingers against the notebook. Within a few weeks, the clinic had added more than a dozen folders, each representing a new patient. Pride in what she and Teena had accomplished so far lifted her chin, although she hadn't a clue how Jeanne would feel. The woman was extraordinarily hard to read. So far, Carolyn had only seen her smile once.

When Jeanne invited her in, Carolyn sat down and presented her report, while her boss peered at her over a cup of coffee. After forty-five minutes of rather uncomfortable questions, a sliver of satisfaction erased the lines normally etched between the woman's brows. *She liked what I said?* Relief filled Carolyn to buoyancy like a burst of helium. Then Jeanne brought her back to earth with a thud. "Remember, we'll soon make our first report to the city, and surgery numbers aren't quite where they need to be yet."

Totally deflated, Carolyn picked up her folders. Low numbers certainly weren't from lack of trying. She'd convinced a few clients to neuter their animals, but most of them downplayed the need. As Rio had predicted, she'd found men to be especially offended by the idea.

"Why would I cut off my dog's balls?" One of her recent male clients had shuddered. "He's got girlfriends to keep happy."

Education is one of my jobs, Carolyn reminded herself with a grim smile before she responded.

"Your dog will be less aggressive and not as likely to roam if he's neutered. It can even prevent certain tumors as well." With words carefully chosen, she slowed her normal tempo of speaking, in hope of sounding more persuasive. "The city has huge problems with so many puppies and kittens being born. Many of them end up in the pound because there aren't enough homes for them all."

"Get real, Doc, there'll always be a market for puppies," the man had shot back at her.

She'd have better luck talking to a rock. There had to be a way of countering such an attitude, though she hadn't found it yet. Dispensing veterinary care was easy. Selling a new philosophy was not, especially when success would be measured by numbers on a graph. Back in her vet-school days, she'd once attended a workshop on helping clients deal with the loss of a dog, but no one had offered any classes on changing the mindset of someone who ignored facts.

Even after she returned to her office, the question wouldn't leave her mind. There had to be an answer—every problem had a solution. But what? Teena opened the door to Carolyn's office, interrupting her unhappy spiral of thoughts. "We've got an injury case—a dog. Can you take a minute to see her?"

Carolyn nodded and rose to wash her hands, hoping the situation wasn't severe enough for a referral to an emergency clinic—a much costlier proposition.

Teena already had the animal on a table in the exam room. A teenage boy with hair cropped close to his scalp and skin the color of coffee with a spoonful of cream had one hand on the dog's back. The boy's height and the way his lower lip trembled made him appear much younger than the sagging jeans and baseball cap cocked to the side indicated.

She turned her attention to the patient, a female Staffordshire terrier who was bleeding from several puncture wounds on her face and neck. Approaching slowly, she placed her hand on the animal's back and felt the dog shiver beneath her touch.

"My name is Dr. Becker. What happened to your dog?"

"Another dog got to her." The boy scuffed a tennis-shoe-clad foot against the tile. "I ran him off."

"What's her name?"

"I been callin' her Stella." His voice seemed whisper-soft.

The dog's ears pricked up, and her tail waved back and forth. Carolyn raised a brow and got out her stethoscope while the boy's fingers plucked at raveling strands from a piece of twine knotted around Stella's neck.

"Good girl." Carolyn crooned. "This won't take long."

Stella appeared young, likely less than three years old. Her coat was black with a bit of white on the muzzle and a splash of white on her chest—like she wore a tuxedo. The tips of her four paws were also white, as though they'd been dipped in paint. Some time ago, her ears had been cropped far too close to her head. Carolyn touched one of the wounds, and she didn't show her teeth, but she did give a soft whimper.

"Looks as though we'll need to clean her up and maybe put in a stitch or two. But her color and vital signs seem good. I think she'll be fine. Teena, give me a hand."

Teena restrained Stella while Carolyn worked. She half expected the dog to lunge or snap, not an unusual response from an injured animal, but Stella lay quietly and flicked her tail whenever Carolyn spoke to her. The boy watched as Carolyn worked, shifting his weight from foot to foot.

After a few minutes, Carolyn announced, "Okay, that does it. I'll put Stella on a course of antibiotics just in case. You'll need to keep a close eye on her and make sure she doesn't chew her stitches. I can give you an E-collar if you want."

"An E-collar?"

"It's a large plastic cone that fits around her neck. When she's wearing it, she can't lick her wounds or pull out any stitches. Can I get a collar for you to take home?"

"Well, um, she ain't exactly my dog."

Carolyn turned to look at the boy. "What do you mean she isn't your dog?"

"I've seen her before on the street. When another dog went after her, I knew she needed help. Some guy I know told me to bring her here. He said you'd fix her up fine."

"Animal control usually takes charge of strays." Carolyn pursed her lips together.

The boy's dark eyes got big, and his words tumbled out. "Don't send her to the pound. They kill dogs there. I'll talk to my mom. Maybe Stella can come stay with me for a while." He stroked the dog's head.

Perhaps it was the quiver in his voice. Or the pleading look on his face. "I'll tell you what. We'll keep her here while you square things with your mom, but remember, if she won't let you take Stella home, then we'll have to call animal control."

Teena rolled her eyes but allowed the boy to pat Stella again before she bustled the dog back to the kennel recovery area. The teen's brows scrunched in a line low over his eyes as Stella disappeared from view.

The look on his face touched her. "Don't worry. Miss Jacobs and I will take good care of her."

"I'll talk to my mom when I get home." He edged toward the door.

"Just a minute, young man. I've got a few questions for you." Carolyn kept a sharp eye on his face. "Stella reacted when you said her name. If she's a stray and not your dog, why would she respond to that?"

He studied his toes. "Well…I guess I seen her before. She hangs out around our apartment building. I give her food and watch out for her. She watches out for me." His chin jerked up in defiance as though he expected to be challenged.

"I see." Carolyn crossed her arms. "Let's get one thing clear. If you want my help, you've got to be honest. From now on, no more making up stories, please. That won't work."

He moistened his lips and uttered a sullen, "Okay."

"First, I've got to fill out some paperwork. I need your name and your parents' names."

He shifted his weight from one foot to the other again. "I'm Coby Jefferson. My mom is LaDonna Jefferson. My dad don't come around much, so I ain't got nothing to say about him."

"All right. What's your address?"

"Not far from here. I live at 2712 Cole." His shoulders rounded. "How much you gonna make me pay for this?"

"Let's take a look. There's today's work, and"—Carolyn decided to eliminate the idea of a choice—"as soon as she's healed, I'll do surgery to spay her." She wrote a list of figures and added them before pushing the paper across the table for Coby to see. He inhaled a healthy gasp of air. Even low-cost veterinary care wasn't as cheap as she wished it could be.

"I ain't got that much money. My mom don't either."

"Maybe we can figure out another way." Carolyn leaned against the table and Coby watched her, his expression lined with suspicion. A dog in the recovery room barked, and a metal crate rattled. "I think I have an idea. A proposal for you."

Coby's eyes narrowed. "What're you talking about?"

"Miss Jacobs and I could use some help. What if you come to the clinic for an hour or two after school to give us a hand with things here? You can work off what you owe by volunteering."

"Doing what?"

"Oh, stocking supply shelves, helping us keep the floors clean, disinfecting kennels, walking dogs. And after your work is done, you can spend time with Stella."

As though she'd written the perfect prescription, a grin spread across his face. "I can do stuff like that. Am I supposed to start now?"

"I think you better go home and talk to your mother first. If it's okay with her, you can start tomorrow."

"That rocks!" He fist-pumped the air and raced from the room. Carolyn followed and saw him nearly collide with a broad-shouldered man who grabbed his arm and laughed.

"Why are you in such a hurry, buddy? Did the doc chase you away?"

"No, Rio. She's nice, like you said. And she's gonna take care of Stella. We made a deal."

Coby sailed past Rio and out the door, heading— Carolyn hoped—for home and not the myriad of problems young people otherwise could easily find.

Dogs in the city had a rough time. So, she decided, did kids.

"Well, Dr. Becker, for a change you seem to have made somebody happy. Tell me, what kind of deal did you cut with Coby?" Rio sounded amused and more than a little condescending.

Her first impulse was to tell him it wasn't any of his business, but she thought about Coby and mellowed. "He's going to work off expenses for a dog's medical care by helping at the clinic."

A satisfied smile softened Rio's face. "I couldn't have suggested a better plan myself. The boy doesn't have an easy life, but he's got a good heart."

"How do you know him?"

"Let's just say I see Coby on the street a lot more than I should. He's only fifteen, but he hangs with an older crowd. When he told me about a dog being hurt, I suggested he bring her to you, though I didn't imagine it would work out this well. He'll be much better off helping a good-looking woman on a creature crusade than running with the riffraff he finds out there." Rio gestured toward the street with his thumb.

His comment and casual machismo stiffened her backbone. "I wish you wouldn't refer to my career as though it's a hobby."

"And here I am, taking time out of my day to give you some important feedback." His eyes grew somber. "Several of my, um, acquaintances, have brought their dogs here. I've heard them complain about you pushing the idea of neutering their animals. All you're doing is turning the subject into a joke. I told you preaching wouldn't fly—not even when the preacher looks as tempting as you do.

Which can, I believe, create an entirely different set of problems."

She brushed aside the backhanded compliment as though swatting a bothersome fly. "Thank you for your opinion, but I know what I'm doing. Is there something else I can help you with? I mean other than being an audience to your patronizing lecture."

"As a matter of fact, I do have a question." His blue eyes bored into hers. "Have you noticed injuries similar to those on Coby's dog with any other animals since you opened the clinic?"

The abrupt change in topic threw her off-balance enough that she answered his question without a second thought. "I've seen plenty of bite cases in vet school, but Stella is the first one I've had in St. Louis. Her injuries were a little more than what I'd expect from a quick run-in with another dog."

"Hmm. Did you notice anything else about her?"

"Nothing extraordinary." She considered it a few moments. "Except I did see evidence of a few older injuries. Seems like the poor thing has had hard times as a stray."

Rio rubbed his chin as though deep in thought. "I wouldn't necessarily assume that dog came from off the street as a stray."

"What do you mean?" She stared at him.

His shoulders lifted carelessly. "Look, you probably aren't in the mood to do any favors for me, but I'm going to ask anyway. Let me know if you run across any other bite cases."

Carolyn narrowed her eyes at him. "Why should I do that?"

"Maybe you've inspired me to follow your lead. I'm out to save the world by neutering one dog at a time." A crinkle appeared at the corners of his eyes.

"Even if I wanted to report anything to you, I don't have your phone number. And frankly, I don't want it."

"Believe me, there's no need for you to call. Anytime I want to talk, I know exactly where to find you." He inclined his head toward her and walked out the door before she had time to think of anything clever yet tart to say. Still debating what could have been a withering response, she jumped when Teena's voice came from behind her.

"Stella didn't have any problem drinking her water, and she's bedded down for the night."

"Thanks. I'll check on her before I leave."

"Excuse me, but what is that gorgeous hunk of a man doing back here again, and why are you glaring meaner than a judge on sentencing day?"

Carolyn shook her head. "He's impossible. I've never met anyone who can get under my skin quicker."

"That's interesting, Dr. Becker. Very interesting."

"He's the one who sent Coby and Stella here. He asked me some questions about her and implied I'm not doing my job properly. That's about the extent of our conversation."

"He actually said you're not doing your job?"

"Well, not exactly." Hammers thrummed in Carolyn's temples, and she massaged them with her fingertips. "It's not so much what he says as the way he says it. Oh, never mind. Will you lock up today, please? I need to go home."

She could tell by the glitter in Teena's eyes she hadn't heard the last of questions about the utterly aggravating Rio. Maybe after a good night's sleep, her patience would be restored enough to handle Teena's inquisition.

At least she hoped so.

Chapter Five

After an overnight drenching thunderstorm, the clinic's front door swelled so much, Carolyn could barely scrape it across the floor. She had to bang her shoulder against it three times before the blasted thing would open. Fuming, she remembered it had been weeks since she'd filled out a requisition form asking the city for help with the issue. It was a simple enough request, but so far, all she had to show for her effort was a bruised arm. She plunked her bag on her desk and marched to the recovery area.

Stella stood nosing the crate's door in a doggie greeting and Carolyn's ire at the city traveled to the back burner. An enthusiastic greeting from a dog. What better cure for any affliction? She unlatched the kennel and removed the plastic cone from around the dog's neck, buckled on a collar, and attached a leash. "Let's go outside, girl."

The pup followed her with only a slight limp and sniffed the ground before she did her business. Carolyn watched the animal while they walked. "You're looking good, Stella.

I don't see any sign of complications." She ruffled the dog's hair and noticed patches of dirt crusted on her legs. "A bath is in store for you soon, my friend. Now let's go back and get you some breakfast."

There certainly wasn't any reason to worry over Stella's appetite. She gobbled every last morsel of food in less than a minute, then licked the empty bowl with dedicated devotion. When satisfied not a speck remained, the dog padded over and pushed her muzzle against Carolyn's leg in an obvious invitation. "You're a darling," Carolyn pronounced, rubbing behind Stella's cropped ears and moving her fingers along the dog's back. "It feels good to have that cone off, doesn't it?"

After the massage stopped, Stella looked at Carolyn expectantly, tongue hanging out from a wide dog-smile. "With any luck, you'll be going home with Coby soon," Carolyn told her, "and you won't have to spend all your time in a crate anymore."

The clinic door rattled and scraped. Footsteps followed by thumps sounded in the waiting area. Teena's entry routine seldom varied. Plop down purse and satchel. Turn on computer. Turn off answering machine. Carolyn could almost time it. She glanced at her watch and waited. Sure enough, in less than five minutes, Teena appeared.

Her windswept hair framed her face, currently bare of any makeup. "Morning, Carolyn. What's up?"

"I came in early to check on this one." Carolyn stroked the dog's head. "She seems to be doing well."

"Stella's a great dog. I can't believe how many people give pits a bad rap, painting them into demons from hell or something."

Carolyn remembered what she'd heard from one of her instructors. "Don't call them pit bulls. Call them terriers. It sounds a lot nicer."

"Ha! I've met plenty of terriers who are terrors. But nice or not, if you ask me, it's people who create the problems by doing whatever it takes to make their dogs look tough and act mean."

"Socialization and training." Carolyn picked up a stack of folders for the day's appointments. "We'll add those to the list of things we need to teach people." She took the folders to her office and settled in front of her computer. Scrolling down a long list of emails, she found one from Jeanne Nevins.

The clinic's first report to the city is due April 30. Let me know when we can meet and discuss.

If only Carolyn had better news to report. It had been more than a month since the clinic opened, and she'd only done five neuter surgeries—counting the one she'd be doing on Stella. She could already picture the quiet glance of disappointment that would take up residence on Jeanne's face when they met.

Teena hollered from the lobby, "Dr. Becker!" Carolyn looked up, hoping no clients were waiting. Shouts from one room to the other wasn't the image she had envisioned for the clinic. She got up and walked to her office door. "What is it, Teena?"

"The printer man's here with information on the machine." Teena sat at her desk, keeping her eyes fixed on a compact mirror while she swept mascara on her eyelashes.

A slender man waited in front of the counter. He had light auburn hair styled into an artfully messy look, reminding Carolyn of a cover model on *GQ*. Mr. Fashion Plate thumbed through a stack of pamphlets on the counter. When he looked up and noticed Carolyn, the dimples on his cheeks deepened. Extending his hand to take hers, he said, "Dr. Carolyn Becker? I'm Jonathan Locke from Realistic Electronics. I understand you need a printer."

"Yes, we do." She shook his hand. "We're looking for something good and reliable, but it has to fit a tight budget. Can you help?"

"Let me think." Jonathan opened his briefcase and shuffled through papers. "Here we are. Based on the specs Ms. Jacobs sent me, I believe this one would suit your needs. It's a top-notch laser printer, but you can also scan documents and make either black and white or color copies with it."

"I see." One printer didn't look any different from another one to her, but she studied the picture and tried to look savvy. "How much is it?"

Jonathan pulled out a colorful slick pamphlet. "This one is our best model. It'll handle your workload and environment without a problem. We also offer toner, ink cartridges, and a maintenance contract to keep it in good enough shape to last for years." He wrote a figure on the paper and handed it to her.

Her eyes widened when she saw the number. Maybe she hadn't been clear enough. "We can't afford that. What about a cheaper model? A lot cheaper," she said, adding the last for emphasis.

"A cheaper model wouldn't be a good idea. In surroundings like this, I'm afraid it wouldn't last you but a year or two." He narrowed his eyes and watched her a moment before snapping his fingers. "Wait a minute. I've got an idea. Since you're affiliated with a nonprofit, I can reduce the cost by half and write it off as a donation. How does that sound?"

It sounded fabulous to her. "Is that possible?"

"My father started this company, and I own it now. It's more than possible. Give me a minute to put together the paperwork."

Jonathan filled in numbers on a one-page proposal before signing the document with a flourish. He handed the paper to Carolyn for her signature. "A copy for you and one for me. We'll do delivery and setup tomorrow. And," he said, pronouncing each word slow as a sacrament, "as part of my donation, I'll personally come by at least once a month to service the machine for you. Animal hair is notorious for clogging office equipment, you know."

The unexpected gift brought a delighted smile to her face. "That would be wonderful. I don't know how to thank you."

A woman carried in a whimpering puppy as Jonathan handed Carolyn a manila envelope of information. "Shall we go over the features? Then I can answer your questions."

She gestured toward the woman. "I'm sorry, but I have a patient waiting."

"Certainly. I know you're busy. We'll discuss it tomorrow when the machine is delivered." Jonathan took her hand and held on longer than necessary. "You asked how you can thank me. I'd love to take you and your husband to dinner tonight so I can hear more about the work my company's donation is supporting."

"I'm not married," Carolyn blurted. Then she wanted to smack her own forehead at divulging more than Jonathan needed to know.

His dimples carved deeper. "Then can I take you to dinner? I'm fascinated by what you're doing."

She hoped he was referring to her work. Dinner with Jonathan Locke felt uncomfortably date-like, yet he'd just given the clinic a very nice donation. Refusing him might be considered ungrateful—or even insulting. What if he withdrew his support? "How nice of you to offer. I'd love to have dinner with you and talk about the clinic."

"Great! And call me Jonathan, please. I'll pick you up at seven thirty. What's your address?"

A sliver of her mother's unending safety lectures lightning flashed through Carolyn's mind. "How about we meet at Stephano's Place at seven thirty?"

"Sure. I'll see you then—Carolyn."

She clutched the packet to herself and watched him walk away. Carolyn hadn't been to dinner with a man since Clay, and even though this wouldn't be an official date, she hovered between aggravation and an odd feeling of gratitude. She'd just met a nice man who had not only stepped up to be her benefactor but also seemed interested in friendship.

The waiting woman's puppy yipped, and she clutched at the squirming bundle of brown fur. "Do you know how long until someone sees my dog?"

"I'll be right with you," Carolyn assured her client, preparing for what she knew would be another day that likely wouldn't allow time for lunch.

She wasn't wrong.

Later in the afternoon, Carolyn looked up from her paperwork when Coby rushed through the clinic door, his open jacket flapping. She glanced at her watch. Three on the dot.

"My mom says it's okay for me to come here as long as nobody calls to bug her about it. She gets pissed easy. You know what I'm sayin'?"

"Sure, I guess so. I'm glad, Coby. And what did she say when you asked about Stella?"

"It, uh, isn't smart to ask favors when she's on the phone screaming about why the power got turned off."

"Oh, dear. Well, why don't you take Stella outside for a walk? But go slow. She's still healing."

Coby took the leash Carolyn offered him. "Cool."

She heard a tail thumping wildly from the recovery area. Stella had undoubtedly heard Coby. It would be good for the two of them to have a little time together before Teena took charge and put the boy to work. The look on his face before he rushed to the kennel told her everything. He obviously came from difficult circumstances, but anyone could see how much he loved that dog.

After an hour tapping on her keyboard, Carolyn looked up to see Coby swish a mop across the floor. Teena's no-nonsense supervision kept him busy, and to her relief, he worked hard without argument, even during Teena's lengthy instruction on the proper way to disinfect. What she said had made it difficult for Carolyn to keep a straight face.

"Anytime you mop in here, you need to use bleach and water. Listen to me, mister—bleach and water. If you don't, germs will grow faster than weeds in the cracks of concrete."

Teena had a way with words and always found an— interesting way of getting her point across. Carolyn smothered another urge to smile and went back to her report.

Not much later, her assistant appeared. "We're finished for the day. I set the answering machine, and I've got everything back where it needs to go. Since you have your little helper here, do you mind if I leave? Believe it or not, I've got another date."

"No problem." She couldn't resist asking. "Are you seeing somebody special tonight?"

"Time will tell. Right now, I'd rate him as a few steps above okay. I might even think about keeping him around if he ever stops making me pay for our meals."

Carolyn raised her brows. "He does? Maybe you should forget to bring your wallet."

"And get sent to the kitchen to wash a bunch of dirty dishes?" Teena's shoulders vibrated in an exaggerated shudder. "No, thanks."

Finished at last. Carolyn stretched a crick from her neck and then shut down the computer. A bucket rattled, and Coby tromped into her office peeling off a pair of rubber gloves.

"I'm finished mopping. Miz Jacobs had me clean the tables and the counter. Anything else I gotta do?"

"No, I think that's all. Thank you, Coby. You did a really great job today."

He gave Carolyn a shy, pleased look, making her wonder how many compliments he got.

"Hold on a minute. Now that I think about it, there is something else. Would you mind taking Stella out before you go?"

The request lit his face. "Sure."

If ever a boy needed a dog, it was Coby. Carolyn wondered whether she should call his mother to let her know just how important Stella was to her son. She reached for the phone, then realized she didn't have the number. Maybe it would be better if she waited. After all, it wasn't her business to interfere in their private affairs, and there really wasn't any need to rush things. Stella could use more time for healing, and she still needed her spay surgery too. As a matter of principle, Carolyn had no intention of letting the pup leave without it.

Stella's toenails clicked across the floor, signaling her return from the end-of-day walk. The door on her kennel clanged. Then someone sprinted through the lobby. Carolyn called out, "Coby, let's take a few minutes to talk about Stella tomorrow."

The front door scraped and banged shut. She wasn't sure whether he heard what she said or not.

Chapter Six

Carolyn examined a cream-colored silk blouse from her closet, puckered her mouth, and tossed it on top of the pile she'd already thrown on the bed. She hadn't given so much thought about what to wear since the party when she and Clay announced their engagement. The reminder made her wonder for the millionth time what had possessed her to accept Jonathan's invitation in the first place. She thought longingly of a good soak in a warm bath with a glass of white Zinfandel in her hand. Maybe she could tell Jonathan a long day at the clinic had completely wiped her out. It wouldn't even be a lie. Her spirits rose for a moment.

You don't have his phone number.

The totally annoying whisper of logic sealed her fate for the evening. If she didn't show up, who knew what Jonathan might think? He might decide to withdraw his generous gift. Not exactly news Jeanne would be happy to hear, since Carolyn had already sent an email to announce her first small success.

Oh, knock it off, Carolyn. This is a business dinner. Don't make such a big deal of it.

The grounding notion provided enough reassurance for Carolyn to choose her black wool slacks, a white silk blouse, and comfortable flats, nixing the idea of high heels—in case heels caused Jonathan to sprout non-business ideas. She brushed her blonde hair until it crackled and put on a headband to keep the loose strands away from her face. Then she strapped on the leather-banded watch she used for work, a much more casual way to check the time than constantly inspecting a cell phone.

Cell phone! The thought gave her a brilliant idea. She called Teena, who answered on the third ring, her voice thick with sleep. "Hello?"

"How'd your date go?" Carolyn asked her.

"I'm at home in my flannel pjs if that tells you anything."

"Ouch. I'm sorry it didn't work out." Carolyn paused to brush a dog hair off her slacks. "Could you do me a favor? Would you call my cell around nine o'clock?"

"Why? I don't work after six."

"I know, I know. But this isn't for work. It's a favor for—your friend. Will you do it?"

Teena exhaled a loud breath into the phone. "Not expecting a night of magic with the printer man, huh? You'll have to fill me in tomorrow."

"Sure. If there are any juicy details to report, I'll save them all for you." Carolyn ended the call, feeling a little smug she'd arranged a way to escape the restaurant gracefully. Being prepared was something she'd excelled at in vet school.

A ten-minute cab ride to Stephano's Place left no time for angst. She paid the driver, squared her shoulders, and entered the crowded restaurant lobby. It appeared to be a popular destination. Tables were full, and the sound of silverware as it scraped across plates accompanied snatches of conversation drifting through the room. Carolyn looked around, trying to spot Jonathan, until the hostess asked for her name. Then the woman pointed to a table near a spacious window where he sat, cell phone to his ear. He'd dressed just as Clay would have done, in dark slacks and an expensive-looking gray wool sweater. The sight pricked her heart with a tiny pang.

As soon as she made her way to the table, he put down the phone and stood to pull out a chair. "You're the best-looking thing I've seen all day."

She laughed off the compliment. "Considering you spend most of your time with office equipment, there isn't much competition."

"Touché," he replied. "So how did your day go?"

"Busy, as always. I can't tell you how much we're looking forward to getting the new printer. The old one jammed with paper and when Teena tried to fix it some plastic piece broke off. She's got a tall stack of documents waiting."

Jonathan put his hand over hers. "Your wait is nearly over. I'll be there first thing in the morning to help set up and make sure you're happy with everything."

Carolyn swiftly withdrew her hand to reach for the menu, keeping her eyes focused on its pages. "Tell me, have you eaten here before? Do you know what their specialty is?"

"I don't know how anyone can come to Stephano's Place and not order their seafood pasta."

She closed her menu. "You're the expert. A salad and some pasta sound perfect to me."

Jonathan nodded in a pleased way and placed their order with a dark-haired waitress who wore the exaggerated smile of an employee in training. Carolyn took a sip of water and considered the best way to be gracious but businesslike.

When the waitress left, she put down her glass. "I spoke with the Humane Society's director today, and on her behalf, I want you to know how grateful we are for your generosity. Our development director will mail you a receipt for tax purposes." She met his eyes levelly. "I appreciate you inviting me to dinner, but it really wasn't necessary."

Her pronouncement sounded prim and overly formal, even to herself.

The tips of Jonathan's ears turned pink. "I'd really like to find out more about the clinic. You're a nice woman, Carolyn, and you're doing good work. I'd like for us to be friends."

He sounded awfully sincere. Flustered, she dropped her gaze to the tabletop. "I'm sorry if I sounded rude. My nerves are wound a little tight today. We're falling short of the numbers we need for the city to let us keep the clinic open. Clients are a lot more resistant to the idea of neutering their pets than I thought they'd be."

"That's a shame. So what are you going to do about it?"

"Keep on as I have been, I guess, by trying to educate people. To keep our grant funding, we have to perform a certain number of spays and neuters. We're bringing in new clients for routine work, but for surgeries, they seem a bit…reluctant."

"I read your pamphlet, and what it says makes sense to me. Surely the powers that be understand it takes a while to push through a new idea."

Rio's blunt remarks returned to Carolyn's mind. "Actually, I'm trying not to push. Truth is, convincing people is going to take more time than I expected."

He pushed his lips together a moment before speaking. "Well, when I have a problem, it helps to brainstorm. Maybe we can come up with some ideas." He put his paper napkin on the table. "Do you have a pen?"

Carolyn delivered a pen and leaned forward while they batted around potential ideas which Jonathan scribbled on the napkin. In school, brainstorming had always energized her. She almost felt like she was working out problems again with the help of her old study group, until Jonathan's hand brushed against her arm as he emphasized a point. His touch felt decidedly un-businesslike, so she scooted a little farther away from him. He didn't appear to get the message and only stretched his arm farther. She couldn't decide if he was coming on to her or completely unaware of her discomfort. *Nuh-uh. Nobody could be that unaware.* The voice of reason made her think of how Clay had behaved the last time they were together. The next thing she knew, her stomach cramped with anxiety.

By the time their waitress returned with two steaming bowls of pasta, heat burned her neck and face. The noodles, shrimp, and scallops were covered in a mix of butter and heavy cream. She stared into the bowl and gulped, figuring it might be wise to excuse herself for a discreet visit to the bathroom.

Just as she opened her mouth to speak, her phone rang from where she'd shoved it into her purse, loud enough to turn heads. She opened her bag and scrabbled past a wallet, a mirror, three bandages, one key chain, and a tin filled with mints before she found it. "Excuse me a moment, Jonathan. Hello?"

Teena's voice sounded muffled. "Here's your nine o'clock escape call, Dr. Becker."

"Oh, dear," Carolyn said. "Yes, I'll be there right away."

"Coward." Teena hung up.

Jonathan cocked his head to look at her. "Is something wrong?"

"It's an emergency call. I need to get to the clinic right away. I don't want to bore you with the details, but I'd better run. I'm so sorry."

"But you didn't eat a bite." Disapproval weighted each word.

"I know, but I need to go now."

He started to rise from his chair. "Can I at least drive you there?"

"Oh, no." Her voice squeaked, and she coughed. "I mean, please go ahead and enjoy your dinner." She jumped up, keeping herself two arms' lengths away from Jonathan. Better to play it safe.

"Well, okay. I'll see you tomorrow when we bring the printer. Maybe there's another evening we can get together," Jonathan said. "I want to help you if I can."

She managed a weak smile and grabbed her jacket. "Thanks. I'm not sure when I'll be free to meet though. Maybe when things slow down a bit."

With her purse tucked under her arm, she dashed toward the door as though the room had caught fire. Discussing the clinic had been sort of nice, but the rest? It felt too much like a date to suit her, even if she hadn't worn heels. A quick glance back showcased Jonathan waving his arm for the waitress. From a distance, he looked benign and more than a little embarrassed. *Maybe Teena had it right. I am a coward.*

Carolyn's belly made an odd gurgling sound and she hurried out the door to fill her lungs with sweet night air. Her stomach settled at once. Thank goodness. It wouldn't look good to have someone think she'd guzzled a cheap bottle of wine. She scanned dozens of cars motoring down the road, eager to reach home and examine the evening's events. Of course, there wasn't a single cab among them. Go figure. Usually they were everywhere. She dug out her cell and called the cab company.

Low-lying clouds had covered the stars, deepening the dark of evening. Her peripheral vision caught somebody moving across the street, and she spun around to look. A man in a leather jacket approached the warm glow of a streetlamp near an apartment building. He stared at her in a deliberate fashion and lifted his hand to his forehead in a mock salute. Then he sauntered away, heading for the apartment's entrance.

She squinted hard, trying to see better. Definitely Rio Medina. Could he be following her? The creepy thought made small hairs on her arms rise. And if he was, why?

Chapter Seven

Morning brought Jonathan to the clinic not long after Carolyn arrived. He pushed the door and then held it open for a delivery man with a long mustache who carried the enormous box as easily as if it had been filled with air. Carolyn pointed at a spot she'd cleared on the counter for the printer, and he hoisted it into place.

"Good morning, Carolyn," Jonathan said. "Did you know your door sticks?"

Only since day one. "Yes. I've been trying to get it taken care of since we opened. I guess we're low on the city's priority list."

"After Ted gets the printer set up and running, I'll have him look at it. He's a master at fixing things."

"Really?" Her voice lifted at the idea of any kind of help she could get. "I'd sure appreciate it. If he can tell me exactly what needs to be done, maybe the city will send someone to take care of it." *Sure they will.* "Or maybe I'll just hire a handyman myself."

"By the way…" Jonathan had something in his hand. "Here's your pen and our notes from last night. You ran off so fast, you forgot them."

She took the items he gave her. "How sweet of you. Thanks."

"Did you get your emergency taken care of?"

"Emergency?" Carolyn felt heat bloom on her cheeks. She'd never been great at fibbing. "Oh, yes. Everything's fine now."

Jonathan nodded—did she detect a note of disbelief in his face?—and turned to help Ted unbox the copier. The two men spent more than an hour fiddling with connections and programming settings. When the machine passed all their tests and printed clean copies with no issues, Jonathan opened the operation manual and called to Carolyn and Teena. "Ladies, let me go over this with you."

While Jonathan talked about the not-so-fascinating topic of a new printer's capabilities, Ted turned his attention to the front door. By the time Carolyn understood how to use digital buttons and program different settings, Ted joined them to announce, "Your door isn't sticking anymore. All I needed to do was adjust and tighten the hinges."

"Are you kidding me?" The long-awaited fix made her happier than an early Christmas gift. "Thank you so much. Let me pay you for your time."

Jonathan held up his hand. "Unnecessary. Let's just call it part of our services. Ted, you go on to your next delivery. I'll finish up here."

Carolyn looked at Jonathan, and guilt shadowed her words. "You must think I'm a magnet for problems." She extended her hand and he took it. To her surprise, she felt no urge to pull away.

He grinned. "I'm leaving this packet for you along with my personal cell number. Call me if you have any problems. And as soon as you're ready to try another dinner, let me know." Jonathan released her hand and glanced toward his knees. A sheen of light-colored animal hair covered the front of his expensive-looking dark slacks. He wrinkled his nose and slapped at his pant legs.

"I'm sorry, Jonathan. It's an occupational hazard wherever there are animals."

Most of the hair remained stuck to him as though magnetized. "I think these pants will need the dry cleaner." He sighed and headed toward the door in a hurry. "Don't forget to give me a call, Carolyn."

Teena, who sat at her desk unabashedly watching, broke the silence. "My, my. A nice new printer and a door that doesn't stick anymore. What other magic tricks are you going to pull off today?"

"It feels good, doesn't it? Maybe things are finally starting to fall into place." She rested her hand on Teena's shoulder. "I have the strongest feeling something else amazing is going to happen."

"The logical Dr. Becker has a feeling about something other than notes and graphs? Well, I hope you're right."

And as it turned out, she was. By closing time, Carolyn had convinced three clients to schedule surgeries, and she couldn't stop grinning. They were making headway. She

silently thanked whatever guardian angel had lent a hand—
and none too soon either, with the clinic's first month of
operating stats due in less than a week.

As Coby moved his mop across the floor, water
splashed from the bucket. The boy wasn't much of a talker,
but he'd proven to be a hard worker. She hated to think
about the time when he'd finish his obligation. With only
Teena and herself to manage, there were usually more tasks
than hands to do them. Coby had been a godsend, and
better yet, he seemed to enjoy being with them, even asking
a few eager questions about animal care.

When she noticed how quickly he consumed the apples
and cheese sticks she kept in the staff room's tiny
refrigerator, she kept it bursting with snacks she knew he
liked. Carolyn hadn't forgotten how much other veterinar-
ians had once helped and encouraged her. Even though she
wasn't a seasoned practitioner, taking on the role of a
mentor to someone else felt delightful, a paying-it-forward
kind of thing. Coby had enough drive and potential to
succeed if he'd stick around long enough to benefit from
the experience. It reminded her of a question.

"Coby, have you talked to your mom about Stella yet?"

"Yeah. We talked about her." He kept his eyes on the
mop's progress.

"What did she say?"

He didn't look up. "She's thinking on it."

She waited for him to say more, but all he did was move
the mop around. "Do you want me to call her? Then I can
let her know how much we appreciate your help at the
clinic."

Coby stopped to scratch his cheek, indecision flitting across his face. Carolyn offered him paper and a pen and waited. Did he trust her enough? When he nodded and bent to scrawl a name and number, she wanted to yell out loud. Victory!

"My mom just got her phone turned back on. She'd probably like to hear something good about me for a change. Five'll get you ten she won't believe it though."

"Oh, Coby. I know she will."

"Whatever." He avoided her gaze. "I have to go home now. See you tomorrow."

She bid him goodbye, wondering why he'd make such a remark. Typical teenage angst, she supposed. Carolyn couldn't imagine any mother would be so negative about her child. Her own mother had given counsel on a daily basis in a cool and modulated fashion—she didn't approve of shouting—for as long as Carolyn could remember. But of all her meddlesome observations, Mother never made her feel inferior. Or her sister, Kat, either. Love wasn't in question when it came to her mother's feelings, despite her suffocating ways of showing it.

Carolyn looked at the paper with Mrs. Jefferson's number. It couldn't hurt to nudge things along. As she picked up her phone, the front door rattled, so she shoved the paper in her pocket. With Teena hard at work in the recovery room, it must be a client. Carolyn rose from her seat and a second later, Rio barreled into her office—with no invitation.

"Hello, Dr. Becker." The words were polite, but his inflection taunted her.

Carolyn's hackles rose immediately. She had a few things she intended to tell Rio Medina, and it would take a monumental effort to keep her voice even. "Pardon me," she said, "but I have a question for you. Is there some reason that no matter where I go, I see you on the street staring at me? Why are you always—standing around?"

Rio folded his arms across his chest. "Do you own the public streets?"

"You know I don't, but I feel like you're following me. Watching me. I don't think it's a coincidence."

"Dr. Becker, I can safely say following you is not the focus of my existence. I've got other things to take care of, and none of them involve you."

"Well, seeing you everywhere is creeping me out. I want you to stay away from me and the clinic unless you have something important to say."

Rio came closer. Despite her instinct to back away, she stood her ground and looked up at him, exuding—she hoped—fearlessness. His swarthy face transformed from amusement to a blank mask. He didn't lay a hand on her but stood so close, she could feel the warmth of his body. It made her knees go a little soft.

"Fair enough. As a matter of fact, I do have something important to say." His mask turned to granite. "Stay away from Jonathan Locke."

"What?" At the startling comment, Carolyn's voice squeaked, and her eyes grew wide.

"You heard what I said. He's trouble you don't need."

Nearly speechless at his audacity, she glared at him. "I'll see who I want when I want. My life is none of your business."

"Maybe not, but I'm giving you a friendly warning all the same."

Rio moved a step closer. This time she did back up, until she bumped into her desk. His eyes gleamed with an intensity she couldn't decipher, mouth quirked up on one side. A voice smooth as warm butter said, "You're acting like a scared rabbit. Should I get a chair before you pass out on the floor?"

She sputtered the first thing she could think of. "You don't scare me."

A lightning bolt of laughter illuminated his face. "Not much. If you were shivering any harder, I'd be forced to behave as a man of honor should and give you my jacket." He shook his head, still chuckling, and left her office without a backward glance. Carolyn willed her heart to slow down, feeling as if she'd just run a marathon blindfolded. Why was she so breathless when he hadn't so much as touched her? God help her if he ever did. She took a few moments to try and make sense of what he said. How had he put it?

Stay away from Jonathan.

She fumed anew. No doubt about it. Rio had just issued what amounted to an order with zero explanation. What right did he have to tell her what to do? The more she stewed, the hotter she got until she had to flap the top of her blouse a few times to cool off while she walked to her chair.

The printer packet from Jonathan sat on top of her desk. He'd printed his contact information on the front page in bright blue ink. She grabbed the envelope and pounded the numbers into her phone, then waited until a bored-sounding female electronic voice instructed her to leave a message.

"Jonathan, this is Carolyn Becker. Call me when you can. Let's set up a time to have dinner, and the sooner the better."

The phone went dark, and she smiled with a blaze of triumph. This time she had no intention of seeing Jonathan as a business obligation. He'd be her first official date since Clay.

Take that, Rio!

Chapter Eight

No sooner had Carolyn put down the phone, Teena pounced. "I was going to ask you about Jonathan, but now I think I'd rather talk about him." She gestured toward the door.

"There's nothing I can say about Rio Medina that's fit for anyone to hear. And as for Jonathan, we're going to our rescheduled dinner—no big deal." She took a moment to compose herself. "By the way, I forgot to thank you for bailing me out last night. I wanted to go, and your call gave me the perfect excuse."

"I bailed you out? So you needed a half-baked excuse to leave?"

"I didn't want to seem ungrateful after he helped us with the printer." She shook her head. "Honestly, I don't know what got into me. Now the whole thing seems silly."

"But not as silly as this. Look at you. Rio's here a few minutes, and you're all fired up and ready to go to war. A pretty peculiar reaction to some random guy stopping in."

"Get that look off your face, Teena. With no exception, Rio is the most infuriating person I've ever met. I hope he never sets foot in this clinic again."

"What's that line about some lady who protested too much?" A knowing smirk accompanied Teena's remark.

"It's Shakespeare and totally irrelevant to this situation. Why don't you go on home, Teena? Please?"

"I've got it figured out. You know what your trouble is? You're skittish as a spooked horse whenever you're around a man. They either scare you or piss you off. I know a guy back home hurt you, but when do you plan to move on with your life? Don't you miss having a sexy man in your bed at night?"

"Since I've never had a man in my bed, how can I miss it?" Carolyn closed her eyes a moment in horror.

Oh, Lord, now I've done it.

Both Teena's brows shot up. "You've got to be kidding. Are you telling me you've never slept with a man before? Who were you engaged to anyway, a priest?"

"It's like I already told you. I didn't have time for a social life, not with everything it took to stay on top at school." She realized how fast words were tumbling and counted to ten before she continued. "After Clay and I got engaged, we decided since we'd waited so long already, we might as well wait until our wedding night to make it special. My mother thinks—"

"Lord Almighty, Carolyn. Who cares what your ex said or what your mother thinks? What are you planning to do now? Be the Virgin Veterinarian forever?"

"I don't know what possessed me to discuss something like this with you. I've got too many other things to worry about to rehash old history."

"You've got plenty of problems, for a fact. And it's exactly why you need to do something besides analyze numbers." Teena's hands went to her hips. "Just when are you going to start living?"

Carolyn felt the zing of truth and pressed her lips together. She'd already said way too much, and she didn't need to hand out any more ammunition than she already had—especially to Teena. "I need to get back to work." She tried to stay cool and entered a number in a column of figures on the spreadsheet still open on her computer. From the corner of her eyes, she saw Teena shake her head.

"Girl, it's plain you've got two guys interested in your fishing bait. Maybe you better take a time-out to figure which one to reel in."

"I'm busy, Teena."

"One more news flash and I'll go. In case you haven't figured it out yet, the walls in this clinic are paper-thin. Whatever you say comes through loud and clear. I heard what Rio told you. Sounds like he's warning you away from his competition. Then I heard you call Jonathan just to get even. Maybe you better think about what that means."

Carolyn kept her face averted. No telling what her assistant might read on it. "Good night, Teena. I'll see you in the morning."

To her relief, Teena finally walked away, shaking her head with every step. Carolyn leaned back and considered her assistant's implication. A first date didn't necessarily mean anything more than two people enjoying each other's company. Getting acquainted. Nothing cryptic about that. People did it all the time. The thought improved her mood. She entered a few more figures into the spreadsheet and then laced her fingers behind her neck.

Normally, the predictable behavior of numbers soothed her, but today they skittered around in her brain wilder than a flock of sparrows, defying logic. She gave up and turned off the computer to check on Stella. From her kennel, the dog gazed up with large soulful eyes that hurt Carolyn's heart. "You're tired of being cooped up, aren't you, baby? Soon we'll get your surgery done and then you can go home with Coby—I hope. You know, it might break the boy's spirit for good if his mother doesn't let him keep you." She opened the kennel door to stroke Stella's head.

The dog nuzzled her hand in silent sympathy. Carolyn patted her again before latching the kennel door. Then she reached into her pocket, pulled out Mrs. Jefferson's number, and went to her phone.

A few rings later, she heard a woman answer. "Hello?" The tone seeped annoyance.

"Is this Mrs. Jefferson?"

"Yeeees." She drew out the word as though dreading what might come next.

"I'm Dr. Carolyn Becker. May I talk to you about your son?"

A heavy breath followed. "What's he done now?"

"Coby hasn't done anything wrong. I just wondered whether he's told you about helping at the Almost Home

Animal Clinic."

"He said something about it, but I figured he was just covering up again. Coby's never where he's supposed to be, and he's full of lame excuses."

"He wasn't lying. Coby's been volunteering for us. He left about an hour ago. Isn't he home with you?"

"He's not here, and he skipped school today, too. The principal calls me all the time to complain. What am I supposed to do about it? I'm only his mama, the last person Coby ever listens to."

"Coby's skipping school?"

"Whenever he feels like it."

"But he's here every day by three." Carolyn figured now wasn't the time to discuss the reason Coby spent his time at the clinic. "He does a great job too." She felt compelled to let Mrs. Jefferson know about his success, especially since she seemed so lost in his failures.

"Being around a bunch of dogs won't help his grades any. He's failing three of his classes."

"I'm sorry. I didn't know about any of this. Do you mind if I try talking to him about it tomorrow? Sometimes kids take things better from people other than their parents."

Mrs. Jefferson's voice sharpened with suspicion. "Why are you so interested in what happens to my child? Seems to me a doctor's got more important things to do than deal with a kid like Coby."

"He's smart and a hard worker. What's more, he really cares about animals. I think he'd make a fine veterinarian someday—if he gets this problem with school worked out."

"And an astronaut to the moon too." Mrs. Jefferson's laugh reminded Carolyn of broken glass. "Even if he wants to go to college, who's gonna pay for it? I'm lucky to keep a roof over our heads." She stopped talking, and Carolyn wondered if she'd hung up, until the woman finished her comment. "Talk to him if you want. You sure aren't the first who's tried to change his ways."

"Thank you, Mrs. Jefferson. Believe me, I'll do what I can." *Might as well get it over with.* "I do have one more question. Has Coby mentioned Stella to you?"

"Stella? Who's Stella? Is that some girlfriend of his?"

Yikes. "Never mind. After I talk to Coby tomorrow, I'll call you back. In the meantime, if there's anything I can do to help, please let me know."

She put down the phone and sank into her chair. If Mrs. Jefferson seemed at the end of her rope, how must Coby feel as the recipient of so much hostility? Yet if he wasn't in school and he wasn't at home, what could he be up to? Even from her sheltered perspective, she knew the streets held temptations. She'd been too busy keeping her nose stuck in a book to do anything even remotely outrageous, yet she remembered some of her own friends who lived a privileged life in prestigious neighborhoods. Even they hadn't been immune to making bad choices. Her own sister had pulled enough stunts for their mother to name Kat as the reason she had to color the gray strands cropping up in her blonde hair.

Then there was the clinic. Common sense told her it might be best to relieve Coby of his volunteer duties. With the eye of city government trained on them, the last thing she ought to do was allow a child who skipped school, failed classes, and defied his mother to come in and work. Yet the thought of sending him away made her eyes watery.

People who were planners shouldn't have to deal with problems like this. And they definitely shouldn't have to deal with contrary people who made a point of complicating every scenario. It's a good thing she'd always preferred animals over the unpredictable behavior of human beings. Her skills weren't nearly up to what the job required.

Chapter Nine

Not even the pleasant dinner date she'd had with Jonathan the night before—or Teena's endless questions about it—could distract her from turning the issue of Coby over and over in her mind like a puzzle. Between each appointment, she found herself directing sage comments toward Fred, practicing what she'd say to the boy. Fred offered no advice, but listened without judgment, his button eyes full of understanding. If only Coby would be half as receptive.

The thought of laying out his misdeeds in a row sounded so much like his mother's approach it made her cringe. But how else could she get through to him? The whole mess made her feel more flustered than she had on the day she took her board licensing exam, but with one big difference. She'd prepared for that test. Not so much for this one.

Teena pinched her eyes together as she handed over a file. Despite her questioning look, Carolyn enjoyed a moment of relief at Teena's presence, even if it did feel a tad judgier than Fred's. Anything was better than fretting over how to get through to an alienated teenager.

When late afternoon arrived, Carolyn stood and stretched a kink from her neck. She glanced at her watch. Twenty minutes after three. Still no sign of Coby.

Teena appeared from the kennel, her hair in disarray and a scowl on her face. She held a tray stacked full of utensils. "I have to sterilize these things. The dogs in recovery need to go outside, and the litter boxes stink. Is he coming in to help or not?"

"I don't know. Let's give him another ten minutes. If he isn't here by then, I'll call his mother." She dreaded adding to his mother's list of her son's sins, but apprehension kept her unsettled and restless. He could be at home. Maybe even sick in his bed. But what if something had happened to him?

After three thirty came and went, Carolyn reluctantly picked up her phone. Mrs. Jefferson answered on the first ring. "Hello?"

"This is Carolyn Becker at the clinic. Is Coby home? He hasn't come in yet, and I'm a little concerned. He's never been late before."

"Why does everyone ask me? How should I know what's going on with him? He didn't bother to show up at all last night, and now I've got the school cop coming here to look for him, all full of threats. He says if I don't keep Coby from skipping, I'll end up in court. Somehow whatever he does is my fault." Years of frustration tarred her words. "I want somebody to tell me how to get him to do what he should when he doesn't listen to a thing I say."

Carolyn sensed desperation and a little fear under Mrs. Jefferson's anger. She could hardly blame her. Where in the world could he be?

"I'm so sorry to hear this. Let me try to help. As soon as I'm finished here, I'll look around for him. Maybe he's somewhere near the clinic." She hoped the notion wasn't as lame as it sounded. "Do you have any idea where he might go?"

"Ain't you hearing me? He lies more than he tells the truth. I'm better off when my phone don't work. Every time it rings, somebody's after me. A bill collector, the school, or the police. I want to work, but bosses don't put up with people whose phone rings all the time. Can't pay bills without a job." She paused a long moment, and her voice dipped. "He's done it this time, and he's not gonna get me in hot water over the crap he pulls anymore. I'm about done with it all."

Carolyn had zero experience with children who stayed out all night without permission and squeaked out the only suggestion she could think of. "Maybe you should file a missing person's report."

"I am not calling the cops. My landlord will throw me out if the police keep showing up here. This isn't the first time Coby's been in trouble, you know."

"Well, try not to upset yourself," Carolyn said, knowing the suggestion to be hopeless. "If we're lucky, he'll be home soon."

She put down the phone. Her appointments for the day were finished, but she still needed to work on reports. After typing a few words, she stopped to nibble her thumbnail, nearly sick with nervous dread. Maybe Mrs. Jefferson had planted the seed in her brain, but Coby had been gone too long for anything good to come of it.

Carolyn shut down the computer and grabbed her jacket. She stepped into the recovery room, where Stella, happy as always, thumped her tail. Another dog barked, and a feline patient hissed. "Teena, I have to go. Can you handle closing today? I'll help you catch up with things in the morning."

"I can manage." She squinted at Carolyn. "You better watch yourself. This town isn't a place to play detective."

Those thin walls again. Carolyn nodded at Teena and hurried to the door.

Her gaze swept the area outside. She hadn't the slightest clue which direction to go, and charcoal gray clouds were approaching at a speed that made her wish for an umbrella and her bright yellow rain slicker—even if the ensemble did make her look like a school crossing guard. What made her think she could find one boy in a city filled with so many people? She planted herself in the middle of the sidewalk to think while combing her mind to remember if Coby had ever mentioned anything that could provide a clue. Someone bumped against her, but she didn't budge.

"Well, look who we have here. Did you lose something, Dr. Becker?"

A familiar voice lifted her chin. She twisted around to see Rio, his hands shoved into the pockets of his leather jacket, mouth twitching with the effort to suppress what appeared to be laughter. Her annoyance at seeing him won out over worry, and she spoke more sharply than intended. "Must you make a habit of sneaking up on me?"

She didn't wait for an answer and tromped away, but rather than leaving, Rio fell into an easy stride alongside hers.

"You looked a little flustered, so I'm disregarding your previous ungracious remarks to offer my help. I'm not sure I've ever seen you so agitated, even when you're cornered into the curse of being anywhere near me. Is there something I can do?"

Rio's attempt at banter made her want to tell him exactly what to do and where to go after he did it. But this issue wasn't about her, so she tamped down her ire. "It's Coby. He didn't show up at the clinic. His mother told me he didn't come home last night either. She's really upset. So am I."

All traces of humor disappeared from Rio's face, and he hooked a hand onto her arm to stop her. "Where do you think you're going to find him?"

"I have exactly no idea, but I told his mother I'd try." Carolyn glanced toward an abandoned building farther down the street where a few boys who wore sagging pants and seemed to be around Coby's age sat on the steps. "But I'm not sure where to start."

Rio pulled her around to face him. "I suggest you don't try. It isn't safe to wander around places Coby goes."

She stared into his pale blue eyes, and a tiny flame sparked in the pit of her stomach. "What kind of places are you talking about? Do you know where he is?"

"I have a pretty good idea. If you promise you'll go home and forget about chasing him around town by yourself, I'll do my best to find him."

He regarded her steadily, waiting for an answer. She thought about telling him she could take care of herself, but the cool hand of reason shut her up long enough to think about the stakes. Coby needed help, and Rio knew the streets far better than her.

"Okay." She pulled a business card from her pocket. "Here. Let me give you my cell number."

He smiled and lifted his hand. "Not to worry. I know how to find you. Go on home now before it gets dark."

And just like that, Rio sprinted across the street, nimbly dodging a cab, before he disappeared around the corner of a crumbling brick building. She stared after him, open-mouthed.

He appears and then disappears. I don't know a thing about him, but he seems to know everything about me and everyone else. Who is he, anyway? Batman?

A man walked around her with a grunt of dissatisfaction, forcing Carolyn from her stance. She shook thoughts of Rio from her head, knowing she ought to feel frantic about Coby. Instead, a sense of relief bolstered her flagging spirit. She'd just transferred a complex problem to someone who seemed confident he could get the job done. Instead of meandering around the city on a fool's errand, she could think up options to help the boy once Rio found him. Funny, she didn't doubt for a minute he'd succeed.

Rio's mysterious capabilities prompted a deliciously inappropriate shiver to ripple down her spine. For once, she noted to herself with astonishment, he hadn't caused her blood pressure to rise. In fact, his presence felt surprisingly—not awful. Maybe she was getting immune to him.

She might as well head back to the clinic and occupy herself by helping Teena close. An abrupt gust of wind blew a tendril of hair over her eyes. Smoothing it away, she looked up. The heavy clouds were moving out, and the sky appeared much brighter than it had before.

Chapter Ten

Carolyn perched on the sofa with her bare feet tucked under her and plucked at a loose thread on the upholstery. It had been hours, and still not a word from Rio. Would he call tonight or would he come by the clinic in the morning? She stopped plucking. Surely, he wouldn't be inconsiderate enough to let her dangle. Or would he? Enough second-guessing. She turned on the television to distract herself. A solemn-looking anchorman appeared on the screen. He stared into the camera and gloomily described the day's events with one dreadful story after another. Would the man ever have anything positive to say? He started his next report. No, apparently not. She turned the set off and shuddered. News about the latest shooting didn't do a thing to decrease her panic level.

Her cell jangled like an alarm through the silence. She leaped from the sofa and rushed to pick it up, her heart in her throat. A glance at the name on her caller ID brought a grimace. "Hello, Mother."

"Hello, darling. I've been so worried about you. It's been forever since we last talked. You told me you'd keep in touch."

The low-pitched elegant Jackie Kennedy voice—with studied enunciation—immediately made Carolyn feel six years old. "I'm sorry. I've been tied up with the clinic. How are you and Daddy?"

"Your father is working too hard, as always. I haven't had much free time either, with planning for the Candlelight Ball. Can you get home a day or two early? It would be lovely if we had time to visit before the event."

Holy Shih Tzu! The Candlelight Ball! "To be honest, Mother, I forgot all about it. I've been totally swamped at the clinic." Her mother said nothing, so she cautiously plunged onward. "I'm afraid I can't make it." Carolyn heard a soft exhale and hurried to explain. "There's too much happening now. I can't possibly get away."

"As chair of the ball, I had hoped to have all my family present to support me."

Carolyn took an instant detour to Guilt City. She silently counted to five before she spoke. "I haven't missed once since you took over as chair. You have Daddy and Kat. Aren't they enough?"

"Kathryn says she's singing in some little coffee shop that evening, but if you're here, I know she'll go with us. She misses you." Mother cleared her throat. "Daddy and I do too. I must say, all of this isn't like you, darling. Throwing away a good job. Moving all the way across the state from your family. I don't understand. You've always been the sensible one."

"We've already been over this. I had to make choices that were right for me."

"What happened is over and finished. You need to stop thinking about it so much and not allow someone else's foolishness to rule your life. Clayton hasn't gone into hiding. Why should you?"

"I'm not hiding and I haven't been thinking much about what happened at all." It surprised her to realize the truth of her words. Then the phone's second line clicked. "I have to take this call. It's important. I'm really sorry about missing the ball, but I promise to come home for Thanksgiving. We can have a long talk then. Goodbye."

Carolyn knew better than to give her mother a chance to hammer holes in her decision. She clicked to access the other line but found only a voicemail. Holding her breath, she listened.

"I wanted to let you know how much I enjoyed your company at dinner last night. I'd like to see you again. Let me know when you're free."

Jonathan. Well, she'd think about him later.

The call from her mother and growing agitation over Rio's failure to keep her posted kept Carolyn on her feet, pacing from one end of the room to the other until she thought she'd lose her mind. He had to know she was worried. Couldn't he at least be obliging enough to give her an update?

After fifteen more minutes of frantic solitude, she gave up and called a cab. As long as she couldn't sit still, she might as well go back to the clinic to finish up a few odds and ends and check on her patients.

It sounded like a far better idea than wearing a path into the floor.

Carolyn opened the door and snapped on the clinic's fluorescent lights. Then she locked the door behind her. One of the dogs barked from the kennel. She heard an anxious whine and a thumping noise. Probably Stella's tail.

"Sssh, guys. It's only me." In the recovery area, she stooped to look at the two dogs who'd been kept overnight for observation. Both were clear-eyed and appeared to be doing well. Stella pressed her nose against the cage wires, begging for attention with a look that tugged Carolyn's heart. She sat on the floor and opened the crate door. Stella moved out to press against her. "You've been locked up too long, haven't you, girl?" She really had to do something about getting the poor dog out of here.

Stella whined again. Carolyn moved her hand from the dog's head down along the soft hair of her back in a rhythmic motion, which seemed to settle them both. No more dirty-dog aroma either, since she'd let Coby give her a bath. She clipped a collar and leash on Stella and led the pup outside. The terrier bounded from place to place, sniffing the ground to investigate what other creatures might have traveled the way before her, filled with the joy of freedom. She didn't bark or growl at anyone they passed, but the few people who walked near them took one look at the leashed dog and hurried to move away. "If they only knew. You're about the sweetest guard dog around."

Carolyn kept moving until the night air made her shiver. At least she felt much calmer than she had before. "Come on. We need to go." Stella turned with her and amiably trotted alongside.

After she checked the dogs one final time, peace settled over the clinic. Carolyn pulled up a report and worked on it until her eyes drooped. When it became pointless to sit any longer, she yawned and shut down her computer. There wasn't anything more she could do tonight. Unless she wanted to wind up asleep on the office floor, she had to get home soon.

A soft knock on the clinic door popped her drooping eyes open wide. Who'd show up at this hour of the night? She thought about ignoring whoever stood there, but with the lights blazing, she couldn't pretend the office was empty. Her heart hammered into high gear, but she straightened her shoulders, keeping her cell clutched in her hand just in case. With fingers poised over the number 9—for 9-1-1—on her phone, she called out, "The clinic is closed. Please come back tomorrow."

A deep masculine voice responded. "I saw the lights on and figured it had to be you, ignoring everything I said about safety. I have somebody with me you need to see."

Carolyn fumbled at the lock and opened the door. Coby stood beside Rio, who kept his eyes on the boy. He put a hand on Coby's back and guided him inside.

"Coby! I've been worried sick about you."

He looked a little resentful but not completely unrepentant. "What's the big deal? I've been with my friends."

Carolyn opened her mouth, then clamped it shut at his terse words. She didn't know much about being a parent, but she'd already been reminded that evening of how it felt to have someone dump a load of guilt on your head. "I only wanted to say—I'm glad you're okay. Did you call your mom? She needs to know you're safe."

"No. Have you talked to her?" If Coby had been a dog, she knew the fur along his back would have risen.

"Umm, we've talked a time or two," she said, dodging the question.

Coby addressed his reply to the pair of dirty red tennis shoes on his feet. "If you talked to her, I guess you already know Stella can't come to our house. Even if she let me have a dog, our place doesn't allow pets. Another stupid rule."

His admission didn't fit with what she'd hoped for, but at least he'd chosen to tell some of the truth. "Coby, you know we have to do something about Stella. She's been here such a long time, and she can't live her life in a cage."

Resentment gone, his gaze lifted to hers, naked with fear. "You can't take her to the pound. I know what happens when dogs go there."

Moisture pooled in his eyes, hardening a lump in Carolyn's throat. Her arms itched to hug him, but she figured a teenaged boy probably wouldn't appreciate the gesture. Out of nowhere, an idea sparked.

"She can't stay here cooped up night and day, but I think I've got an answer. After her surgery, she can come home with me."

Coby's jaw dropped. "What?"

"I'm not taking Stella to the pound. I'm taking her home with me. I'll keep her until we can figure something out."

Joy lit Coby's face, followed swiftly by a shadow. He swiped his shirt sleeve across his nose. "I guess I won't see her no more."

"Not necessarily. If you'll work hard at staying out of trouble, I want you to continue paying off your debt with volunteer work. I'll bring Stella with me to the clinic every day. She'll be our office dog, and you can see her as much as you like."

Coby's face made the overhead lights appear dim. "Sweet!"

"Remember though, this means no skipping school or staying out all night. You've got a great future ahead of you if you don't throw it away."

It took a moment before he nodded.

"Do your best. That's all I'm asking." With the evening's terrors receding, Carolyn's heart swelled. She couldn't help herself, and reached to grab Coby's shoulders, pulling him in for a hug. He held his arms tight to his sides at first but soon relaxed into her embrace. She liked it when he wasn't trying to act like a tough guy. "You don't know how happy Teena will be to have you back. You've been a huge help. We'll see you tomorrow, same time as always. Okay?"

When he didn't answer, Rio nudged him, and Coby said, "Okay. I'll be here."

She'd almost forgotten Rio. He'd been leaning against the door with his arms crossed, a silent observer to the conversation. A corner flick of his mouth evoked a spark of connection before he finally spoke.

"I'm taking him home now, and I'll talk to his mom when we get there. Let's go, pal."

There were many things she could have said, but she finally decided to keep it simple. "Thank you, Rio."

"*De nada*. Which means, my non-bilingual friend, you're welcome."

"I know that much." She lowered her voice to a whisper. "Where did you find him?"

"I'll tell you later. By the way, if it does any good for me to give you advice, don't even think about wandering around tonight alone. It's late. Call a cab and keep the door locked until it gets here."

He turned to leave but she grabbed his arm, warm and solid as steel. "Will you let me fix dinner for you tomorrow? As an apology and a thank you for finding Coby."

"An apology?" He lifted a brow.

"I said things I shouldn't have, and I want you to know I'm sorry."

"That's worth the price of admission any day. I can be at your place by eight o'clock if that works for you."

She nodded, closed the door, and leaned her forehead against it. Making dinner for a friend. Nothing complicated about it—except for the cooking part, that is. Yet she couldn't help wondering, if an evening with Rio meant nothing more, why did the pulse in her neck pound so hard? She considered the issue and then locked the door. It had to be—Coby. Rio obviously had a rapport with the boy. Staying on good terms with Rio could be a major help in figuring out the best way to help a teenaged boy. Tomorrow night she'd ask him for advice.

At once, her chin jerked up and her mouth dropped open. She'd forgotten to give him her address. Carolyn scrambled to open the door, hoping he'd still be outside, when a high-pitched giggle erupted from her. One of the dogs in the back barked at the sound.

Give Rio her address? How ridiculous. She'd bet her last penny he already knew it.

Chapter Eleven

Carolyn walked past rows of salad dressing, trying to decide which one to grab, when her grocery cart banged into another one. "Oh, I'm so sorry," she said with a limp wave. The woman pushing the other cart acknowledged her apology with a dip of her head before squeezing between Carolyn and a mountain of bagged croutons. Grocery shopping reminded her of texting and driving. How in heck could anyone keep their eyes on what they're shopping for while guiding a cart at the same time? And why did stores make the aisles so ridiculously narrow? To make matters worse, her cart wheels kept jamming, which didn't help her ability to steer.

She'd taken off early to shop for food and then get to work on preparing dinner. But faced with the reality of putting a meal together, she wondered if it would be bad form to suggest they find a nice restaurant instead. Cooking had never been one of her talents, and learning how had never entered her radar. She admired people like her mother who could throw together a scrumptious meal for twelve without disturbing a single hair on her neatly coiffed head. Surely it couldn't be difficult to sear a steak, toss a salad, and bake a couple of potatoes. She'd chosen the menu because Teena advised her it would be the perfect meal for a macho—Teena's word—man. Carolyn reached the freezer section and paused, contemplating whether to buy a lemon meringue or key lime pie for dessert.

Her phone rang, and a glance at her caller ID brought a sigh. She put her cell to her ear while juggling the frozen key lime. "Hello, Jonathan. I'm sorry I haven't had a chance to call you back."

"I was beginning to think you were avoiding me. How about having dinner tonight?"

"I'm afraid I already have plans, but thanks for asking."

"What about tomorrow?"

"To be honest, Jonathan, keeping up with everything at work and settling into the apartment doesn't leave much time for a social life." She plopped a pie in her cart. "You understand, don't you?"

"No, I really don't. It's been nice spending time together, and I thought you enjoyed it as much as I did. Have I done something to offend you?" He sounded hurt, dang it.

"Look, I'm at the grocery store right now, and I can't talk. There's just too much going on for distractions."

"Distractions?" The silence that followed spoke volumes. "I see. Well, regardless, I'll be stopping by to check on the printer. I guess you must have had a long day. Maybe we can talk after you've had time to relax."

A refrigerator case filled with what appeared to be identical packages of meat prompted her to end the conversation fast. "Sure, okay. We can talk when you come by the clinic."

She tossed her phone into her bag. The steaks were enormous. Did men usually eat more than one? Better safe than sorry. She tossed three sirloins in her basket and moved to the produce section. There she gathered two potatoes, a head of lettuce, an onion, and a tomato before pushing her cart, which had unjammed but developed a limping wheel, to the checkout line.

Delighted to be finished navigating the rebellious store cart, Carolyn drove home and hauled two bags from her car up the steps to her apartment. Plopping the groceries on the counter, she glanced around the room, trying to see it as a stranger would. Her place looked neat enough, although...She hadn't realized it until now. The apartment looked practically the same as it had when she moved in. She hadn't even hung a picture on a wall. There'd been no need to decorate since she was the only person who ever saw it, yet the open area of the living room and kitchen did look somewhat—clinical.

Well, there wasn't anything she could do about it now. Carolyn preheated the oven and scrubbed the potatoes. Then she tossed the greens together and examined her bowl of salad. The lettuce seemed brown at the edges. Hopefully, a stint in the refrigerator would perk everything up. A loaf of frozen garlic bread sat on the counter, ready to heat. She put the potatoes in the oven and looked at the next item on her list. The stove-top grill. According to

Teena, steaks didn't take long to cook, so there wasn't any need to turn on the contraption until Rio got there—assuming she could figure out how the dratted thing worked.

At least she felt confident about the bottle of white Zin she had on ice. Her favorite brand never disappointed—until a thought occurred to her. What would Rio think? The evening didn't really call for wine. Besides, didn't men usually prefer beer? Or maybe he didn't drink at all and would suspect she had latent alcoholic tendencies. Holy Shih-Tzu, what to do?

Before she could make up her mind, she heard a knock. Carolyn grabbed a paper towel to blot the sheen from her forehead, smoothed her hair, and peered through the security peephole. Rio—right on time. In his usual black leather, he looked attractive and more than a little dangerous. Her heart skipped a beat when she opened the door.

"Come in," she said. "I'll take your jacket, and you can have a seat." She gestured toward the sofa and noticed her palms were damp. She scrubbed them down her pant legs before she took Rio's leather jacket, warm from the heat of his body, and hung it on the back of a chair. Why did she feel flustered when he appeared so calm? It wasn't fair.

"Can I get you something to drink? I have water. Or wine."

Rio chuckled. "How Biblical of you. I'll take the wine, please." He followed her to the refrigerator. "You have a nice apartment."

"Thank you. I'm thrilled with it. One of these days, it'll look more lived in."

She fumbled with the corkscrew, and it dropped to the counter with a bang.

"Here, let me." Rio took the bottle from her and expertly peeled back foil, attached the wine opener, and twisted out the cork, all in less time than it took to tell. Carolyn put two goblets on the counter. Rio filled them and they lifted their glasses. Rio surprised her by clinking his glass against hers. "To a better life for Coby."

"To Coby," she said and studied Rio over the rim of her drink. Her apartment paled into boring vanilla against his—quite robust—presence. This evening he wore the same dark jeans and buttoned-up shirt as was his custom, and she knew the terms Teena would use to describe him. The notion formed a knot between her shoulder blades. She took an extra-large swallow of wine to steady herself and then put her glass down. "How do you like the Zin?"

"I usually prefer a red, but it's not bad."

"Sorry about that. I guess red does go better with steak." Ack! Why hadn't she picked up a bottle of red wine? "The potatoes are probably getting close to ready. At least I think so."

"I'm not in any hurry." Rio glanced around the room. "Where's Stella? I thought you'd have brought her home by now."

"She has her spay surgery in the morning, and she'll come here after I get off work. I needed to set up a few things for her first."

"Stella's a good dog. I'm glad she won't have to be kenneled anymore."

"I hope she does as well at my apartment as she has at the clinic." Carolyn's rigid shoulders loosened at the thought of Stella's move to a more home-like setting. "If we're lucky, maybe Coby's mom will decide to move someplace where he can have a dog. I know he'd love that." She opened the oven door to peer at the potatoes. "By the way, where did you find him last night?"

"Not far from his apartment building. With a gang of kids. He came along without any problem though. He said he left home because he and his mom had another argument."

"I wish I could do more to help him."

"Putting him to work is the best thing you can do. He needs to be busy."

"It seems like he's got so many problems."

Rio put down his glass. "It's the situation and where he lives. Some things can be controlled but others..." He shrugged.

"I hate it that I can't come up with the right answer."

"Don't be so hard on yourself. Believe me, you're doing plenty."

His remark coaxed the hint of a smile from her as she poked the potatoes with a steak knife. "This is all so different from where I grew up."

"St. Louis doesn't seem like a place you'd settle. I'm curious. Why'd you leave the lap of luxury in Kansas City for an area teeming with trouble?"

Carolyn stopped fussing with the potatoes and turned toward him. "Who told you I came from Kansas City?"

"Your assistant is very helpful. When she talks, I listen."

"I should have known," she said ruefully. "The fact is, I had a great reason for coming to St. Louis. I wanted to do something useful. Helping to set up the clinic seemed like a perfect opportunity for me."

"That sounds quite noble, but I suspect you had more concrete reasons than benevolence."

"Wait a minute." She put her hands on her hips like a principal preparing to scold a wayward student. "You seem to know way more about me than I do about you. That's hardly fair."

He picked up his glass and turned it to make the wine swirl. "What would you like to know?"

"Your story." She smiled again. "Everybody has one, you know."

"I suppose that's true, but mine isn't nearly as pretty as yours." His lips tightened like a stretched wire. "My mama raised me by herself after being foolish enough to have an affair with a man she thought loved her. He ran out on us not long after I was born."

"Oh." The smile left her face. "I'm so sorry."

"I'm not. My mama did a damn good job. I'd even call it a *muy bueno* one."

"That's another thing. Where'd you learn to speak Spanish so well?"

"Mama came from Mexico. Can't you tell by looking at me?" He spread his arms and grinned.

"I suspected as much, but your eyes…"

"The only gift my father gave me." His gaze dropped, and he swallowed a deep drink of his wine.

What could she say to that? By the slight hitch of his shoulders, she could tell the abandonment had hurt him, although she didn't notice any bitterness. "It must have been hard for your mother—for both of you."

"More her than me, I think. Like most mothers, she wanted to give her boy whatever she could, so she worked two—sometimes three jobs, while I spent my time trying to prove nobody on the street could beat me in a fair fight." His hand went to his nose. "I've still got the scars to prove it. After she got sick, bringing in the money fell to me."

"Where's your mother now?"

"Dead." His eyes carefully filtered out any emotion. "Not long after I graduated from college. She hung on just long enough to see me get my degree." Rio drained the remainder of his wine.

A glimmer of pain flashed again in the stony exterior of his face and then it was gone. He put down his glass and poured more wine into both goblets.

She moistened her lips, heart squeezing in sympathy. "Do you have any other family around, or someone in your life you care about?"

"No family. I've dated plenty of women, though, if that's what you mean. But in my line of work, I don't want entanglements. A short and sweet fling generally works out best for everyone."

"Oh," she said. She waited for more, but he only stared at his glass as though lost in thought. She hurried to fill the silence. "Where do you work?"

Diverted from his reverie, he looked at her with a smile tight at the corners. "Construction projects here and there. I'm an independent contractor and take care of the headaches no one else wants to deal with. But enough about me. Now that you've heard the short dull version of my life, tell me what else happened with you."

She ached to ask him more questions but, with an effort, restrained herself. "My background is really simple. Just normal average family stuff. What else is there to say about it?"

His blue eyes pierced her. "Let's start with the *real* reason you came to St. Louis."

A flush rose from her neck to her face, and she took another long sip of her drink. Wine on an empty stomach. She could literally feel it spread to her limbs and loosen her tongue. Confession time. Good for the soul, right?

She force-smiled. "It's the perfect cliché. A broken love affair."

He didn't return her smile. "What happened?"

"During the years I spent in vet school, I got serious with a man I'd known for a long time. After we both graduated, we got jobs at the same clinic, and my parents planned a ridiculously grand wedding. A week before the big day, things happened, and we decided to call it all off."

"Things?" He didn't take his eyes off her. "What kind of things?"

"Well, actually, it was one thing." Her mouth felt dry, so she took another drink to bolster her courage. "A week before our wedding, Clay slept with my best friend, Lisa. I walked in on them myself." The scene replayed in her mind. Shock. Anger. Bewilderment. Pain.

If Rio felt any surprise, he didn't show it. "And I suppose he begged your forgiveness?"

Could this man read her mind or what? Even Teena didn't know the whole story, so she couldn't have told him. "Yes. Clay and Lisa both apologized all over themselves and said it was a terrible mistake, that one thing led to another." The usual pinch of pain that came with the memory of Clay's face and Lisa's wide eyes didn't hurt quite as much as it had before.

"That's when you called off the wedding, quit your job, and moved here."

She raised her glass toward him. "Bingo. My parents tried to convince me to forget what happened and give him another chance, but I couldn't even bear to look at his face. All I wanted was to put it all behind me and move on. Our families have always been so entwined, it seemed best to start over someplace new."

He rubbed his chin. "And I'll hazard a guess they gave you a ration of grief over leaving?"

"Oh, yes," Carolyn said. "But it was only the latest thing I'd done to disappoint them. Daddy always felt veterinary school was a waste of time. He thought medical school would be a better investment. More money and prestige in doctoring people, you know."

"And yet, here you are. Any regrets?"

"None at all. Don't get me wrong, making the move was hard. But now I feel needed. Not just another white jacket taking people's money."

Rio threw back his head and laughed. It sounded so full and honest, she hugged her arms across herself to keep from reaching out to touch him.

"I'd say there's a man in Kansas City who needs his head examined. The clinic's lucky to have you. Word on the street is good. I've heard people say—sometimes a little grudgingly—they respect what you're trying to do."

"I hope it means they'll use our services."

"I wouldn't worry too much about that. They'll come. You just have to give it time."

If only we had more time. "That's what Teena keeps saying."

"Not to change the subject, but do you remember when I asked you about bite cases? Have any come in?"

"No. It's mostly been basic exams and immunizations, but we're starting to make a dent scheduling more neuter surgeries—in spite of your warning." She considered his question. "Why are you so interested in bite injuries, anyway?"

"Just wondered if it was a problem. And for the record, I am glad to hear you're having success with surgeries."

His abrupt change in attitude warmed her. "Does this mean you're developing the heart of an animal lover at last?"

Mirth twitched his lips, and it alarmed Carolyn to recognize the tug of irritatingly powerful attraction.

"I enjoy dogs and cats, though I've never owned either. Inner-city apartments don't allow it."

"You mean like Coby's?"

"Exactly. I hate to destroy fairy-tale endings, but I'm betting he'll never be able to take Stella home. You're the dog's best bet for a happy life. If she's turned over to the pound, we both know what will happen."

She knew. "I really didn't plan to have a dog at this point, but I won't send her to the pound. At least my apartment building is pet friendly."

"Why don't you want to keep the dog? Isn't it unheard of for a vet to have no animals?"

"I always had dogs growing up, but during years of school and then starting a career—the timing just hasn't been good. Besides, Coby loves Stella so much."

Rio poured them both a third glass of wine. Carolyn felt a little woozy, but utterly relaxed. She took another swallow. Since wine tended to go straight to her head, she usually kept to a one-glass limit, but tonight, she didn't seem to care. "I guess I ought to put the steaks on. It's probably not good for us to drink without eating."

"A matter of opinion."

"What did you say?"

"Never mind." Rio drained his entire glass and put it down. He moved so close to Carolyn, she had to look up to see his face. It seemed a little blurry.

"A reminder, Dr. Becker. If you run into anything unusual, tell me."

She tried to focus. "You mean at the clinic?"

"I mean anywhere. I've noticed you tend to run hell-bent into situations you don't know anything about. It's a good way to get yourself in a world of trouble."

Carolyn mulled over his comment. "I wouldn't do anything stupid."

"All the same, take care."

He certainly didn't have much confidence in her good sense. It ought to make her furious. Instead, her body tingled. Was it the wine? She wasn't sure.

Rio moved closer. So close, she could feel his warm breath on her face. His expression remained impassive, yet she detected something within the silvery depths of his eyes. His palm cupped her cheek and he said, "Are you sure it's wise to trust me?" She didn't have an answer since blood pounded through her veins in a most disconcerting way. Rio's eyes held hers, and he leaned closer. Her lips parted, and she let her eyelids close against the magnetic attraction of his gaze. Would he kiss her? She waited.

A cell phone shrilled, and her eyes flew open. Rio uttered a soft curse and pulled his phone from his pocket. He glanced at the screen, and his face darkened.

"What is it, Rio?"

"Sorry. This is important. I've got to go."

"But..." She felt disembodied, as though abruptly awakened from a deep sleep, and pointed toward the oven. "What about dinner?"

"We'll have dinner another day, but next time it will be on me."

With one wicked grin, he retrieved his jacket from the chair where it hung. She watched until the door closed behind him, then pondered how to interpret what he said. Dinner? On him? What did he mean by that? A sudden burst of giggles erupted, which quickly turned into hiccups.

She held her breath and counted to twenty. The hiccups disappeared, but a wisp of smoke curled from the oven. Carolyn leaped up and raced for the kitchen.

Chapter Twelve

Carolyn pulled off her surgical cap, tightened her ponytail, and slung her stethoscope around her neck.

One spay and three neuters done.

Morning surgeries finished, all four patients were sleeping off anesthesia, oblivious to the world, snuffling softly in their kennels. She put pen to paper and recorded her surgery notes on each. A glance at the clock on the wall told her she didn't have any time to waste. Her first appointment of the day would arrive any moment.

Teena stomped into the recovery area, hands fisted at her side. "As if we're not busy enough, he's here again. And he wants to talk to you."

"Rio?" Carolyn's pulse picked up speed.

Her assistant's scowl deepened. "No, not Rio. Jonathan."

Carolyn's heart steadied back into its normal rhythm. "Tell him I'm with patients right now."

"I already did. He says he'll wait as long as it takes to see you."

"Perfect. And on a day like today too." She waved the chart she'd been holding. "Send him to my office in about ten minutes."

"Fine. Guess I'll go take Stella out for her potty break while you two talk." Teena grumped and grumbled her way from the room. Carolyn finished her notes on a sweet-looking, orange tabby cat's chart. Then she changed from her scrubs, slathered lotion on hands chapped from scrubbing, and dropped her paperwork on the desk in her office.

She sat down and her feet thanked her. The clinic's workload had picked up substantially with new patients, and as much as the fact pleased her, she found herself with little energy or patience for entertainment. Jonathan apparently hadn't taken the hint when she nixed his invitations with one excuse after another.

He was a persistent man. It didn't surprise her when he showed up again. What she hadn't expected, though, was for Rio to vanish. She hadn't seen or heard from him in two weeks, ever since the evening he left her apartment so abruptly. Maybe he couldn't wait to leave and used the call as an excuse. But who'd use a gimmick like that? Oops.

Carolyn remembered the evening at her apartment, and her chest felt so tight it hurt. How could she have been such an idiot? The thought of what had (almost) happened between them reminded her of how easily Clay and Lisa had betrayed her. Didn't she learn her lesson? Rio even made a point to ask if she should trust him. Good question.

Now it all sparkled clear as a summer sky. He had the power to hurt her all over again—if she let him.

Jonathan strolled into her office with a cheerful "Hello, Carolyn. I thought I'd stop by to see if you've had any problems with the printer."

Carolyn shuffled the stacks of paper on her desk impatiently. "You really ought to ask Teena. She's the one who uses it."

Cold as the cut of a scalpel, she had efficiently wiped away his grin.

He leaned over her desk, his brows knitted together. "Won't you tell me what's wrong? You haven't been yourself at all lately."

"It's been a bad few weeks." The spicy scent of his aftershave wafted toward her, and a twinge of guilt made her say, "I'm sorry. I didn't mean to take it out on you."

"I've got an idea to make you feel better." His face smoothed into a smile. "I want to take you out to dinner and then to the theatre the day after tomorrow if you're free."

A look at his face, alight with eagerness, soothed her battered soul. For the past two weeks, she'd spent her evenings laboring over paperwork while hoping the phone would ring. How ridiculous. Did she really want to become another one of Rio's casual flings?

Jonathan stood before her, his face puckered with anticipation. This was a man who would never do anything to complicate her world. "The theatre? That sounds intriguing. What's the play about?"

"It's the touring company of *Cats*. I figured since it's about, well, cats, you ought to enjoy it. Before the show, I thought we'd have dinner at a restaurant on The Hill that has the best authentic Italian food I've ever tasted."

"Nice." She pushed aside her stack of paper. "I think I deserve one evening to just relax. You may not believe this, but I've never seen *Cats*. It sounds like fun." She jotted on a slip of paper and handed it to him. "Here's my address."

He took the note, and his fingers brushed against hers. "You won't be sorry. I'll pick you up at five o'clock."

Jonathan left her office with a decided bounce to his step, and despite herself, she couldn't help but smile. A night out sounded better by the minute. Of late, most of her outings consisted of walking Stella to the park, waving at people she didn't know, and holding on to the brim of her favorite pink wool hat whenever the wind gusted.

The dog had become a steady and amiable companion. She'd settled easily into her temporary home with only one accident on the door mat and not a single bout of frenzied barking that might send her neighbors complaining to the landlord. She couldn't have picked a better roommate. Carolyn glanced fondly at Stella's empty bed, and opened the file for her first patient of the day.

A bucket rattled in the recovery room, catching Carolyn's attention. A long work day had nearly come to an end. Why not lay the groundwork now? There was no time like the present to launch her—admittedly somewhat vague—plan. She called to him, "Coby?"

He peered through the doorway to her office. "Yeah?"

"Have you finished mopping yet?"

"Yep, it's all done."

"Would you come into my office, please? I need to talk to you for a minute."

"Okay." He sounded much less enthusiastic at the request and stepped in with his hands crammed into his pockets.

She pointed at the chair next to her desk. "Have a seat."

He deposited himself where she indicated and stared at a place over her head where the wall met the ceiling.

"How are things going with school?"

He returned his gaze to meet hers. "I ain't missed school in two weeks."

"And your grades? Are they coming up?"

"I'm working on it." His eyes shifted back up to the wall.

"Look, I'm not trying to pry. I've got a reason for asking."

He looked at her again and scratched the back of his neck. "You don't want me workin' here anymore, do you?"

His words were so quiet, she had to struggle not to leave her chair and comfort him. Instead, she leaned back. "You're wrong, Coby. Having you here has been a bigger help than you can imagine. I've seen how good you are with our patients, and I also know you're smart and a hard worker. As a matter of fact, I think you'd make a fine veterinarian someday."

He slid lower in his chair. "I can't do that. College takes a bunch of money. My mom is always telling me we ain't got enough cash to pay the bills."

"But if your grades are good, there's scholarship money and student loans. Believe me, it's possible, but you need to know there are requirements for anyone who wants to go to veterinary school."

"What kind of requirements?"

A tiny light in his eyes warmed her to the topic. "First, you need decent grades in high school with classes like biology, chemistry, and calculus. Second, after high school you need to get into a good undergraduate program where you can take anatomy and physiology, plus classes in zoology, microbiology, and animal science. Third, you have to get involved in activities where you can demonstrate leadership skills." She watched Coby's eyes glaze as she ticked the items off on her fingers. "Fourth, you'll need hours of volunteer work with an animal shelter or veterinarian. Fifth, letters of recommendation are required. If you're accepted, then you can plan on another four years of classes after you finish your bachelor's degree."

"What?" His eyes resembled an owl's. "How can I ever do all that stuff?"

"The same way I did, Coby. By reaching one goal at a time." She tapped at the pile of papers on her desk to straighten them. "I'll help you track the hours you work at the clinic. There are people I can introduce you to at the school I graduated from. And if all goes well, when the time comes, I'll write a letter of recommendation."

His chin dipped downward. "I don't know."

"I've seen the ability you have working with animals. Remember when I let you observe surgery? You were a champ. I've seen vet students pass out the first time they witness a scalpel cut into flesh." She could almost see the wheels turn in his head.

"I wish I could be a vet someday and help animals like you do. Dogs and cats are cool. I'd rather be around them than people."

Silently, Carolyn agreed with his assessment but said, "If you want it badly enough, you can do it, and I'll help in any way I can. What do you say? Will you shake on it?" She reached toward him and held her hand out until he took it. "Perfect. I know you can do this."

The boy's abashed grin arrowed straight into her heart.

Her spirits considerably higher, Carolyn shot a sneaky thumbs-up toward Fred and then went back to do a final check on her patients. Fading light from the window showcased how much shorter the days were getting. Stella and she would need to get outside earlier in order to take their after-work walks—a necessary thing for any dog with the boundless energy of a young terrier. Their strolls to the park carried another benefit too. It helped her forget silly romantic notions and allowed her to focus her energy on what was important. The one thing which brought her more satisfaction than anything else ever had.

Her career.

Chapter Thirteen

The black sheath dress had clean lines neatly designed to hug the curves of Carolyn's body before falling in a narrow silhouette to her knees. The sales lady had raved a little too much about how nice the dress looked on her, but the tactic worked. Carolyn ignored her budget and spent an outrageous sum on a purchase she might not otherwise have bought.

She studied herself in the mirror from every angle. It was an extravagance, true, but worth it. The new dress fit better than if it had been custom made. She'd clipped her hair to the back with a tortoiseshell comb in favor of the ponytail she usually wore, and a mother-of pearl beaded necklace hung halfway to her waist. Low-heeled pumps completed her chic ensemble. It had been so long since she'd seen herself wearing a dress; even her mirror image looked startled at the metamorphosis. It reminded her of an evening not so long ago when Clay complained over her outfits, which were mostly comprised of slacks or jeans.

"You've got great legs. Why don't you show them off?" he'd asked her.

Well, why not indeed? She applied a rose-colored shade of lipstick and blotted her mouth with a tissue. Stella watched her, patiently waiting for her own favorite event— mealtime.

"How do I look, girl?" She twirled, model-style.

Stella's ears rose, and she tilted her head with an expression that implied *I hope you're saying it's time to eat.*

"You'd tell me exactly what you were thinking if you could, wouldn't you?" Stella's tail brushed the floor. "Okay, let's go get dinner."

The dog's face beamed approval as she padded to the kitchen. Carolyn filled a bowl and placed it on the hardwood near the refrigerator. Stella gobbled like she hadn't seen food in a century, licking the empty bowl with so much vigor, it scooted around the floor. If it weren't for their frequent walks, this dog would need to go on a diet. Or at least not receive as many of the treats she adored so much.

When several raps sounded at the door, Carolyn left Stella to her favorite activity and checked the security peephole. She watched Jonathan straighten the lapels of his sport jacket and then smooth his hair. Stella joined Carolyn, licking her chops to find any remaining crumbs of dinner, her ears perked to attention.

When the door opened, Jonathan gave a low whistle. "Wow. You look like a million bucks."

The whistle prompted Stella to bark, something she'd never done before, and the comment brought a flush to

Carolyn's cheeks. The curse of being fair-skinned. "Quiet, Stella." She covered her self-consciousness with chatter. "Thank you. I'm almost ready. Come in while I grab my sweater."

Jonathan strolled through the front door and looked down at Stella. "Is this the pup Coby brought to you?"

"Yes, that's Stella." She handed her sweater to Jonathan and slipped her arms in the sleeves while he held it for her.

"She seems to be healing up pretty good. Did you ever find out what happened to her?"

"An attack from another dog is all I know."

Jonathan bent and put out his hand to touch her. "Hi there, pooch."

The dog retreated a few steps and the hair between her shoulders ruffled.

"Stella!" Carolyn's voice rose. Stella folded herself to the floor and put her head on her paws at the rebuke.

"Not very friendly, is she?" Jonathan withdrew his hand.

"She's usually quite sweet, but this is the first time anyone's come into the apartment since I brought her here. I'll bet she's feeling a little territorial. Remember, she's never had a place of her own." Carolyn bent to pet Stella's head. "Don't be offended. She's been through a lot. It'll take her some time to get adjusted." Carolyn straightened and brushed a few Stella-hairs off her dress. "Do you have a dog, Jonathan? Maybe she smells other animals on your clothes."

"I don't have any pets, but I do see a lot of dogs when I'm working. It would surprise you to know how many people take their pets to work."

"A great idea, as far as I'm concerned." She smiled. "Let's go."

Carolyn gave Stella a bone to chew on—okay, she'd start limiting treats on another day—and went with Jonathan downstairs to the street. Late afternoon lengthened shadows. It wouldn't be long before the automatically controlled streetlights flared on.

He held the door open for her. "My car's in the lot next door. Maybe you should wait inside the lobby, and I'll pick you up."

She found his consideration oddly endearing. "There's no need for that. It's a nice evening, and I enjoy walking."

The trees near her apartment glowed with beauty. Gold, scarlet, and pumpkin. She glanced across the street at a spectacular sugar maple, when she saw a man step from the parking lot and head toward the curb. He stopped to look in her direction. She pressed her lips tight together and deliberately tucked her hand into the crook of Jonathan's arm. He put his hand over hers, obviously delighted. As they strolled along, she didn't waste a second glance on the man in a leather jacket.

After an extravagant dinner of creamy lobster pasta topped off with a slice of decadent white chocolate cheesecake and a bottle of vintage champagne, Carolyn and Jonathan arrived at the Fox Theatre. The outside seemed rather ordinary, but once she walked through the door, she couldn't stop craning her neck to take it all in. She'd never seen such an opulent place. It had colors of crimson and gold accenting wooden walls carved into intricate gargoyles and lions, all gleaming with the patina of age. As they ambled down the aisle to their plush red velvet seats only five rows from the stage, her gaze bounced from the carvings to an enormous chandelier to colorful glasswork. But when the show began, she forgot everything and lost herself in the costumes, songs, and stories of stray and abandoned cats. During the final tune, she sniffled, and Jonathan handed her a handkerchief to dab her eyes and wipe her nose.

"I don't know how to thank you," she told him on the ride home. "I can't remember when I've had such a wonderful evening. The show was fun and the theatre—it's absolutely fabulous!"

Jonathan grinned. "You bet it is." He drove his sleek, dark Mustang fast around a bend in the road. She had to grab the door's armrest to steady herself. "Trust me, the evening was entirely my pleasure. I enjoy having a beautiful woman on my arm."

He rounded another curve, and the tires squealed. Carolyn kept her death grip on the door while stomping an invisible brake on the passenger-side floorboard, but he didn't slow down. As soon as the car screeched to a stop at her apartment building, she unbuckled her seat belt with a barely suppressed sigh of relief. "Thanks again for everything. It was an amazing night."

Jonathan reached for her arm. "I'd love a cup of coffee before heading home. Do you mind if I come up?"

"Gosh, it's so late. I have early morning surgeries, and I really need to get to bed." She stifled a yawn. "Maybe another time."

His fingers gave her arm a gentle squeeze before he released it. "All right, I understand. I'd sure like to see you again. Would tomorrow be too soon?"

"I'll be at the clinic until after closing tomorrow, and I don't want Stella to have another night alone. Why don't you call me later, and we'll talk about it?"

Jonathan drummed his fingers lightly on the steering wheel for a moment before he nodded in agreement. "All right. I'll call you tomorrow."

"Or maybe the next day," she hinted.

"We'll talk soon. Goodnight, Carolyn."

"Good night. I truly did enjoy the evening."

She got out and pushed the door shut. The Mustang's engine revved, and its tires squealed again as Jonathan sped away. She hoped the neighbors wouldn't gripe.

Once his car disappeared, silence ruled over the evening. It made her think of sitting in the back yard at her parents' house late at night, where crickets chirped and sometimes the hoot of an enormous barn owl could be heard. She took a look up and then down the street. Nothing but parked cars, lights shining from windows, and lonely looking trees. Not even a cat scampered in the darkness, as they'd done in the play, and certainly no one peered at her from the shadows. The area couldn't be any more peaceful.

But she didn't feel as tranquil as her surroundings. Splinters of resentment she'd so far managed to hold in surfaced, until she fairly steamed with aggravation. How could Rio Medina have the gall to vanish without a word for weeks, and then show up again like some weird meddling stalker? If he thought she'd be at his beck and call, he had another thing coming. He could find his flings somewhere else and stop sneaking around to watch her every move. Who did he think he was?

Mood completely ruined, she hoofed it into her apartment and turned on the computer for a web search with the query: Why people spy on other people.

It pulled 55,400,000 results.

Chapter Fourteen

Carolyn rubbed the young Rottweiler's head, and the dog's stub of a tail wagged hard enough to set its entire rump wiggling back and forth.

"Gretchen looks good, Mrs. Perry. All her tests came back normal, and her spay is scheduled for next Wednesday. Remember, no food or drink after midnight the day before surgery."

Mrs. Perry pulled the leash to control her ecstatic dog. "We'll be here."

Carolyn wiggled her fingers in a wave as Mrs. Perry went out the door. Gretchen bounced along at her owner's side, a four-footed atomically powered rubber ball. She scribbled a note in the dog's chart and handed it to Teena. "Are we finished for today?"

"Yes, we are. And a good thing too." Teena tucked the file folder under her arm. "I've got a date tonight, but how I'm gonna thrill him when my feet hurt is anybody's guess."

"Well, I wish you good luck. Why don't you go on home so you have more time to get ready? I'll lock up."

"You aren't going out tonight?"

"Nope. Stella and I are looking forward to a long walk and a nice quiet evening at home."

"Lord. You must be going for sainthood or something. Why don't you call good ole Jonathan instead of making me take messages from him all day long?"

"He only called twice, and I was busy. Shoo! Go on now and have fun. I'll expect a report in the morning."

Teena rolled her eyes, mumbled a few additional pointed remarks on the dismal state of Carolyn's love life, and walked away.

Sheesh. Staying at home didn't sound bad at all, especially since she planned to spend the evening strategizing. Surgery numbers had picked up but not nearly as much as needed. A glance around the kennel proved at least the clinic looked great. Coby had mopped floors earlier, and Teena had everything in its place. No overnight patients to check either. Locking up would be easy, although she could always work on reports…

Her cell rang, and she scurried to her office. She glanced at the caller ID and picked up the phone. "Hello, Mother."

"Darling. I called as soon as I heard the news."

Carolyn's heart dropped at the quiver in her mother's voice. "What news?"

"It's Clayton and Lisa. They ran off to Las Vegas and got married."

"Wait. What? Did you say Clay and Lisa are married?"

"Yes, dear. Can you imagine? Clayton Harper had a wedding in some tawdry little place in Las Vegas. His poor mother is sick over it."

After everything that had happened, this latest bulletin shouldn't come as a surprise, yet her heart still stuttered. "Well, it's apparently what they wanted to do, so be it."

"You mark my words. This 'marriage' won't last." Carolyn could hear the quotation marks in her mother's voice. "Clay was miserable without you. For the longest while we thought he was biding his time until you changed your mind and took him back. I guess he got tired of waiting."

"As he should. It's over between us. If Clay and Lisa want to be together, there's nothing I can do but wish them well."

"When I think of how happy the two of you could have been together. Oh, if only—"

"Mother, please. I have to go now." Carolyn interrupted, in no mood to hear anything more about Clay and Lisa's viva-Las-Vegas wedding. "Thanks for letting me know. Goodbye."

She put down the phone and felt a sting prickle her eyes. Even though she knew she'd done the right thing by leaving, the reminder still smarted. Lisa had once been the person with whom she shared secrets. And Clay—the first man she ever loved. Would it have been better if they spent the rest of their lives in sackcloth and ashes regretting what they'd done to her? Maybe. Was it too much to ask? Evidently so.

Oh, well. She wasn't going to accomplish anything more today. Might as well turn off the computer and go home. "Come on, Stella."

The pup lifted her head with a doggie smile. Carolyn clipped on Stella's leash, gathered her jacket and purse, and reached to turn off the overhead light. Her hand touched the switch, and the front door opened.

Bold as a marauding pirate, Rio walked in as though he had a right to do so.

Stella jumped up to greet him, her tail a dizzying blur of happiness. Rio scratched the dog's ears while Carolyn ordered herself to remain calm.

"Looks like I caught you just in time. Are you free for dinner, or does your new boyfriend already have all your evenings booked?"

The snarky comment stirred her up faster than Jonathan's speeding car. "Boyfriend? I have no idea what you're talking about."

He ignored the jab. "What's Stella doing here? Isn't she staying at your place?"

"She lives with me, but I bring her to the clinic every day." Carolyn paused. Why was she explaining anything to him? "And I don't intend to have dinner with you, now or ever. Stella and I are going home."

Rio's hand vigorously rubbed Stella's neck until the dog collapsed on the floor in a puddle of canine pleasure. As his hand moved, his jacket sleeve exposed his wrist. Fresh bright blood on it caught her eye. She inhaled sharply.

"What happened to you?"

"Just a scratch. I tried to help a friend catch his dog and got nipped in the process."

Something didn't sound right about his explanation. She rushed toward him and pushed up his sleeve. There were puncture wounds on both sides of his wrist. "This is more than a scratch. Did you see a doctor?"

"I washed it off." He shrugged indifferently. "It'll be fine."

"Men are such colossal babies." Without a trace of her usual bedside manner, she ordered, "Come with me and I'll take care of it."

With a bemused look, he followed her into the examining room. She helped him remove his jacket and doused cotton with antiseptic to dab his wounds. He only flinched once before holding his arm rock-steady, even though she knew from experience how much the stuff burned.

"You'll have some bruising, but you don't need any stitches." She applied antibiotic cream liberally and wrapped his wrist with sterile gauze. "Does the dog have all his shots? Are you up to date on your tetanus boosters?"

"The answers to your questions are I think so and yes, in that order." Rio pulled on his jacket.

"The dog that bit you needs to be quarantined."

He shook his head at her prim announcement. "He was healthy enough to bite me with no problem, so I'm not too worried about it. Thanks though. I appreciate your concern."

"It's not concern. It's common sense."

Stella lifted her head with ears pricked up and Carolyn realized how the pitch of her voice had raised. She cleared her throat and tried again. "You really ought to take this more seriously. People die of rabies, you know."

"I'm too thick-skulled to lie down and die. You, *querida*, should know that better than anyone. So how about dinner?"

She gave him as hard a stare as she could muster. "Never mind dinner. Why don't you explain why you were standing across the street from my apartment last night?"

"I was wondering how fast you'd get to that. My plan was to come by and talk to you." His hands went to his pockets. "But Jonathan got there first. How heartwarming to see the two of you becoming so close."

"My friends are none of your business." She sounded like a fishwife. Why couldn't she rein in her temper when dealing with him?

"Didn't I specifically say you should stay away from Jonathan?"

"I'll see who I want to see." She crossed her arms. "Who are you to order me around? I haven't heard a single word from you in weeks."

"Ah. So that's what this is about. It's the nature of my job, Carolyn. When a problem happens, I need to be there and stay for as long as it takes to fix it. I don't have time to make phone calls to soothe an overactive imagination."

"Is that what you call it? Haven't you ever heard of common courtesy?"

"Only most of my life. But that, I'm afraid, would be most uncommon from me."

Carolyn slammed the supplies she'd used to treat his wounds into a drawer. He took her arm and pulled her around to face him. "Look, Carolyn, whether or not you believe me, I *am* sorry. If I'd been able to call you, I would have." The usual baiting quality of his voice was remarkably absent, and the timbre turned her knees to pudding.

She took a deep breath and then exhaled to steady herself. What did she expect? It's not like he owed her anything. "I guess I understand. Things have been hectic for me too."

Without missing a beat, he asked her for the third time. "How about dinner?"

Carolyn answered grudgingly, "Oh, all right," and then hoped she wouldn't be sorry later.

"Good. I wish I could take you farther west. There are some nice places in St. Charles. But since Stella can't come with us, we'll have to pick her up after dinner. It's better we stay close to home base. I happen to know a nice restaurant with decent food."

Carolyn nodded and gave Stella a pat of reassurance, along with a treat from the jar on the counter. She locked the clinic door and followed Rio to his car, a dusty black Jeep Cherokee that had evidently been around for a while. A sizeable dent in the door looked like someone had driven it through a demolition derby. Carolyn looked from the dent to Rio.

"Say what you will, but this old girl always gets me where I need to go."

He opened the door and she climbed inside. "My parents never keep a car more than three years. Daddy says any longer and repairs come too frequently."

"It depends on maintenance, I guess. If you take care of a car, it'll generally last a good long while."

"Similar to a relationship, isn't it?" Horrified, she clamped her mouth shut, wishing she hadn't uttered such a coquettish remark. What would he think?

Rio didn't seem to notice. "I suppose so, if you can compare a relatively predictable car with the completely unreadable factors found in a woman's head."

Enough of that subject. She sought a safer topic. "Were you able to take care of what needed to be done on your job?"

"We had problems at an older building. I finished a few things, but there'll be a lot more to do later."

She adjusted herself in the seat. "Might they call you away again tonight?"

Rio pulled out his phone and pressed the button to turn it off. "No calls tonight. I'm officially off duty."

She felt smugly satisfied and then annoyed with herself for it. This called for another conversation detour. "You'll be glad to know Coby's doing much better in school. He showed me an essay he wrote on veterinary medicine. He did a great job on it."

"You're giving him a dream, motivating him. That's something he doesn't get enough of."

"I've often wondered about his family. His mother seems to be unbelievably angry at him."

"Things are different here, Carolyn. When you're trying to pay bills and keep food on the table, school doesn't always stay at the top of the list."

"Well, I hope he's not getting in any more trouble. I'm afraid if I ask too many questions, he'll get mad and stay away."

Rio chuckled. "I'm sure he could do better, but he's a teenager in a tough town. Small steps are better than none."

"Does he talk to you?"

"Sometimes." Rio lifted his shoulders. "When he's in the mood."

She slanted a glance in his direction. Ruggedly male and decidedly not the type of man she was used to being around, it seemed out of character for him to look out for a misguided young boy. "It's good of you to take an interest in him."

"Coby reminds me a lot of myself at his age—like a lost ball in high weeds. Not a child and not a man. Mad as hell at the world. And all that rage must spill over somewhere. For me, it was on the person I loved most."

"Your mother?"

"Yep. My resentment didn't help her much."

"But all young people test boundaries, don't they? Some mothers are able to tough it out better than others. You can't blame yourself for that."

"Maybe. At least I learned to appreciate her before the end came. I thank the angels on both knees for that." He hesitated a moment as though considering the matter. "Anyway, chalk it up as another life lesson, a reason it's best to keep other people from getting too close. Everybody stays safe, and no one's life gets screwed up."

She'd never heard him speak so openly. "Rio, I know I don't have any right to ask, but I'd take it as a special favor if you'd keep watching out for Coby. And if there's anything you know that would help me understand him better, I'd appreciate you telling me."

Rio stopped the car in a parking space and grinned at her. She'd been so immersed in their conversation, she couldn't believe they'd already arrived. "He's gotten under your skin too, hasn't he, Doc? Well, I aim to please—usually."

He came around to open her door, and they walked side by side toward the restaurant. Through the massive wooden entryway, there were booths lined against crimson-colored walls and lights burning in a soft glow. The hostess pointed at an open booth next to exposed red brick. A candle on the table burned and sputtered, casting shadows on Rio's face that danced with the flame.

A blonde girl who didn't look much older than Coby appeared at the table. Rio didn't even open the menu. "Salad and pizza?"

"Sure." Carolyn felt her stomach drop and tighten. *Probably hunger.*

"So tell me. How did your evening with the ever-eager Jonathan go?"

The remark thinned her lips. She'd nearly put the image of Rio watching them from her mind. "Must you say such things?"

"You sure are a skittish woman. I'm only teasing. I didn't intend to ruffle your feathers."

"What is it with you showing up out of nowhere? It seems like you're always waiting for something—or someone."

"Opportunities happen for those who keep their eyes and ears open." Rio leaned back in his seat. "Which brings me to something else."

She took a sip of water and waited.

"It's about your good friend, Jonathan."

"That's another thing I don't understand. What do you have against him? I know he can be a bit overbearing, but he's harmless, and he's been very nice to me." She hoped he got her implication.

"Just don't let yourself get all muddled up with him."

"Give me one good reason why I need to watch out for Jonathan."

"Hear what I'm saying." He put his hand on hers. "I'm not telling you to watch out for him. I'm telling you to watch out for yourself."

"Cryptic comments with no explanation are great for my peace of mind, you know."

The waitress brought their salads to the table, and Carolyn pulled her hand away from Rio's.

"Your pizza will be ready soon," the girl announced before she hurried away, wiping her hands on a tomato-sauce spattered apron.

"I'm only giving you a heads-up because I feel a little responsible for you."

His comment caused another flip of her stomach. "Why should you feel responsible for me?"

"Just a figure of speech. I'd hate to see you disillusioned again. Now, calm yourself and try this salad. Remember, we still have to pick up Stella."

She picked up her fork, and after one bite, she found the food delicious enough to finish not only her salad but a large slice of pepperoni pizza with a crust so thin it snapped with each bite. Finally, she pushed away her plate.

Rio paid the bill and gave their young waitress a tip that made the girl's eyes go wide with delight.

He led Carolyn outside. The stars had disappeared behind clouds. If not for a street light to guide them, it would have been hard to see the Jeep. Carolyn sank into her seat and buckled the safety belt. Filled with food and a lulling sense of contentment, she put her head back and closed her eyes. Rio didn't speak, and the next thing she knew, the car stopped.

"Time to wake up, Sleeping Beauty."

Her back straightened in a hurry. "I wasn't asleep. Just resting my eyes."

Rio snorted and got out of the car. He walked Carolyn to the clinic door, keeping his hand on her elbow. She fumbled with the key and heard Stella scrabbling across the floor in her eagerness to greet them. "Well, thanks for dinner. Good night."

"Not good night just yet. It's late. Do you have your car?"

"It's in the shop. Maintenance."

"Then I'll drive you home."

"You don't need to do that. I'll call a cab. They only charge a children's fare for a dog, speaking from previous experience."

"No argument. I'm taking you home." His tone didn't invite debate.

At least it would save cab fare. "All right. Thanks."

Rio drove them the few blocks to her apartment. Stella bounded from one window to the other in the back seat. Blows and puffs punctuated by an occasional grunt of joy clearly showed how she felt about watching cars pass by them.

After Rio pulled his Jeep into the parking lot near her building, he twisted to rummage in the back seat. "Just a minute, Stella." He moved his arm and laughed, apparently searching for something despite the slobbery sound of dog kisses. When he finally found what he wanted, he lifted a bag. "I have a bottle of Cabernet from a new winery in Mexico. It's a brand I've grown to like a lot. Interested in trying it?"

This could be dangerous territory. Rio was the most exasperating and unreliable man she'd ever met. He sent her good sense screaming from the room any time he spoke to her. But with his mouth curved up enough to crinkle the corners of his eyes, she heard a treacherous—and rather alluring—voice drift from her own mouth. "Why not?"

Chapter Fifteen

The apartment still smelled vaguely of lemon. Luckily, she'd done an early morning cleanup before work, so thankfully no need to sneak-spray air freshener around the room. Not even a random book or paper could be found lying about. She hated disarray. Only one small bowl loaded with bright red apples sat on the counter, near where her laptop connected to an outlet on the wall.

She handed Rio the opener and watched him twist and pull out the Cabernet's cork. Then he poured the dark rich wine into two glasses she gave him. When they were full, she reached for one, but he held up his hand.

"Wait. Let it breathe for a few minutes first," he said.

Neither of them spoke as the silent room layered itself with ambivalence. It made her jumpy as a nervous cat. "I think I'll turn on some music." *Drat*. Would he take the comment as suggestive? She gave him the side-eye, but his attention remained on the wine.

Carolyn moved away from Rio which made her feel more in charge of the situation. She booted up her computer and selected an album she'd downloaded. After a few adjustments to the volume, Nat King Cole's mellow voice filled the room. One of her favorite songs too—*Unforgettable*.

Stella leaped into a chair with her tooth-pocked bone and contentedly chewed along with the beat. Nothing occupied that dog's attention more thoroughly than food.

Rio handed Carolyn a glass of wine. "You've got good taste in music," he said.

"I must have been born too late. I'm totally out of touch with Teena's music style. It's so *jarring*. Hip-hop sets my teeth on edge."

"That's because hip-hop is meant to energize the soul, not soothe it." A grin flashed briefly across his features. "So give it a try and tell me what you think of the Cab."

She took a mouthful of wine, swallowed, and her throat spasmed into a coughing fit. Once she could breathe again, she choked out, "It's definitely full-bodied." A little like Rio.

Stop it, Carolyn!

"This is a brand that takes some getting used to. It's best to drink it with food."

"I can understand why." She put her glass down. "I'd better stick to my tame little Zin. I have a bottle in the refrigerator already open."

"Let me take care of it for you." He took her goblet to the counter. Rather than pouring her wine into the sink, he lifted it to his mouth and drank every drop before rinsing the glass. He refilled it with Zin.

The intimate act made her cheeks flame. If this kept up, she might set off the sprinkler system. *Think about something else.* "Uh, how's your wrist? I don't see any blood on the bandages, so that's a good sign."

He handed her the Zinfandel. "It's fine." He moved his hand. "I don't feel a thing."

"Liar," she said to him. "Let's sit down." Carolyn kicked off her shoes and moved to the sofa, sinking into its plush softness. Rio sat beside her and swirled the dark wine in his glass a moment before he lifted the goblet in Stella's direction.

"She seems to be doing well."

"Yes, she is. I was worried about how she'd adapt to such a different way of life than what she knew, but I can't complain at all. Coby still hopes his mom will move to another place so he can take her. They're so fond of each other."

"Stella's lucky to have you as her guardian angel. A lot of people won't have anything to do with pits. They claim they're dangerous."

"And I suppose they can be, in the wrong hands." Carolyn emptied her goblet.

Rio lifted a brow and fetched both bottles from the kitchen and set them on the coffee table. He refilled her glass and observed. "You're a vet. I'm sure you know there are some people who use animals for entertainment or profit."

She lifted her glass and examined it, wondering idly why her arms seemed heavy when the rest of her felt so glorious. "What are you saying?"

"Come now, don't tell me you've never heard about dogfighting."

"Well, of course I have. It's a repulsive thing, but the police are cracking down on it."

"They try," Rio said, "but it isn't an easy thing to pin down."

"I know. Dogfights are held out in the middle of nowhere, so others aren't around to catch them."

"I disagree. The city sees its share of dogfights too."

"Oh, I'm sure you're wrong." She gazed at him over her glass. "How could anyone get away with dogfighting in the city? Police officers are everywhere."

Stella left her chair and trotted to Rio. He smoothed his hand across her head. "I can assure you they do. Every single day."

"I've seen no evidence of it." Her chin tilted up with conviction.

"It's not likely you would, unless there's a reason for you to become involved."

"Me involved? That's ridiculous." She dissected his observation. "How do you know all these things about dogfighting?"

"My job takes me many places around town. And across the river too. I hear about it."

"Well, if you learn about people involved in dogfighting, you should report it to the authorities." Her voice sounded stiff and possibly a little preachy. She waited for a zinger from him.

"Thanks for the sound advice. I'll keep it in mind." He chuckled. "You know what? I've noticed something about you. The more we talk, the more your face tenses up. When will you learn to relax? You're wound tighter than any woman I've ever met."

Carolyn regarded him warily but saw only genuine interest. She put her glass to her mouth again. Maybe he was right. Maybe she should loosen up. Downing another glass of wine helped, and she leaned back to enjoy how it made her feel. Warm and nearly carefree. Tension over betrayals, the clinic, and troubled teenagers were no more than wispy summer clouds drifting away. "I admit to being a worrier. So many unexpected things can happen. That's why I like to solve one problem, then move on to the next."

"Even worriers need a break." He examined her face. "And may I add you look great with that splash of wine on your chin."

"A splash of—oh!" Her heavy eyelids flared open. "I'm sorry. Maybe I'm getting a little too relaxed."

Rio touched the tip of his finger to the wine drop. She found she couldn't move and searched her memory. Was wine known to cause paralysis? He moved his finger down to trace the side of her cheek and under her jaw. The scent of wine and outdoors and the antiseptic she'd used on his wounds made the room lean. She closed her eyes but sensed him coming closer.

When she couldn't stand wondering one minute more whether he'd kiss her, Rio brushed his mouth against hers, light as a feather's touch. His cheek, stubbled with five-o'clock shadow, set off an array of fireworks in her chest. He paused a moment, then growled deep in his throat and pulled her hard against him. As though some invisible force had willed it, she lifted her arms and put them around his neck, woozy with wine and emotion, every heartbeat a jolt of sensation throughout her body.

When he finally spoke, his voice sounded unsteady—so unlike him, she opened her eyes to stare.

"Carolyn, we should stop this right now."

"No," she whispered. She hadn't the courage to say aloud what kept running through her mind. Not only did she want him to continue what he'd started, she feared she might die if he didn't.

His lingering glance held a trace of regret. "I'm sorry to admit it, but tonight I'm not gentleman enough to take the high road." He scooped her up as though she weighed no more than a kitten and rose to his feet. Carolyn kept her arms around his neck and rested her head against the strength of his shoulder.

Lost in a sea of sensation—that's how she felt. He carried her into the bedroom where the overhead light still burned.

The better to see you with. Head spinning a little, she wondered what he'd do next. Desire showed so clearly in his eyes, her insides twitched with anticipation. This was it. The Big Moment. Should she make a witty remark? Purr something sexy? What was the etiquette for the first time?

He placed her gently on the bed and then reached for the light switch.

"No," she finally managed to say. "Leave it on."

The glow of a street lamp filtered through the window and glistened off Rio's moist skin. She trailed her fingers down his muscled bicep, but he rolled away from her and off the bed. With his back turned, she had no idea what he was thinking. He'd been gentle and considerate—sweet even. Lovely. That's how she'd describe the experience. If only he'd turn around so she could judge whether his reaction matched hers. For even with a parched throat, her heart leaped and danced in a ridiculous rumba of delight.

Rio pulled on his discarded jeans with tight deliberate motions that pinched her forehead together. If only he'd say something to reassure her he felt as giddy as she did. But when he finally turned around, her heart sank. His jaw was squared hard and a muscle in it twitched as though he meant to measure his words.

Rio's expression made her wish she could grab her own clothes, but they were scattered on the floor like an F4 tornado had torn through the room. Lack of clothing put a person at a certain disadvantage. She gathered her blanket around herself and stared at the sheets, waiting for him to speak. When she noticed a few spots of blood dotting the linens, she pulled the blanket's edge to cover them.

Too quiet. Too quiet! This isn't good. The air in her room all but shimmered with resentment and—accusation? She picked at a fuzz ball on the blanket and tried to figure out a way to gracefully break the silence when Rio's voice sliced through the air like a knife. "Why didn't you tell me?"

Tell him? Tell him what? She replayed what had transpired between them and blushed. "Can you enlighten me? Exactly what was I supposed to tell you?"

"The truth."

His face etched into lines of fury. He so seldom showed emotion, it startled her. "I don't know what you're talking about."

"You know exactly what I mean. You've never been with a man."

Her eyes widened, and she clutched the blanket tighter around herself. A pointless gesture since he'd already had a full view of her body, yet it still made her feel somehow less—well, less naked. "Why on earth should it matter to you whether or not I've been with a man before?"

"For the love of God, Carolyn. Do you think I make a practice of seducing virgins?" He ran his hand through his hair, ruffling it even more than before, and glared at her.

"Seducing virgins? I can't believe you just said that. What century are you from, anyway?"

"Tell me this, Carolyn. How is it possible for any woman in today's world to finish eight years of college and nearly make it to the altar without ever having sexual relations? That's hard to believe."

"Yet, as you discovered, it's the truth. Why are you acting like I've committed a crime?" Her temper erupted at his mindset. "I'm nearly twenty-eight years old. I knew what I was doing."

"Did you? Well, I obviously didn't, which is my point. This is a big deal to me, Carolyn, and something you should have mentioned before we made such a mistake. I was under the impression you were more—experienced."

She hardened her words to ice. "I don't know what you're getting at, but if you're wondering whether I might be sorry about this in the morning, don't worry. That's how I feel right this second. And by the way, how very gallant of you to make sure my first time is so memorable."

His attitude cut her, and she intended to let him know it. But Rio only jerked his arms into the sleeves of his shirt and fastened the buttons, his face a thundercloud.

What a miserable state of affairs.

Tears misted her eyes, but there was no way she'd give him the satisfaction of knowing how horrible he'd made her feel. She stared at the ceiling and blinked her vision clear. Part of her wanted to smack the judgmental look off his face, while the rest of her wished he'd flash his enticing grin and climb back into bed. Such an awkward tangle of emotions. She drew her knees to her chest, tenting the blanket, while she tried to decide what to do next. Could his attitude become any more uncivil?

Apparently so. "I didn't plan on this happening, and I guarantee it wouldn't have if you'd been honest with me."

"Pardon me, but I didn't know you expected a report of my romantic history. Did you plan to paste a label on me? Yes, I think I can see it now. Warning: You are approaching a woman who's never had sex. What am I, some kind of carnival exhibit?" The glow from being with Rio—the feeling of total indulgence—faded into a familiar gut-punch of loss. But if he was looking for an apology over the situation, he'd wait a long time to get it.

"Think, Carolyn. Among other problems with this scenario, I didn't use any—precautions. I don't intend to do to you what my father did to my mother. Do you understand what I'm trying to say?"

She narrowed her eyes at him. "Yes, I catch your drift. How naïve do you think I am? May I remind you I'm a doctor?" *Is he for real?* "Let me assure you, there's no need for you to worry. I've taken birth control pills for years, so it isn't likely you've impregnated me, although what you've done to other women, only you can say. There. Is that enough to relieve your conscience?"

Rio must have sensed the undertone of something other than anger in her words. He sat on the bed with a resigned look on his face. "The last thing I want to do is cause pain for anybody, especially you. You've already had more than your share of grief from a man who was nothing less than a jackass. If my life wasn't already so—problematic—I'd be back in this bed in a heartbeat, just to make sure you don't run away from me like you ran from him."

Carolyn searched his face. Maybe he did care about her. At least a little. But he sure had a funny way of showing it. Uncertainty kept her from admitting the budding—no, blooming—attraction she had for him. Safest to keep the secret locked in her heart. She smoothed a wrinkle on the sheets. "Maybe we both let things get out of hand tonight."

He reached out to stroke her cheek. "Listen to me, Caro. You're a beautiful, passionate woman. You need the type of man who deserves you, not someone like me."

The sweet nickname brought splotches of color to her cheeks. Yet despite the caution sign her mind had erected, she couldn't quite restrain herself from testing the water. She swallowed and then asked the obvious question. "Why not you?"

He stood and walked toward the door. When he turned toward her, something flickered so swiftly on his face she couldn't quite catch it. "I've never done well with things like this. It isn't you, it's me. For many reasons, I can't get tied up with anyone, and I'm leaving because it's the right thing to do. For both of us."

And with that emphatic and unarguable point, he left. She heard the tap of his heels across the living room, then the low whine of contentment Stella made whenever anyone scratched her ears. The front door opened and closed.

Carolyn lay back on the bed and curved her body into a question mark. Her eyes felt scorched, and a tear squeezed out to roll down her face. I'm not upset, she told herself firmly. It's only the aftermath of a long day—plus a gigantic misunderstanding. And let's not forget all the wine. She pressed her eyes shut for a moment to calm herself and then sat up.

That's when she became aware of it. Her body smarted with a distinct twinge here and ouch there in her southernmost region. So this is what it felt like? Between the emotional roller coaster and the physical discomfort, she couldn't figure out what anyone got from making love but misery. And yet...

Distant thunder rumbled, and lightening forked in the sky. Within minutes, raindrops pattered, then drummed down hard against her window. Even though it wasn't open, she could smell the sweet wet scent. She used to love falling asleep during a rainstorm—all cozy and snug under the covers, while the soothing sound splashed from the roof.

But tonight? All she felt was the cold snub of an empty bed.

Chapter Sixteen

The next morning, rain sprinkles still drizzled off and on, which eliminated the idea of walking. Carolyn leashed Stella and called a cab. Determined to focus on practical tasks she knew would help settle her mind, she threw herself into the clinic routine. Affectionate slurps from some of her patients helped, like the rotund cocker spaniel she'd just put on a diet. If the dog knew his future lack of treats and table scraps came at the order of Dr. Becker, things would change fast between them. She'd just finished going over instructions with the dog's owner and sent them on their way when Teena forwarded a call to her office.

She rushed to pick up the phone, and Jonathan's cheery voice inquired, "How about seeing a movie after work?"

His tone untied the knot between her shoulders. Unlike Rio, Jonathan wasn't an enigma at all. Last night she'd spent hours picking apart Rio's remarks, trying to understand what he meant, until she fell asleep on the sofa no wiser than before. At least Jonathan didn't consider her deceitful or a pariah. In fact, his obvious interest soothed the battered state of her self-esteem in a most agreeable way.

"I haven't been to a movie in ages," she told him and glanced toward Stella, who lay on her overstuffed pet bed, snoring blissfully. "I can leave early enough to take the dog home and grab a change of clothes, then finish things up at the clinic. How does that sound?"

"Fantastic. Do you need a ride from your apartment back to the clinic? I can come by and get you and then you won't have to deal with your car."

"Don't bother. My car's been in the shop, but it's ready. I'll get it and take a cab or the MetroLink back to the clinic. You can meet me here around six if that's okay."

"Absolutely. See you then, Carolyn."

Her gloomy state of mine lifted a fraction. Talk about perfect timing. Dwelling on a history of foolish missteps in the romance department wasn't getting her anywhere. Some people simply weren't destined for love. True—the twinges reminded her—there were advantages to a relationship. After all, as much as she loved her career, she had to admit it didn't keep her company at night. A dependable and caring man in her life would be nice. Someone she could talk to about her day or laugh with over dinner. Yes—her cheeks warmed—and even share her bed from time to time. That is if he stayed all night with his arms wrapped around her instead of racing away like he'd seen a hobgoblin.

The front door rattled, pulling her back to the present. Stella leaped from her bed and galloped to greet her best buddy, Coby. Carolyn could see them from her office door, the boy holding Stella's head with both hands and giving the dog's ears a thorough rub. Stella's body wriggled with joy as though it had been weeks since they'd seen each other, rather than hours. Coby's face didn't register a smidgen of sullenness or distrust. He had the same tender expression when he interacted with any of the clinic's patients, whether canine or feline.

He reminds me of myself when I was young.

A wisp of familiarity teased her brain. She thought about it and then remembered Rio saying practically the same thing. Swiftly, she shoved away the bothersome image to concentrate on Coby. "How was school today?"

"Okay," he said, keeping both his hands on Stella's head. He didn't even look up at her. She wondered if something bothered him.

"Are you caught up with your schoolwork? Remember, getting into vet school means you need good grades."

"It's going all right, I guess." Coby seldom elaborated on his activities, and she decided it best not to pursue the matter with more questions. At least not now. "Teena's in back with the new surgery patients. She's got a list a mile long of things for you to do. Get yourself a snack from the fridge first and then give her a hand. I have to run home for a few minutes, but I'll be right back." She picked up her bag.

After Carolyn retrieved her car, dropped off Stella, and returned to the clinic, she hunched over her computer to puzzle out figures on the dreaded statistical reports. Numbers mired her in deeper than the Mississippi. She penned paragraphs of explanations to justify what the clinic had done and what it could still do given enough time. Who knew grants required such a mountainous level of creative writing? When her eyes gritted with the feel of sand, she pressed her fingers on the bridge of her nose and glanced at the clock. Nearly six already?

The clinic door opened and closed with a rattle. Jonathan sauntered through the doorway into her office, dressed to kill in a white polo shirt and khakis with a sharp crease down each pant leg. His appearance made her painfully aware of her own disheveled look—uniform covered with evidence of the day's work, and hair straggling from a ponytail.

"Are you ready, Carolyn?" He sounded a bit incredulous. No wonder.

"Give me a minute. I just need to change and comb my hair."

She rose as Coby came into the office with a bucket and mop. He saw Jonathan and ducked his head to dip the mop and plop it on the floor. She'd never seen him scrub so hard.

Jonathan spoke to the boy in the hearty voice of someone who was trying too hard. "Hello there, young man. Are you doing a good job today?"

"Yeah," Coby replied, speaking to the floor.

"Well, that's just fine. See to it you don't get yourself in any more trouble now, okay? I don't want you to make Dr. Becker unhappy."

Carolyn saw a flush rise on Coby's neck and winced. She wished Jonathan would be more discreet, and apparently so did Coby, as he hurried from the room, bucket sloshing water to the floor with each step.

Jonathan lifted both his hands in an I-told-you-so gesture. "See? You just need to know how to talk to kids."

"I guess so." She dropped her voice to a whisper. "I know you're trying to help, but please be careful what you say to him. I don't want Coby thinking I've broadcasted his troubles to everyone."

"Don't worry about it. I'm sure he'll do the right thing. And if he doesn't, he'll have to pay the consequences."

"Can we discuss this later? I'll be right back." She went to the clinic's closet-sized bathroom to change.

However inelegantly phrased, Jonathan could have a point. Wasn't life basically a menu of choices? Do the right thing and you're rewarded. Do the wrong thing and you're punished. A carrot or a stick. What you chose determined your fate. But, she argued with herself, the problem became more complicated when other factors were added in. Things like unfortunate circumstances and hard-to-resist temptations.

Oh, if only life could be simple!

She tossed her scrubs into the wicker laundry basket and looked at the tiny mirror hanging over the sink. Her face appeared to have aged about a decade from a few short weeks ago. A dab of powder and fresh lip gloss made the necessary repairs in her rather anemic appearance. She released her ponytail, ran a brush through her hair, and gave herself a smile of encouragement.

Situations could change. It happened all the time. People could change too.

The movie, an action epic, featured fast cars and blazing guns. Their seats were next to a speaker turned up so loud, she wondered if her ears would ever stop ringing. Jonathan analyzed each scene for her, excitement edging his voice. Thanks to the booming sound system, she couldn't hear most of what he said. Just as well. Action movies weren't her thing, so she nodded while he spoke as though it all made sense. People near them shot disapproving glances at the running commentary.

Afterward, the much more pleasant restaurant atmosphere improved her outlook. The dining room, high on the forty-second floor of a downtown building, offered a sweeping view of the riverfront where light dappled the water. The restaurant remained pleasingly dim, accented by votives that sent a warm glow flitting from each tabletop. Music played—barely noticeable, thank goodness—in the background. Jonathan ordered them both filets with cognac cream sauce, a sautéed lobster tail, and a salad piled so high with cheese, she could only eat half of it.

The office supply business must be lucrative indeed. Carolyn knew such an evening would stretch her own salary, and the thought prompted her to speak up. "Just for the record, Jonathan, you don't have to wine and dine me this way every time we go out. Simple things and simple places are good too."

Jonathan raised a glass of sparkling champagne. "But you deserve the best, and you'll get nothing less from me."

He took a sip, and Carolyn followed his lead. Unbidden, the idea came to her of how her parents would compare Jonathan's obvious success with the austere life Rio apparently led. She knew who'd come out on top in their eyes.

Jonathan put down his glass and steepled his fingers. "I hate to bring this up, Carolyn, but I had a disturbing conversation with Teena the other day. She mentioned you've spent time with a man named Rio and she made it sound like the two of you are quite an item."

Note to self: Tell Teena it isn't a good idea to broadcast a friend's or coworker's personal information. "Believe me, we're not an item. Any time we do talk, it's about Coby. Rio knows his family."

"I'm sure he does. I've heard of him. He spends a lot of time with the locals. Fits in well too, always skating on the edge of the law."

Curiosity raised her brows. "What's that supposed to mean?"

"Some of my customers talk about him. Doesn't he strike you as kind of shady?"

She opened her mouth to argue on Rio's behalf but stopped herself. The experience she had with him made her wonder if Jonathan might be right. So she said nothing, even though the uncomfortable silence might tell Jonathan more than he needed to know. He looked at her, and his eyes tightened as he took another sip of champagne, so she deftly guided the subject toward one she knew would make him happy—a recap of the movie.

When Jonathan took her home after dinner, she didn't invite him to go upstairs even though he dropped enough hints to make it obvious how much he wanted her to ask him.

"It was a lovely evening, but I'm awfully tired tonight." Truth. She'd barely slept at all. The escape still made her feel a little guilty. Yet it couldn't be helped. The thought of bringing any man near the room she'd shared with Rio last night made her cheeks scorch with shame.

One thing she knew for sure. The next time she invited a man into her apartment, it would be on her carefully considered terms and not anyone else's agenda.

Chapter Seventeen

Teena leaned forward, her eyes studying Carolyn's face. "So, lay it on me. What do you think?"

Carolyn swallowed the bite of chicken mushroom casserole, patted her mouth with a napkin, and looked heavenward before she pronounced the verdict. It was kind of fun to see her assistant squirm. "Delicious! This is so good. I'd like to have the recipe, and you know how much I hate to cook."

Delight spread across Teena's face. "Sam-fran-tastic! I wanted to be sure before I spring it on Sketch."

"Sketch? That's an interesting name."

"It's a nickname. His daddy was an artist. Anyway, you know what they say about catching a man by feeding him good food."

The altered idiom made Carolyn smile. "All I know is if the only way to a man's heart is through his stomach, I'm sunk. I'll be single for the rest of my days."

Once upon a time, a thought like that would have disturbed her. It went against every dream her mother had ever envisioned for her future. Yet, what's wrong with being the mistress of your own fate?

"You staying single? Ha! Ain't gonna happen. You've got men chasing after you like flies follow honey, even if you never serve them anything but potatoes burned to charcoal."

The tab under which she'd filed the meal she had tried to make for Rio pinged open. It had been so long since she'd seen him, she wondered if he packed up and left town. Mysteriously missing again. Even after the things he'd said to her, she half-expected him to appear at the clinic as he'd always done before. When he didn't, she couldn't help but feel curious. And yes, maybe underneath it all a little disappointed too. It would be nice to get the last word in with Rio at least once.

"You're right, Teena. Burned potatoes are exactly what anyone would get from me." Carolyn stood to wash her plate. "I pronounce this meal a winner. Sketch will love it."

Teena grinned and all but pranced away, a woman with a plan—and maybe very soon, a man.

Carolyn had no plan yet, but she wasn't lonely either. She'd seen Jonathan twice during the previous week, and they'd spent all day Sunday wandering through the zoo. Both of them had laughed when a polar bear dived into the water, his massive body gliding along as he played with an empty plastic barrel. Never underrate happiness. It felt good. Lately, Jonathan had been more relaxed and less persistent, which made the idea of spending time with him one that appealed to her as it hadn't before.

She put away the dish and returned to her desk when Coby traipsed through the door. Her watch read twelve-thirty. "You're really early today. Didn't you have school?"

"We had a half day. Can I do my work right away so I can meet up with my friends? Is that okay?"

Carolyn couldn't remember having a short day at school unless a major snowstorm approached, but schools did many things different now. "Sure, that's fine. Teena will get you started."

As she watched him move away, a peculiar feeling troubled her. Maybe she ought to call Mrs. Jefferson, just to be sure. As soon as she heard the clangs and bangs of Coby working in the kennel, she shut both her office doors and lifted the phone. After two rings, Coby's mother picked up. "Hello?"

"Mrs. Jefferson, it's Carolyn Becker." Carolyn cupped her hand around the phone. "I'm sorry to bother you, but I was wondering something. Did Coby have a short day at school today?"

"Oh, he had a short day, all right. Short because he made it that way. He skipped out just before noon. The principal called me again and says he'll probably have to suspend him this time."

"Oh, no. He showed up here a few minutes ago to work. He told me he needed to come in early because he had plans with his friends."

"Is that so? Plans with his friends means nothing but trouble. Did he say what they're up to that's so important he has to skip?"

"No," Carolyn said. "He's still pretty close-mouthed about what he does."

"Between his stuff and bill collectors, my nerves are shot. Maybe I should just come down there right now and whip that boy's butt every step of the way home."

"No, please don't do that, Mrs. Jefferson. I have an idea. I'm going to talk to him right away and not tiptoe around this anymore. I think we've built enough of a rapport for him to level with me. If you'll wait before you do anything drastic, I'll call you back." A long, breath-holding pause followed.

"Well...I've got an appointment in an hour. My doctor says all this trouble is messing with me. If you keep an eye on him, he can't get into anything too bad. I'll deal with it when he comes home."

"Thank you. I'll call as soon as I can."

Relief flooded her. The last thing they needed was a screaming scene at the clinic. She put down the phone. All she had to do was convince Coby to be honest with her without scaring him off for good. Easy peasy, right? But how in the heck could she get him to spill information about things he clearly didn't want anyone to know? She chewed her lip and opened the door that led to the kennel. *Don't worry. The words will come.*

They didn't. Coby bent over a kennel to clean it, and Carolyn's mind offered nothing pithy. Teena knew Coby as well as anyone. Maybe she had an idea. Carolyn gestured toward her assistant. "Could I speak to you for a minute in my office?"

Teena followed, her arms filled with freshly washed towels. "What's up?"

"There's a problem, and I need your help. Coby skipped out of school today, and I'm going to have a showdown with him. He may get upset, so if he leaves, let me know right away so I can follow him."

"Say what?" Teena's voice was incredulous, and Carolyn put her finger to her lips.

"Shhh," she whispered. "His mother said she's at her wit's end. If he won't talk, then the only way I'm going to get to the bottom of this is to follow him and find out where he's going."

"And you think you can do that without him noticing?"

"You know how crowded the streets are with people walking every which way, especially this time of day. I'll stay far enough back just to observe. With that bright-red T-shirt he wears, it shouldn't be hard to spot him."

Teena rolled her eyes. "It's pretty sad when somebody like you decides to play detective. Go ahead and be a sucker if you want, but my money's on Coby. I'll bet he leaves you in his dust."

Carolyn curled her lip at Teena's lack of faith in her plan, but enlisting someone's help at least put her halfway to where she needed to be. "I want to at least try. Please?"

"This is a lamebrain idea, but call me crazy. I'll go along with it." Teena left the office, shaking her head. It wasn't five seconds later when she reappeared.

"Too late. He's already gone. I'll bet he heard us through these stupid thin walls."

"Cancel my appointments." Carolyn didn't wait for an answer, grabbing her jacket and bag before she scurried outside. Her gaze swept the mix of pedestrians on the sidewalk, and she shaded her eyes to look for Coby. Nothing. He must have gotten too much of a head start. But then she caught a glimpse of a boy in red disappearing around the corner at the end of the block. She picked up speed and dodged past the other walkers. After accidently bumping into one of them, she muttered a swift, "Excuse me," and kept moving.

Right around the corner, a MetroLink station appeared, where a large group of people gathered near the platform awaiting a train. She spied Coby among them. He didn't appear to be with anyone in particular, and spent his time kicking at an empty can. She pressed close to the building, pretending to look through a window. A woman inside the building at a desk near the window stared right back at her. Not knowing what else to do, Carolyn gave her a distracted wave.

A train whooshed into the boarding area, and Carolyn turned to watch. Coby moved along with the other passengers to get on. A digital sign on the train flashed its new destination—East St. Louis. The doors closed, and the cars rattled away.

It wasn't much of a clue, but it was something. She nodded at the woman, who was now on her phone— probably calling security. Carolyn dashed to the curb and held up her arm until a cab stopped. She opened the door and jumped inside.

The cabby asked, "Where to, lady?"

Carolyn spoke to his eyes reflected in the rearview mirror. "Take me to the MetroLink stop in East St. Louis, please."

The cabby's shoulder twitched. "Whatever you say." His cab jerked away from the curb and merged into heavy traffic. Slow heavy traffic.

She knew the glacial pace wasn't likely to get her near the station before Coby did. "Can't you go any faster?"

"Hey, traffic is what it is, and the ride will take as long as it takes. Why are you in such a hurry to get over there, anyway? You do know that station isn't in a great part of town, don't you?"

It figured she'd get a chatty driver. "I'm beginning to get a glimmer, but it doesn't matter. That's where I need to go."

Obligingly, the cabby punched his foot on the gas and weaved around other cars. Holy Shih-Tzu! If he wanted to scare her, he'd certainly succeeded. It appeared only inches separated them from vehicles in the next lane, not to mention the one in front of them. Compared to this, Jonathan's driving habits were exemplary. She wanted to close her eyes but instead held on to the door's armrest and prayed she'd live to see another day.

After a few hair-raising minutes, the traffic thinned to a trickle, and the cab picked up speed to cross the long expanse of bridge over the Mississippi River. The cabby made a few turns to the right and then to the left before he stopped at a MetroLink station where only a small knot of people stood waiting. A train pulled in, and a group of passengers exited while new ones climbed on board. She hadn't the slightest idea whether Coby's train had arrived already or whether he'd ridden farther along the line.

"Could you drive around the area a little bit while I look around?"

In the mirror, she saw the cabby's brows reach toward his hairline, but he didn't object. "If you can pay the fare, I can drive."

They cruised up and down the blocks nearest the station where an abundance of old warehouses stood, most of them covered with graffiti. Billowy-looking letters spelled out names and messages, and colorful spray-painted images struck her as oddly beautiful. They were part of urban culture—and part of Coby's world.

Three blocks away from the MetroLink station, a parking lot held dozens of cars and trucks parked in a makeshift gravel lot near one of the warehouses. Small groups of men walked toward the large, rusting structure. They talked and laughed, reminding her of fans heading to a baseball game.

"Could you drive a little closer, please?"

The cab crept to the outer row of parked cars, and Carolyn said, "This is good. Stop here."

She clutched her purse and watched. Most of the men were in jeans and T-shirts, with all skin colors represented. Many had stubbled cheeks or full beards. Most of the faces were shaded by ball caps. Some men dragged coolers behind them. Clearly the warehouse held some sort of attraction, but she didn't see anyone around Coby's age. Curiosity kept her staring. What could be going on inside to draw such a crowd?

She'd just about decided to abandon her spying mission when a boy in a red T-shirt came out of the warehouse. Her eyes grew wide. Coby. He held the leash of a cinnamon-colored pit bull and walked the animal behind the warehouse. Then two men exited from the same door as Coby, both walking pits. The dogs snarled at each other, and the men yanked leashes to keep the animals just beyond each other's reach. Carolyn's heart twisted.

Dogfighting—and Coby? She thought of the boy she'd grown to care about, the one who always had a gentle touch with animals, who seemed interested in nothing more than helping them. It was impossible to believe he could be involved in anything so horrific—an activity it made her stomach kink to think about.

She couldn't accept the evidence playing out right in front of her eyes. It didn't make sense. There had to be more to this than she knew. Jumping to conclusions wasn't smart or logical. Except...

The day she had met Coby. He brought Stella to the clinic, bleeding from puncture wounds. Not only did the dog have fresh injuries, she had old ones too. Carolyn's hand covered her mouth. Could Stella have been involved in what apparently was going on here this very minute?

Two of the men near the warehouse glanced in the cab's direction, but Carolyn ignored them, keeping her attention on the place where Coby had disappeared. The cabby turned around to look at her, a fine line of perspiration on his forehead.

"Lady, you need to make up your mind. Either get out or stay in the cab, but I have to drive."

She bit her lip, wondering what to do. She didn't want to leave without Coby but feared a confrontation. If she asked him to come with her, what if he refused? She couldn't grab his arm and drag him away. Besides, if Coby felt humiliated, she'd probably never see him again, whether Stella was at the clinic or not.

As she analyzed her options, Coby returned to where she could see him, still walking the same dog. She reached for the door handle, ready to leave the cab and at least try to reason with him, when she noticed a tall imposing man at Coby's side. A man who looked frighteningly familiar. He threw an arm across Coby's shoulder, said something, and laughed.

Then Rio Medina opened the battered door to the warehouse for Coby. He steered the boy and the dog inside. The door closed.

Carolyn returned the cabby's look. "Let's go now, please. Back to St. Louis."

She didn't need to ask him twice. He took a white-knuckled hold on the steering wheel and wasted no time slamming his foot on the gas pedal. The cab's tires threw bits of gravel in the parking lot, reached the paved road, and cut swiftly around a street corner. Carolyn had to place both her hands flat on the seat to keep from being flung from one side to the other as she sat in stunned silence. After a few moments, she squeaked out a question. "Do the police ever cruise this area?"

The cabby glanced at her from the rearview mirror. "The cops don't come here much. They got enough trouble in other places to deal with. Besides, if nobody calls for help, it's a sure sign people want to be left alone. Sometimes it's best not to make waves."

She remembered Coby's rapport with the animals at the clinic. How excited he'd been at the suggestion of becoming a veterinarian. This wasn't his doing. It was the work of men who had no qualms about taking advantage of a vulnerable boy. He wasn't meant to throw away his life like this. Someone needed to do something, and it looked like that someone would have to be her. She'd make waves, all right. Enough to sink a ship.

"You okay, lady?" The cabby looked at Carolyn in the rearview mirror. Something he saw in her face must have alarmed him.

"I'm fine, I guess."

To think she once felt drawn to Rio. How easily he'd fooled her. The thought made acid rise in her throat and her hand ball into a fist. She wished she had the nerve to pop him right on his chin and wipe the smug look he always wore off his face. Her sister, Kat, wouldn't have hesitated, but Carolyn had always been the agreeable one, the even-tempered one, and never let herself be a part of anything that might cause problems. Hadn't Mother said so to both her daughters, dozens of times?

Look out, Mother. Things are about to change.

She seethed a few more minutes, then cooled off enough to concede. Okay, she might not actually hit him. If she did, he'd probably have her arrested on assault charges, and a felon couldn't keep a veterinary license. But she'd sure find some way to make him pay for his part in getting Coby involved in such a world of evil.

Interesting the way connecting two dots led to more. No wonder Rio had asked her questions about dog bite cases. He was looking for inside information on what went on with his competitors. Now she understood the reason he remained so inscrutable—and why he knew the streets better than anyone else. She remembered the bites on his wrist. The injury must have been due to his involvement in this nightmare. And what's more, he had the audacity to lure a child into the same life of crime.

For a moment, she wished she hadn't taken care of his wrist. He didn't deserve any better treatment than he gave to animals. He should suffer, she thought, the same way these dogs did. Permanent exile to a backyard doghouse? Solitary confinement? Graphic details began to form on a fitting punishment. Some of the images would have swiftly uncurled her mother's beautifully coiffed hair. Unspeakable. That's what he was.

Breathe, Carolyn. Just breathe.

By the time the cab crossed the bridge toward St. Louis, she'd calmed herself enough to think more rationally. Flabbergasted agitation had nearly lowered her standards to Rio's level. How incredibly unethical to have misgivings about helping anyone or to pass judgment. Denying compassion made her no better than him. Besides, she had someone more important to think about. Her attention turned to the phone call she'd promised Mrs. Jefferson. How would she ever explain this to Coby's mother? And by what miracle could she convince Coby to salvage his future without driving him away forever?

There was nothing left to do but will herself to approach the issues in a clearheaded way, just as she would with her cases at the clinic. Buildings blurred past her, a trucker honked, and after a few minutes of thought shrouded in clouds of fog, a potential solution began to materialize.

Chapter Eighteen

Teena spoke to the back of Carolyn's head, her voice rising with indignation. "I hope you know when I didn't hear from you last night, I thought you got yourself in all kinds of hot water. You didn't even answer your phone. I almost called the cops out to check on you."

Carolyn looked up from the files she'd been sorting through. Why had she left them in such a jumble? "I'm sorry, Teena. I turned down the volume on my cell, and I forgot to turn it up again. There were a lot of things I had to think about yesterday, but you're right. I should have called you."

"Well, what happened?"

"I found out Coby's gotten himself involved with some people who aren't good for him at all, exactly what I was afraid of. I spent all evening weighing the possibilities over what to do about it." She lowered her head and went back to the files, knowing her face had flushed. Carolyn felt a twinge of conscience over being evasive. Worse than that, when she'd called Mrs. Jefferson last night, she hadn't told her the whole truth either, in hopes Coby's mother wouldn't blister her son's ears out of total frustration. Carolyn had been spinning more webs than all the spiders on earth put together.

Teena cast a suspicious eye her way and grunted "humph!" before stepping away to work in the kennel.

Carolyn sighed. If she intended to keep practicing so many deceptions, she really ought to become a more accomplished liar. She turned her attention back to her files and the more important matter at hand—Coby. How best to approach him with what she had in mind? Assuming, she reminded herself, he came in to work at all.

The front door banged. With Teena busy in the kennel, Carolyn stuck her head out the office door to see if her first appointment had arrived.

Jonathan stood next to the printer. As soon as he saw her, he beamed. "Good morning, Carolyn. I stopped by to check on things. Any issues with the machine to report?" He angled his head to look at her and his expression changed. "More to the point, what's on your mind? You look like you were up all night."

Maybe she should have used a little more concealer under her eyes. "I'm fine, I guess," she said. "The printer's fine too."

"That doesn't sound very convincing. What's going on?"

"Nothing," she said. "Things have just been off-kilter is all."

"You don't seem yourself when you're not smiling." He walked to where she stood and in a possessive way ran his hand down her arm. "I've made dinner reservations for tonight, hoping you'd be available. Why don't we talk about what's bothering you then?"

"Tonight? That won't work for me. I have things to discuss with Coby."

Jonathan's eyes narrowed slightly. "Oh? Are you having problems with that boy again?"

"No, well, yes. I mean, there are some issues we need to address."

"Anything I can help you with?" Jonathan kept his sharp gaze pinned to her face.

"Thanks for the offer, but not right now. After I talk to him, I'll let you know what he says. Actually, it might be helpful to get a man's opinion."

Jonathan nodded. "I'll do whatever I can. This all sounds quite—interesting. I'm looking forward to hearing more at dinner tonight. Pick you up at six?"

Only half-listening to him, Carolyn gathered her files. "Sure. I'll see you then."

He took a handkerchief from his breast pocket and flicked it over the top of the printer before he nodded at her. The cleaning effort wasn't necessary. Teena kept the equipment spic-and-span to avoid anything imploding from hidden fluffs of animal hair.

Teena marched back to the waiting area, obviously still disgruntled, and dropped into her chair behind the counter. "Him again?" She basted her words with a healthy dollop of sarcasm.

"He came by to check the printer."

"Again? Seriously? Never in my life have I seen anyone as interested as Jonathan in keeping tabs on a piece of office equipment. Duh! You're the reason he comes by here all the time."

"Don't be silly. We've become friends and sometimes we go places together. That's all." She could feel warm spots of color high on her cheeks. "He's a nice guy. Unlike some other men I've met," she couldn't help saying.

Teena didn't waste a moment before an impish gleam entered her brown eyes. "I don't need three guesses to figure out who you're referring to. All of a sudden, the mention of Rio puts a stick right up your spine. Your face gets all squished together like a prune. As a matter of fact, you look like..."

Carolyn held up her hand. "Enough. I get your message, and I can honestly assure you Rio is…" She breathed slowly in and then out. "Not who I thought he was. I don't plan to see him ever again."

Her assistant smirked in an irritating you-can't-fool-me way, so Carolyn gathered the rags of her dignity and stalked back toward her office. At least there, she could shut the door. She sat at her desk, and a sudden vision of her handing Rio over to the police appeared. Victory! A judge would hear the evidence and decide what to do. But then what? How would such a grand-slam conquest play out?

First, she'd be forced to testify in court. Even though the legal system was her father's domain, not hers, from the television shows she'd seen, a defense attorney would try to make her look like an idiot. Then he'd prove it by telling the world she'd slept with the suspect. Not a headline she—or the clinic—needed.

Maybe an anonymous phone call would be better—as a concerned citizen. Then she could keep both Coby and herself out of it. Her father! She could call him for advice. But wait a minute. If he or her mother had a clue what was going on, they'd be knocking at her apartment door before the sun set.

Jonathan? She tapped a finger on the desktop. He seemed to know a lot about the law. He'd discussed ordinances with the city and contacted the police when matters arose in his job. She could lay out the whole affair to him at dinner. He'd know what to do. She sagged with relief and moved on to her next problem.

Coby should arrive any moment. Time to launch her plan.

At three thirty on the nose, Teena lurched into Carolyn's office with a sponge in her hand and a yowling pregnant tabby cat tucked under her arm. "Do you know that boy still hasn't come in? Is he skipping out on us again?"

Heart sinking, Carolyn said, "I'm not sure what's going on. I've been sitting here wondering whether to call his mother."

"That'd be a waste of time." Teena dropped the sponge and stroked the cat's head. The yowling stopped, although the animal's striped tail still whipped back and forth. "You can bet your last dollar he isn't at home. Maybe he decided not to come back anymore since you went snooping after him."

"I'm sure he didn't see me." Carolyn picked up the phone. "I guess I'd better call."

She dialed Mrs. Jefferson, and an electronic voice informed her the number was no longer in service. With a sinking feeling, she started to put down the phone, then changed her mind and punched in another set of numbers. After a few rings, a man's voice said, "Hello?"

"Jonathan? It would be great if we could meet earlier. Coby didn't come in to work today, and I need you to help me figure out my next step."

Carolyn took a sip of her wine before she finished her story. "So I'm absolutely certain the people Coby has been seeing are involved in dogfighting. And I strongly suspect Stella's injuries happened because of it. She's got too many old wounds for them to be accidental."

Jonathan cut a slice of his steak. "Well, you do know all of this is completely circumstantial. I can't imagine the police would bother to investigate even if you did call them."

"But dogfighting is illegal. They'd have to look into it, wouldn't they?"

"Trust me." He pointed his fork at her. "The police don't get involved in things like this. They're too busy taking reports on real crimes."

"*Real* crimes? What do you mean by that?"

"I just mean that when you've got shootings and burglaries and carjackings to deal with, dogfighting comes pretty low on the list."

"But, Jonathan, this isn't only a rumor. Look at Stella. Remember what I saw on the east side. Isn't that evidence?"

Jonathan covered her hand with his own and spoke in a honeyed voice as if to an impatient child. "All you've seen is a dog with bite wounds and people walking in and out of a warehouse. Stella is only a stray. Coby told you that himself. Bad things happen to street dogs all the time. You're reading way too much into this and letting your imagination run wild."

"But what happened to Stella in combination with the place where I saw Coby has to mean something."

"Look at it this way." Jonathan's voice remained low and patient. "You start saying things about Coby to the police, and they're bound to check with his mother. You can bet she'll give them an earful. Who do you think will be on the hot seat then?" Jonathan put a bite of steak into his mouth.

Carolyn had a strange feeling she'd been out argued. If she called the police, she didn't doubt for a minute the problems Coby already had would be multiplied. "But I have to do something to help him."

Jonathan rolled his eyes. "For God's sake, Carolyn. Leave the kid alone. You need to stop trying to be his mother. He's already got one of those."

Wounded, she lifted her chin. "I'm not trying to be his mother. He's a decent boy with a tough life. I only want to help make things better for him."

"You're a very tolerant person, Carolyn, but when people are too tolerant, they can get burned. Why don't you forget about this and concentrate on what you came here to do? Take care of animals and the clinic. If dogfighting is going on, you can bet it's been happening for a long time, and you're not going to be the one to stop it. Several of my clients look at dog fighting the same way they do baseball or football or horse racing."

"But dogfighting is illegal." It felt like she was battling her way through a mist to find something impossible to see.

"You are such an innocent. A lot of things that go on are technically illegal."

His words reminded her of Rio. Since she knew how much it would irk Jonathan, she refrained from bringing up his name. "You don't seem to care about this at all."

Jonathan put down his fork and patted her arm. "I didn't say any such thing. I'm only giving you my opinion because I don't want you to tear yourself up trying to do the impossible. Not only that but running around to places where you haven't been invited isn't very smart. There's money involved here, and people get mean when it comes to money. And even meaner if they find out somebody brought in the police."

She pictured Rio with his arm around Coby at the warehouse and stiffened her posture. "I'm sorry, but I can't pretend this doesn't exist. And I refuse to give up on Coby.

I know he loves animals, and right or wrong, I intend to use how he feels to keep him away from—whoever got him into this nightmare."

Jonathan refilled her wine glass. "You forget he's a teenager, not some sort of mama's boy. You may not want to hear this, but if you insist on trying to figure out some way to reach him, it'll take a man to do it. So here's my offer. Why not concentrate on your job, and let me concentrate on Coby?"

Carolyn sipped her wine in thought. True, Coby didn't have a single positive male role model in his life. Only self-absorbed men who took advantage of his youth and circumstances. He obviously tuned out anything his mother said. Carolyn, herself, had become entangled in the boy's woes with little success. As if that weren't enough, she'd neglected her duties at the clinic over trying to find an answer. Where were her priorities? It wouldn't come as a surprise if Jeanne decided to fire her.

"All right. I guess what you said makes sense. I do need to take care of business, so I won't confront Coby and I won't call the police. I'll stay quiet—for now anyway—and leave it up to you. But promise me you'll be careful how you talk to him this time."

Jonathan's eyes met hers as he raised his glass. "Don't worry about a thing. I took classes in law enforcement when I was in college, and I did some volunteer work with a community youth group too. I know how to handle kids. Give me a little time, and I'll straighten him out once and for all."

Chapter Nineteen

Carolyn decided to close the clinic for lunch so she and Teena could walk to a nearby sandwich shop. "My treat," she told her, still feeling a twinge of guilt over the anxiety she'd caused her assistant—and friend. It was high time they had a hard talk about the clinic's situation too. Teena deserved at least that much. Even if at this point Carolyn didn't have answers, only graphs and excuses.

They placed their orders at the counter, picked up their trays, and found an empty booth.

"This is my favorite." Teena took a bite, her face blissful. "They have the best meatball sandwiches in town."

"They do. We should come here more often." Carolyn picked at her own sandwich, in search of the right words. "Teena, I wanted to talk to you about something. I have a meeting with Jeanne to discuss the clinic, and she isn't going to be at all happy about what I have to report."

"Oh? I've been too busy to keep a count, but from the look on your face, I guess we're not hitting the numbers the city wants." She squinted at Carolyn. "Or is something else going on?"

"Nothing else I know of, but you're right. We've scheduled surgeries, but not the number they expect. I hope they'll be willing to give us more time. Anyway, that's going to be my argument."

Teena pushed away her half-eaten sandwich. "More time? Not the way the city's been eyeballing our building. Ha! Guess I better dust off my résumé. I have a feeling I'm going to be looking for a new job soon."

The resigned expression on her assistant's face, moved Carolyn to say, "Let's not jump to the worst-case scenario yet. Jeanne wants the clinic to succeed. I don't believe she's going to give up on it without a fight."

"Maybe so, but it still comes down to what the city decides, and we don't have any control over that." Teena crumpled the paper around her sandwich. "Why don't we head back. I'm not hungry anymore."

Carolyn nodded. She felt as gloomy as Teena looked.

At three o'clock, Carolyn checked her watch. Would he show up or not? The muscles in her neck ached as she glanced from her paperwork toward the door of her office and back again over and over. It was practically impossible to concentrate. Then the front door rattled, and she got her answer. Coby bounded in as though nothing had happened. It took all of ten minutes before she called him into her office. She couldn't keep her mouth closed any longer. In theory, she agreed with Jonathan's advice to stay silent, but there were points she simply had to make. Things any employer would say to an employee—or a volunteer.

"Why didn't you come in yesterday, Coby? You know how much we depend on your help. Not to mention when you leave without a word or don't call us when you're not coming in, we worry about you."

He squirmed under her steady gaze. "Uh, well, I forgot about a school project I had to work on." A light flush tinted his cheeks. "You said my grades had to come up, right?"

There were so many other issues she wanted to bring up, she had to bite her tongue until it hurt before she spoke. "You know I want you to do better in school. But what I'm saying is you must let us know what's happening. In a way, being a volunteer is like a job. When an employee doesn't call and doesn't show up, it's likely he'll get fired. Make a habit of communicating whenever there's a reason you can't work. Then you won't risk losing a job. Also," she couldn't resist saying, "Stella waits all day to see you. You don't want to let her down, do you?" Carolyn had learned the art of planting seeds of guilt from an expert. *All's fair,* she told the reproachful voice in her head.

Coby's face became a little less guarded. "Sorry. I'll call if I gotta miss work again."

"Good. That's all I'm asking." Stella meandered from the kennel to greet him, her tail at full speed. Coby bent to put an arm around her neck, and the dog's tongue slurped across his cheek. The clangs and thumps of Teena working in the kennel area guaranteed Coby would have plenty to do. "Would you take Stella out first before you ask Teena what she needs?"

"Okay." He snapped on Stella's leash, and the two of them bounded out the back door.

The conversation had gone better than she hoped. No sooner had she congratulated herself on a job well done, Teena appeared in her office with an expression that promised trouble.

"Something weird is going on here," she announced. Teena tended to complain in generalities.

"Can you explain what you mean?"

"I sure can." Her hands went to her hips. "I noticed something a couple of weeks ago. Some of our supplies were missing. At first, I thought maybe I made a mistake. I could have counted wrong or something. But it happened again. I just inventoried our supplies."

"What's missing?"

"Before it was gauze and antiseptic. Now a bottle of antibiotic pills is gone too."

"Are you sure?"

"I checked out the supply room, drawers, and cabinets before I said anything to you."

Carolyn frowned. "I can't imagine how that could have happened. Between the two of us, we keep pretty close tabs on things."

Teena stared at her pointedly. "Hello. The only ones with access are you, me, and Coby. I'm pretty sure it's not you or me taking things."

Carolyn rubbed her hand against her cheek. Coby? She wasn't naïve enough anymore to believe it wasn't possible. "Well, I guess from now on we keep the supplies locked. Since we don't have controlled substances on site, I didn't think it would be necessary, but I guess this proves me wrong." Carolyn pulled a key from her desk drawer. "Have a duplicate made for you and one for Jeanne. No one else."

"Carolyn, are you going to say anything to him about this, or should I?"

"No, Teena. Neither one of us are going to talk to him about it. I have someone else in mind."

"Rio? You told me Coby likes him."

"I was wrong about that." Carolyn's voice notched higher, and she cleared her throat. "I don't think Rio is a very good influence on Coby at all."

One problem after another. Crestfallen by the latest distressing news, she picked up her phone and called Jonathan. He answered right away. "It's Carolyn. Is it possible for you to come over now? I don't want to wait. Coby's here and we've just discovered something else that needs to be handled."

Within an hour Jonathan appeared at the clinic, his hair slightly damp as though he'd just gotten out of the shower. Sometimes she wondered how he could possibly run a business and still answer her every request. Today, however, she counted his availability in the plus column.

"Hello, ladies." He nodded at Teena who grunted something unintelligible before returning to tap on her computer keys. "I got here as soon as I could."

"Let's go to my office. Coby's walking dogs right now, so we can talk." She closed the door and perched on the edge of her desk.

Jonathan sat in a chair and leaned back. "Well, what's the young hoodlum been up to now?"

"Please, don't talk that way about him. Something peculiar has been happening. We've discovered some of our supplies are missing."

"And I take it you think young Coby is responsible?"

Carolyn nodded her head sadly. "I hate to say so, but yes."

"What kind of things are missing?"

"Little things—gauze, antiseptic…some antibiotics." Carolyn's eyes grew wide. "Wait a minute. If he's been going to those dogfights—a place where dogs get hurt—I can see him wanting to have supplies on hand. He's such a tenderhearted kid. I'll bet that's it."

"Carolyn, Carolyn." Jonathan stared at her mildly. "You keep looking for ways to justify whatever he does."

"I'm not trying to justify anything. I'm only trying to understand. Maybe I'm jumping the gun. I don't have any proof Coby's done anything wrong, though I don't know who else could be responsible. It's only a guess, but it's the best guess I have right now. When you talk to him, can you ask about the supplies, too, and help him understand we're all accountable for what goes on here? Maybe between what you say and locking everything up, it will be enough to get the message across."

"I'll talk to him, but if he doesn't listen to reason, then in my opinion, it would be best for everyone if you tell him not to come back. Kid or not, if he can't be trusted, he needs to go."

"But trust comes from respect." She startled a little at the ferocity of her own words. "I understand, at least a little, about Coby's life. He's been faithful about working hard for us, and I respect him for doing the best he can, in spite of all the—stuff he deals with every day."

"Tell me, are you planning to make a police report on the stealing that's been going on?" Jonathan crossed his arms.

Stealing. What a harsh word. "No. I don't want Coby in that kind of trouble. He'll never get into vet school with an arrest on his record. I'm sure we can work things out somehow."

"That sounds like a wise idea to me. Keep the police out of it. I'll talk to him now while he's outside, away from all the interruptions here."

Jonathan gave her a reassuring smile and then forged away. *Please let him be tactful.* She got up and felt so edgy, she paced from her office to the lobby and back. Then she entered the kennel to look at the gray long-haired cat waking up from surgery and filled his water dish. The pregnant cat in the next kennel showed no signs of labor yet. She'd taken the animal at the pound's request. How could she refuse when they'd said there wasn't enough room to keep Mama Cat until her kittens were born?

Inhaling a deep breath, she let it out slowly, and wandered back to her desk. A report needed work, so she tried to concentrate on it, feeling jittery as her father had the time he tried—unsuccessfully—to give up caffeine. But she simply couldn't make herself focus. How long did it take to talk to a teenager, anyway?

When Jonathan finally reentered her office, he wore his usual dimpled smile. She looked at her watch and felt a jolt of shock. He'd been gone only twenty minutes? It felt like hours.

"What did you say to him?"

"Not too much. You know how kids are. They tune a lecture out fast, so I just told him he needs to use his head, that he'd been seen going places where he had no business being. I also pointed out you and Teena keep track of every single thing that comes in or goes out of the clinic. He's a smart boy. I'm sure he got the message."

She wound a strand of her hair around her finger. "How did he take it? Did he seem mad or upset?"

"No. He acted the same way he always does, like he was hearing fingernails on a chalkboard. But I'm quite sure he heard what I had to say."

"Well, I hope this does some good. I'll keep a closer eye on him when he's here, but when he's on the street? I don't know what to do about that."

"For one thing, you can stop worrying so much. I'm willing to bet your young man is going to be a lot smarter about what he does from now on."

Chapter Twenty

For the next week, Coby emptied trash cans, mopped the floor, and helped Teena in the kennel. He didn't once come in late or miss a single day of work. Carolyn put in a quiet call to his mother midweek, just to check in. Aside from a few grumbles about life in general, Mrs. Jefferson voiced no complaints about anything of significance. After she hung up the phone, Carolyn felt a little smug. It looked for all the world like Jonathan had been right. He'd accomplished what she couldn't. Apparently, all Coby needed was the intercession of a man—something his life sorely lacked. Now she felt comfortable moving forward with her idea. She intended to make Coby an offer.

Following her final appointment of the day, she found him in the kennel area bent over a deep sink scrubbing litter pans the way Teena had taught him.

"You're doing a great job. I couldn't do it any better myself."

"Thanks," he mumbled, and ducked his head in teen-age embarrassment.

"You've been working hard for a while now, and I want you to know something. You don't owe another penny for Stella's medical care. I'll take responsibility for anything else she needs."

He looked up at her with incredulous eyes. "You mean I'm done?"

"Yes." She smiled. "If you want to be. But I'd love for you to continue volunteering with us. One of the things vet school requires is proof of community service hours, and I'll be happy to document them for you. Besides," she said, "we really could use your help."

He gave the pan in his hand a scrub, evidently considering the matter. Her heart tugged in sympathy as she waited, hoping he'd say what she wanted to hear.

After a few moments, he answered. "I want to work. I like it here."

She nearly laughed out loud. "That's fantastic. I'll start a spreadsheet for you and enter the time you put in today. We'll talk to Teena and figure out a weekly schedule that works for you."

"Okay." The tiny light in his eyes made Carolyn lower her own. She didn't want Coby to see how watery they'd become.

"You're finished for the day, so you can go on home if you want."

"Okay, soon as I dry these." He pulled a litter pan from the sink and toweled it. Stella sat near his feet, waiting patiently—Carolyn felt sure—for her best buddy's attention.

"You know what, Coby? I'm finished too, and I'm starving. Before I go home, I need to grab something to eat. I'd like to buy you dinner—if it's okay with your mom, that is."

Coby finished drying the final pan. "I can't call. Her phone got shut off again. But she won't care. Most nights I'm on my own for eats anyway. Mom don't cook on bad days. She just goes to bed."

The guileless statement made Carolyn swallow. "Well, I don't cook much either. There's a good pizza place down the block. Or would you rather have something else?"

"My favorite is McDonald's." His lips turned up.

"Excellent. Let's go. I'll pick up Stella after we're done. We can even save a little treat for her. But whatever you do, don't tell anyone I'm the kind of veterinarian who lets a dog eat french fries once in a while."

His grin broadened. "I won't."

As they walked the three blocks to McDonald's, Carolyn chatted to Coby about her hopes for the clinic—she didn't mention her fears for it—and made a point to praise him again for his hard work. When his eyes sparked with pride, so did her heart. If ever she'd met anyone who needed an ego boost—an inoculation against the rest of the world—it was Coby. They walked a few minutes more before she brought up another topic. "I understand Jonathan talked to you last week. Did what he had to say make sense?"

The shy animation in Coby's expression disappeared. "I guess," he replied. Then he clamped his lips together in a thin line.

It figured. No one in the history of being lectured ever wanted to rehash a lecture. She tried to think of something more neutral to say, but the restaurant came into view, so she decided to point out the obvious. "There it is. Good. It doesn't look busy at all."

Coby followed Carolyn to the counter and stared at the overhead menu. She ordered a salad while Coby chose a supersize Big Mac meal with a large chocolate shake. Her question certainly hadn't affected his appetite. A client once told her teenage boys could eat more than their weight in food. From the looks of it, she wasn't kidding.

They took their trays to a table near a large window. Good mood restored, Coby dug in right away. Carolyn watched him, amused. "Don't eat so fast. You'll make yourself sick."

"No, I won't," he managed to say around a mouthful of food.

Curiosity piqued her again. "I've been wondering if your mom mentioned anything about moving."

Coby bit off a large mouthful of hamburger and washed it down with a pull of his shake. "She's always scared about getting thrown out because she don't have money to pay the bills. I guess that means she don't really want to move. Otherwise she wouldn't care." He put down his half-eaten burger. "You said you don't want to have a dog right now. You ain't thinking about taking her to the pound, are you?"

"Absolutely not. I couldn't do that to her." She hated the way Coby had stopped eating, as though he'd lost his appetite. "I had a feeling it might not work out for you to take Stella. At first, I wondered whether I should try to find her a good home, but the truth is, I've gotten pretty fond of her. Since she comes to work with me every day, she's become our unofficial greeter. Clients love to visit with her. And I must admit she's good company for me at home." Carolyn smiled. "I've decided to keep her, and the best part is with you volunteering, you can still see her any time you want. If anything ever changes and you can take Stella home with you, we'll figure out a way to make it happen. How does that sound?"

Coby's eyes sparkled. "That's freakin' awesome! Thanks, Dr. Becker. If I can't keep her, having her stay with you is the next best thing."

The boy's delight made her even happier than she thought it would. Coby eagerly dug back into his meal, resuming his vacuum-style method of eating. It struck her as impressive, given his small stature. Carolyn put a bite of salad in her mouth and then glanced up. Standing near the door she saw the last person on earth she cared to look at. She shot him a dirty look, but he stepped toward their table anyway.

"Hi, Coby." Rio patted the boy's shoulder and nodded an acknowledgment toward Carolyn. "Dr. Becker."

Coby beamed as though he'd won the lottery. "Guess what, man? I'm gonna keep volunteering at the clinic, and Stella's gonna stay with Dr. Becker. I still get to see her whenever I want."

Rio chuckled. "I can't say I'm much surprised. The doc and Stella seem to be getting along quite well together."

Coby shoveled the remaining food in his mouth, with the exception of three French fries. "I need to go, but I saved these for Stella. Would you give them to her?" Carolyn nodded, and Coby moved his fingers over the fries, until he'd touched every one of them. "There. They have my scent now. I want her to know the food came from me. Thanks for dinner." He jumped up from the table and sprinted for the door.

"See you tomorrow, Coby," she called to him.

"Eat and run," Rio said with a grin. "He sure is all boy."

Her attention turned toward the enemy. "Yes, and that's exactly what he is. A *boy*." She snapped out her words with as much venom as she could manage in a public place without creating a scene.

Rio frowned as he studied her. "You trying to tell me something?"

"A child shouldn't be put in any situation where he'll get in over his head with trouble."

His eyes narrowed. "How about being a little more specific? I'd like to know what I'm being accused of this time."

"Never mind." She gathered the trash on the table. "I need to pick up Stella."

Rio caught her arm. It was the first time he'd touched her since the evening they'd spent together. His hand immediately brought images of what had happened between them. It infuriated her to realize how her body swayed in response. Face flaming, she yanked her arm away. "Let go of me."

Lifting both hands as though in surrender, he said, "Look, Carolyn. The last time I saw you, the evening didn't end the way it should have. I was tough on you, and I'm sorry for that. I don't want to make you unhappy."

"Really?" She bristled with fury, working hard to keep from spewing the unpleasant things she was thinking.

"You don't believe me?"

It was hot on her tongue to mention the many ways he'd already made her unhappy—and hurt Coby too—but until she sorted out in her own mind how she'd handle Rio's part in what went on at the warehouse, saying anything more would be a rotten idea. She inhaled deeply to calm herself.

"Here's what I believe, Rio. I don't know you at all, and I'm pretty sure I don't want to know you."

With that, she turned and marched to the garbage can, balancing Stella's fries in one hand while dumping crumpled paper, napkins, and the remains of her salad. Some of the trash missed its mark, and she had to stoop over to pick it up off the floor—spoiling a bit the self-righteousness of her exit.

Yet despite the pure outrage she felt, Carolyn couldn't resist sneaking one final peek at the look on Rio's face before she stalked out the door.

Chapter Twenty-One

Carolyn looked at the man who brought in a bleeding pit bull dog. "How did this happen?" The man grunted as he lifted his pup to the table and offered no explanation. The animal had dirty dark brown fur, matted with blood from a few bite wounds on his face. Some time ago, the dog's ears had been cropped close to his head, and he wore a wide spike-studded leather collar around his muscular neck. None of the injuries appeared serious, Carolyn noted with relief. Head wounds tended to bleed in a spectacular way that often made an injury look worse than it was. She soaked gauze with antiseptic and set about the task of cleaning. The man held his dog as she worked, and Carolyn repeated her question. "What happened to your dog?"

"Jake got into a fight with some mutt in the neighborhood. My boy's quite the scrapper. He won't let another animal get away with coming near our property. Since one of the bites is close to his eye, I wanted to have him checked. Nothing major, right?"

"I can clean where he's hurt and prescribe some antibiotics to guard against infection." Carolyn continued to dab as she spoke. "I'm seeing some older scars here too. Does Jake get in a lot of fights?"

"A few. He's a tough old fella though." The man plumped with pride. "Nobody can beat him."

Carolyn finished with Jake to home in on his owner. "You know, your dog would be a lot less prone to fighting if he was neutered. He'd be healthier too. We have a low-cost program I can offer you." She worked hard to keep judgment from poisoning her tone. Jake's owner looked to be the type who'd need sweet talk and a lot of convincing.

The man's voice rose in disbelief. "Are you kidding? I'd never do anything like that to my dog. It's not normal. Besides, you and I both know all neutering does is turn dogs into pussies." He chortled. "Get it, Doc? Turn dogs into pussy cats?"

It took zero effort to keep her lips from turning up. "I can assure you there's not a shred of truth to that idea. Before you decide, will you at least take this pamphlet? It outlines all the advantages of neutering. Please look it over and think hard about calling us to schedule surgery for Jake. It's a very simple procedure."

"Fine. I'll take your pamphlet." He shoved it into his shirt pocket.

His expression didn't give her high hopes the information would go anywhere but into the nearest dumpster. "Sir, I really can't stress this enough. You need to do something to stop Jake from getting into fights. Next time he might not be so lucky."

"Dogs have been fighting with each other forever. They're descended from wolves, you know. It's part of their nature. Only the strongest survive."

"When their ancestors were in the wild, that may have been true, but dogs have been domesticated for a long time. They don't need to fight to survive anymore."

"You don't think so?" The man ran a hand over his dog.

Carolyn wrote in Jake's chart, and a thought struck her. "Mr., uh, Smith, I have a question. You haven't been here before. How did you find our clinic?"

"Oh, a guy I know sent me. He said you were good at fixing up dogs who get hurt, and you did do a nice job with Jake. I'm going to make sure all my friends know where to find you."

Something didn't feel right about this, but she couldn't put her finger on what. Mr. Smith lifted his dog off the table and to the floor. Jake shook himself, tags jingling. He followed his master toward Teena, who waited at the front desk.

Carolyn wished she could shake off the weird vibe she'd gotten as easily as Jake had shaken off his trip to the clinic. What if this guy sent a slew of dogs with similar injuries to her? She wasn't about to deny treatment to an animal in need, yet an influx of dogs who'd been attacked by another dog brought only one thought to her mind—the warehouse across the river. She rested the file folder against her chin and considered calling the police, even though Jonathan had counseled her not to.

If she did call, what proof did she have to report?

Mr. Smith—she ought to put air quotes around the name "Smith"—said a friend sent him. It had to be Rio. He'd probably start sending all his criminal cohorts her way. If she took them on as patients, it practically made her an accessory.

Teena appeared in the exam room with disinfectant and paper towels. Carolyn stared at Jake's chart until Teena sprayed the table and started to scrub. "That man is mean as a striped snake. When he paid his bill, all he did was brag about how tough his dog is and how Jake always comes out on top."

"That's the second one this week. Teena, I have a serious question for you, so please tell me the truth. Do you know anything about dogfighting going on around here? The staged, organized kind of dogfighting?"

Teena finished wiping the table before she looked up. "I don't know any details, but I do know it happens. I also know there are people who think the way Mr. Smith does about them. Some look at it like uptown people do when entering any dog competition. It's a prestige thing. They want to prove they have the best animal."

"What am I missing here? How could anyone get a thrill out of seeing animals fight?"

"Because they enjoy watching it. Because they make money at it. Because it gives them a feeling of power when their dog wins." Teena threw the damp paper towel in the trash. "There's a lot of things that happen on the street. I'm not saying any of it is right, but that doesn't make it go away."

Carolyn's chest felt like a brick had taken up residence in it. "Have you ever gone to a dogfight?"

"Not me. I don't have the stomach for it. But I know men who go to fights with their buddies, and sometimes they bring along the wife and kids. It makes a heck of a family outing, doesn't it?"

"But the whole thing is so brutal. On top of that, it's illegal—plain and simple."

"You won't get an argument from me. And as far as illegal goes, I can walk you down near the riverfront right now and point out more illegal stuff going on than you've got fingers to count. It's just the way it is in a big city."

"Well, don't you think it's time to do something about it? What's happening to these dogs is inexcusable. The idea of anyone standing around and watching it turns my stomach. Am I the only one who cares about this?"

"Maybe somebody will make a dent in it one of these days, but no one will ever stop fighting entirely. Look at boxing and MMA and those crazy cage fights. People love watching that kind of stuff, and there's a lot of folks with dogs who think they've got something to prove."

"But at least people have a choice." The entire conversation nauseated her. Carolyn turned back toward her office. She felt more exhausted than any full day of work had ever made her. Was it foolish to think anyone would take a stand on the issue? Both Jonathan and Teena seemed to think it impossible to stop.

And Rio? His name slipped into her mind far more than it should, despite what she'd learned about him. She sank into her chair, knees still a little weak, when she remembered. Maybe she'd developed an addiction. What was it called again? She turned on her computer and Googled "women who are attracted to criminals." Hybristophilia, that's what it was called. She read on. Apparently when so afflicted, women became particularly attracted to serial killers. She shuddered at the idea. Could Rio be only the beginning? Did she have a long line of shifty men in her future?

Well, if the clinic closed tomorrow, at least one thing had been confirmed. She was lousy at choosing men.

She closed out Google and pulled up the report she'd been laboring over. Time to get to work and focus on her job, at least as long as she had one. Her meeting with Jeanne loomed like a specter. Carolyn felt pretty sure it wouldn't end in a handshake or congratulations.

"Carolyn," Teena called from the kennel. "Can you give me a hand?"

"I'll be right there." She gave a defiant shake of her head. Well, maybe she couldn't do anything about Clay, or Rio, or the things people in the city chose to do, but all hope wasn't gone yet.

Before everything around her crumbled, she could still do something to change things for Coby.

The next afternoon, Carolyn took Stella for a walk and picked up a late lunch. The stroll past glorious fall colors and pumpkins on display cleared her mind and gave her a much-needed boost of pep she hadn't had in a while. It felt so good, she walked farther than she intended, admiring the beauty around her. She glanced at her watch. *Holy Shih Tzu!* They practically had to gallop back to the clinic, and still arrived twenty-five minutes later than planned. Barging through the front door, she called, "Sorry, Teena!"

Teena stood behind the counter, arms crossed and glowering. "He's at it again. I was busy and didn't pick up the phone when it rang. Coby left a message. He said he won't be in today because he has another school project to do."

Carolyn removed Stella's leash. "You think he's lying?"

"What I think is he's playing hooky again, but at least he called like you told him to. I'll give him credit for that. I guess he's learned to be politer about skipping out of work."

"Remember, it is a volunteer job, and he did call to say he couldn't make it. Why shouldn't we believe him?"

Teena snorted. "For an educated lady, you sure don't have much in the way of common sense. I consider a person's track record before I trust 'em."

The seed of doubt Teena planted took root in Carolyn's fertile mind. A sprout grew three inches tall before she could pick up the phone. "I think you're wrong, but I'm calling his mother anyway to see what she says. Cross your fingers her phone's back on."

She punched in numbers. After several rings, a voice said, "Hello?"

"Mrs. Jefferson? It's Dr. Becker again. I was wondering if I could talk to Coby for a minute."

"He's not with you?"

"Well, no, but he did leave a message. He said he had a school project to work on today."

"Here we go again with the same old story. He told me he'd be at the clinic to visit that dog he's so crazy about. You see how it is? Like I ain't got enough on my plate today, dealing with bill collectors."

"I'm sorry to hear this." Carolyn's heart squeezed. "Maybe he'll stop by later. I'll call you if he shows up."

"Uh-huh. And maybe pigs will grow wings and start flying around too."

Carolyn didn't feel optimistic either. As much as she tried to stay upbeat, a charcoal lump of dread sitting in her stomach grew bigger by the second. She practiced deep breathing. It didn't help. *Maybe he's testing the water.* Her sister used to do it all the time. And how did their father respond? He didn't ask questions. He went out and got her. Carolyn turned off the computer and grabbed her purse. Right or wrong, she didn't intend to sit around and wait.

"Teena, I need to leave. Our last afternoon appointment canceled, and I can finish up my paperwork this evening. Would you mind locking the clinic when you're done? I'll be back to pick Stella up later."

The corners of Teena's eyes tightened. "Where are you heading in such a fired-up hurry this time?"

"I'm going to get Coby. He probably won't like it, but at least he'll know somebody cares enough to try."

"Don't get yourself into trouble you can't get out of. The city's full of rotten apples."

"I won't take any chances. I'm not going by myself."

Teena's lip curled. "You're taking Jonathan along, aren't you?"

"When he talked to Coby before, it seemed to help. He said I could call him any time, and he'd do whatever I needed to make things better."

"I still say he's more interested in you than he is in Coby."

Carolyn gave Teena a reproving look. "At the moment, I don't care what his motivation is. Anyway, it's refreshing to have him around. He's only a phone call away whenever I need him." Why was she trying so hard to convince Teena? "The reason why he helps doesn't matter, as long as he does it."

"Where men are concerned, you're soooo dense. What happened to your head, girl? Jonathan's a little too available if you ask me."

"Which I didn't," Carolyn said pointedly as she started out the door, phone to her ear.

Teena called after her. "Just you be careful. Jeanne won't like it if she has to hire a new vet."

Or has to fire one. Too keyed up for more of Teena's remarks, Carolyn waited outside, checking her watch repeatedly. Nothing out of the ordinary here. Pigeons stalked near the curb looking for a handout, and walkers dodged past her. Maybe drastic measures were what it took to settle things. She tapped her foot with impatience, longing to see Jonathan's Mustang appear.

Fifteen minutes later, she did. He pulled his car next to the curb, and Carolyn jumped in.

"At your service, pretty lady. Where are we heading?"

"To get Coby. I want to check a warehouse across the river that isn't far from the MetroLink station. It's by an old apartment building. I don't know the exact address, but I can find it."

Jonathan's eyes narrowed to slits. "A warehouse, you say? Do you have a plan in mind for what we're going to do when we get there?"

Carolyn chewed the tip of her thumb. "Find Coby and bring him back here."

"Do you really think he'll hop in the car just because we say so?" Jonathan's fingers drummed on the steering wheel as he drove.

"I hope you'll convince him. He seems to respect you more than me or his mother."

Jonathan shook his head. "Maybe you should forget about this. The kid's obviously a mixed-up mess. Why do you keep wasting your time?"

Carolyn twisted her hands in her lap. "I won't give up on him. If you don't want to help me, then pull over and I'll call a cab."

Jonathan's knuckles whitened on the steering wheel, but he didn't stop driving.

Chapter Twenty-Two

At least one good thing came from the state of Carolyn's frayed nerves. This time she wasn't even a tiny bit agitated about Jonathan's speed or the hair-raising twists and turns he hurtled the Mustang around. As far as she was concerned, the sooner they got to the warehouse, the better. Bridge supports blurred as they traveled over the river, and Carolyn closed her fingers into fists.

"Don't be so uptight," Jonathan said. "If he's not there, maybe we'll find him someplace nearby."

"I wasn't wondering about that as much as whether anyone will take offense at us coming to get him." Somebody like Rio, she added to herself.

"Do you think I can't handle it if we run into a problem? It's not like we're the police swarming in or anything." The dimples on his cheeks deepened. "If he's there, we'll pick him up and then be on our way."

"I'll be grateful if it's so easy." Jonathan seemed pretty cavalier, all things considered. Fortunately, not everyone launched as quickly into panic mode as she'd been doing lately.

He glanced her way and reached across the seat with his free hand to take her fingers and squeeze them. "I hope this proves I'd do anything to make you happy."

Carolyn saw a truck approaching too close for comfort and yelled, "Be careful!" as they went around a tight curve. She snatched her hand away. At the hair-raising speed they were traveling, he needed full control of the wheel and his eyes on the road. Jonathan's face scrunched into a frown, which made her feel guilty. He didn't have to help her, she reminded herself and offered an olive branch. "I'll owe you dinner once this is over, as long as you don't mind taking your chances on the food. I'm the world's worst cook." An understatement.

Jonathan's face smoothed, and he leaned in her direction. "You're perfect the way you are. Don't believe anyone who says different. I can't wait to finally see your place. It's a lot easier getting to know each other in private than at a restaurant where there's noise and too many people."

"Yes, I guess that's true." Carolyn felt a little uncomfortable, remembering—again, darn it—how easily Rio and his confounded blue eyes had gotten her into bed. Of course, nervousness, culinary incompetence, and a few glasses of wine hadn't hurt his chances any either. "Actually, maybe I'll order food for us from someplace instead of cooking."

"Whatever you want is fine with me. I don't care if we have food or not."

Why did his comment grate on her? *Remember everything he's done. Look at what he's doing now.* She hung on for dear life as they raced around another curve.

Jonathan spoke to her as casually as if he drove at break-neck speed every day. "You know, I respect what you do for a living. Anybody can cook and clean, but not everyone can be a doctor."

"I suppose so." Carolyn scanned the area, eyes squinted, moving her head to the right and then to the left. She pointed. "This area looks sort of familiar—yes! There's the apartment building I told you about."

Beyond the apartment stood the warehouse. Once again, people flocked toward the door. Men went through what appeared to be the main entrance and other men came out. Several dogs were being walked, pulling against their leashes. Then she saw a young boy in a familiar red T-shirt. He had a large canvas bag, and she wondered what he could be carrying in it. A heavyset man beckoned to him, and Coby followed the man inside the building.

Jonathan pulled his car to a stop at the back of the parking lot. "All right. I'm going to lock the car. I want you to stay inside it while I get him."

She had already grabbed the door handle. "I think I should go too. Coby barely knows you."

"It will look a lot less suspicious if I do this without you. Do you see any women around?"

"Well, no."

"All right then. You can see it's best if I go by myself. Anyway, if you're sitting here, it'll keep anyone from messing with my car. A Mustang as nice as this one attracts a lot of attention."

"Okay, fine. Just hurry, please. Is there anything I should be watching out for? Something I should do?"

"Just keep your eyes open and observe."

Carolyn didn't spare him a glance. Her gaze was glued to the activity near the warehouse. Jonathan tramped away over gravel and weeds growing between the rocks until he reached the warehouse door. He opened it and went inside. She sat still as a stone and waited.

A truck pulled up beside the Mustang, and three men got out. Heeding Jonathan's request, she tightened her eyes to monitor them, but no one did anything more than give his car an admiring glance. One of the men passed so close to the window, she could read a message on the camouflage-colored cloth holder surrounding his beer can. It read "Real Men Use Duct Tape."

She turned her full attention back to the warehouse, and noticed a half dozen men who'd gathered near the door. They exchanged something she guessed might be money. Gambling. She'd heard betting happened at dogfighting events. The thought made the skin on the back of her neck crawl in an uncomfortable way.

Then she saw him. A tall man who had shoulders wide as the pickup truck sitting next to Jonathan's Mustang. Rio strolled from the warehouse, casual as could be, toward the group of men. Several of them handed him something that looked like paper. She squinted to see better through the darkness of Jonathan's tinted window, but Rio had already pushed whatever it was into his pocket. He must be taking bets from the other men. Bile rose and the strong desire to vomit in Jonathan's treasured sports car made her clamp a hand over her own mouth. She closed her eyes and swallowed hard a few times until the feeling passed.

When she felt a little better, Carolyn opened her eyes again. The men were gone. Only Rio stood by the door, staring straight at the Mustang. She slid lower in her seat. With the distance and dark-tinted windows, he couldn't possibly see her. Yet he remained there for at least a full minute looking in her direction. Then he moved away to enter the warehouse. Carolyn emptied her lungs with a soft whoosh once he was out of her sight.

More minutes ticked by. Her muscles were so rigid her back ached. It shouldn't take this long to go inside and get one fifteen-year-old boy. Something must have gone wrong. What if some huge caveman-type punched Jonathan? What if he was on the floor and unconscious? What if she lost her own mind worrying?

It didn't take a lot of imagination to know any number of things could have happened, and Carolyn was no slouch in the imagination department. She shifted in her seat and looked at her watch again. Finally, she made up her mind. Five more minutes. If Jonathan didn't come out in five more minutes, she'd go inside herself. She's the one who asked him to come here, and she certainly couldn't just sit by while who knows what went on.

She kept her fingers clamped around the door handle, ready to launch herself from the car. *Four minutes. Three minutes. Two minutes. One minute.* Hand shaking a little, she lifted the handle just as the warehouse door swung open, revealing Jonathan and Coby. Carolyn went limp with relief and watched them walk through the lot toward the Mustang. Jonathan's face appeared smug and a little arrogant, but she couldn't read Coby's expression, although he still had the bag. They got to the car and Jonathan opened the driver's door. He moved his seat forward so Coby could slide into the miniscule back seat.

"Here's your young man, delivered safe and sound as promised."

Carolyn twisted around to look at Coby. "What in the world is going on? Why did you come here?"

Coby remained stubbornly silent until Jonathan prodded him. "Go on. Tell her what you told me."

Voice emotionless, nearly robotic, he complied. "Rio brought me here. He comes to the fights all the time. And he goes to fights at other places too. He helps run them."

As a child, Carolyn had once fallen off her bike to the pavement. The spill knocked the wind from her lungs and made the world spin. Hearing what she had suspected spoken aloud had the same effect. When she could talk again, she said, "Coby, you know this is wrong, don't you? Dogfighting is cruel and dangerous and illegal. After everything we've talked about, I can't believe you'd do anything to put animals in jeopardy. And jeopardize your own future too."

She saw a hint of what looked like remorse on his face.

"I don't want any dogs getting hurt."

Her mouth dropped open in surprise. "But this involves fighting. Dogs *do* get hurt. That's what happens."

"I don't come to watch. I come to help them. If a dog gets bit up, I fix him. Some of the guys have been teaching me, and I've been learning from you too, Dr. Becker. Any dog that gets hurt bad, I send him to somebody else. Someone like you."

Good Lord. Her gaze slid to the canvas bag. "Coby, this may not be the right time, but I have to ask. Have you been taking the clinic's supplies to work the fights?"

He squirmed in the seat, then nodded his head. "Yes'm."

"There you have it, Carolyn, the answer to the mystery." Jonathan nodded with conviction.

Her heart sank, and she turned her face forward for fear disappointment would be too clearly displayed on it. "This is really serious. Stealing and involvement in what goes on here. I'm not sure I can avoid making a report of what's happening, and I didn't want to have to do that."

Coby spoke up fast. "I wouldn't steal from the clinic. All I did was borrow stuff. I figured on coming in to work extra hours for what I took. Here." He shoved the bag at her. "You can have it back. When they pay me for working the fights. I'll give you some money."

Carolyn felt in over her head and massaged the ache at her temples. Perhaps she'd taken on more than she could handle. "It isn't quite so easy. Give me time to think about this. The clinic must be repaid, of course, but I'm not sure you can work it off. One thing I am sure of, though, is your involvement here"—she waved her hand toward the warehouse—"is not the answer."

Silence in the car hung like storm clouds, heavy with unsaid words.

Jonathan shattered it with an announcement. "Well, Carolyn, I saw your friend Rio Medina here. I hope this shows you what kind of person he is."

She stared straight ahead. "You don't have to convince me. I blame myself for a lot of this. I shouldn't have encouraged Coby to see Rio."

"Don't act like I'm not here when you talk." Coby's voice carried over the sound of tires on the nearby highway. "Rio's a friend."

Jonathan shot a glance toward the back seat. "He certainly hasn't done you any favors, has he? Or Dr. Becker either."

"I'm afraid Jonathan's right," Carolyn said, "but I don't want to talk about Rio now. He isn't important. I want to talk about you. We're going to figure this out, and we'll find a way to do the right thing."

"You ain't gonna keep me away from Stella and the clinic, are you?" The undercurrent of pleading in his voice muddled her thoughts, yet this wasn't a time to waver. *Tough love, Carolyn.*

"I can't answer your question right now. I want you to come to the clinic tomorrow after school and we'll discuss it. That should give me time to make up my mind on how this will be handled." She backed off a little at the look on his face and said, "Look, I know you love Stella, and she loves you, but something has to be done before your future implodes. One thing I can say for sure. Whatever I decide, it will include a meeting with you, me, and your mom."

Coby's chin dipped toward his chest. He didn't speak another word during the rest of the ride home.

Chapter Twenty-Three

Coby's apartment building reminded her of the old structure near the warehouse with its grimy glass, missing screens, and rusted air conditioning units mounted in windows. Carolyn got out of the car with Coby, intent on walking him to his door, but he shook his head.

"I don't know if Mom's home. And if she is home and she's mad, it's a bad time for me to bring anybody in." He scuffed his tennis shoes toward the entrance with his shoulders bunched. The dejected way he looked made her wish she could follow him.

Jonathan didn't have much to say on the ride to the clinic. He was letting her stew in her own foolishness, Carolyn supposed. She left him in the car while she ran inside to gather Stella, who barked and leaped with excitement at her return. After a moment's thought, Carolyn grabbed a towel for the back seat. No sense in risking any accidents on the Mustang's spotless upholstery.

As soon as they pulled up to her building, Jonathan looked at her and smiled. "Do you have coffee on hand?"

"I owe you more than coffee, but I don't feel very well. Not to mention the only thing I want to do right now is get in the shower and scrub myself clean." She managed a weak smile. "Let's plan on tomorrow. You bring some wine. I'll figure out dinner. We'll relax and have a long talk."

Jonathan's mouth broke into a grin. "I'll be there. I've got a vintage wine I've been saving for a special occasion. I think this is a good time to open it."

"That sounds great." On an impulse, she leaned over and pressed her lips experimentally against his. The skin on his face felt smooth as a baby's, but his touch didn't generate the same bone-jarring jolt of current Rio's had. It wasn't a bad thing. Electricity killed people, didn't it?

"Wow," Jonathan said, "thank you. I have a few things to do first, but I'll see you tomorrow at seven."

Carolyn nodded wearily. She and Stella got out of the car and walked into the apartment. She unhooked Stella's leash and moved to the sofa where she promptly dropped like a cinder block. The day's events seemed impossible, and she couldn't for the life of her make sense of them.

After lapping from her water bowl, Stella picked up a tennis ball and dropped it at Carolyn's feet. Muscles tense with anticipation, she backed away, pricked up her ears, and waited.

"You're right." Carolyn said. "I think a little playtime would be good for us both."

She tossed the ball into the kitchen. Stella's nails clicked and slid across the floor as she scampered to grab it. They repeated the process over and over until Carolyn lost count of the number of times Stella fetched the ball. Finally, she said, "Sorry, girl. If I don't get in the shower, I'll fall asleep mid-throw." Carolyn ran her fingers through the tangles of her hair, and grabbed a towel from the linen closet. Only two clean ones left, which meant time to do laundry. A quick study of her apartment pointed out a light layer of dust on the furniture. Her home looked as dirty as she felt. With company coming to dinner, a cleanup would be in order. If only she had a Mrs. Caldwell. Her mother's meticulous housekeeper was exactly what she needed. Someone who could turn disarray and grime into organization, cleanliness, and—what did Marie Kondo call it?—a place of joy. Wouldn't that be nice?

Several insistent raps at the front door stopped Carolyn mid-stride. She never had visitors unless they'd been invited and wondered if a salesperson had sneaked through the security door again. It wouldn't be the first time someone tried to sell her a service or a cruise or hand her a booklet to help save her soul—even though the apartment manager had assured her when she moved in, it would never happen. Carolyn's feet pounded to the door in a mood to say what she thought about uninvited solicitors, but when she looked through the security peephole, she saw Rio standing there with his hands jammed into his pockets.

She considered letting him wait until hell froze over when a burst of righteous anger flamed hot enough to burn away fatigue. She yanked the door open. "What are you doing here?"

"That's what I like best about you, Carolyn. Don't bother with pleasantries, just get right to the point." His lips curved. "Since I tend to be the same way, I'll forgive you. Now, may I come in, or would you rather have a discussion in front of your neighbor?"

Sure enough, Mrs. Manafee, who enjoyed nothing more than getting into other people's business, had just gotten off the elevator with a bag of groceries in her arms. It wasn't lost on Carolyn how long the woman stood by the door balancing the bag and fiddling with her key.

"Come in." Carolyn hissed out the words and then waved at Mrs. Manafee, who appeared miffed the conversation would continue without her.

Rio came inside, and Carolyn pushed the door shut behind him. Stella the Turncoat came on the run, racing toward Rio in tail-wagging joy. He reached down to scratch her head while Stella pushed against his leg in bliss.

"It's nice to know somebody's glad to see me."

Stella's legs turned into noodles, and her body collapsed to the floor in complete surrender.

Carolyn cleared her throat. "Would you mind telling me what you want? I have a lot to do."

Rio's face sobered. "You want me to get to the point? All right, I will. You were at a warehouse on the east side today. Why?"

She planted her feet in defiance. "How would you know where I was today?"

"I saw you sitting like a princess in Jonathan's Mustang. It's a rather conspicuous vehicle to hide in. He left you alone somewhere you had no business being in the first place. By all that's holy, what makes you so intent on doing reckless things?"

"Is that what you came here to say? First of all, let me remind you it's none of your business where I go, who I see, or what I do." Furious, Carolyn slammed her hand on the counter for emphasis, then wished she hadn't. Her palm stung like the devil. Stella tilted her head at the unexpected noise and pricked her ears forward.

"Temper, temper, Dr. Becker. I've told you before Jonathan isn't the most trustworthy soul in town. I'll be glad to give you names of people who agree with me, since you seem so reluctant to take my advice."

"Jonathan has done more for the clinic than I can say. He also never hesitates to help when I need him, and he's always a perfect gentleman."

"A gentleman perhaps, but not for lack of trying to be otherwise, I imagine."

The remark made her sputter with renewed rage. "What right have you to criticize him when you're up to your neck in illegal dogfighting? Not to mention taking Coby along with you and encouraging his involvement too."

Rio cocked a brow. "Who told you that?"

"Coby told me himself, after Jonathan brought him to the car."

"I see." Rio folded his arms over his wide chest. "That explains the long talk Jonathan had with the boy before he took Coby away."

"Are you accusing him of something?"

"Make of it what you will, Carolyn, but I can assure you I had nothing to do with Coby being at the dogfights. Actually, when he does show up, I do my best to keep an eye on him."

"Keep an eye on him?" Carolyn wanted to shout, but then—ever aware of Mrs. Manafee—spoke in a softer voice. "He's already in over his head. He's apparently been stealing supplies from the clinic to play amateur doctor with the dogs."

"I'm sorry he resorted to such tactics, but I'm not surprised. I've seen smart young kids used in similar ways before. Dog owners appreciate having a youngster around who has some savvy handling animals. They let the kid take care of little things while the owners handle business."

"That's obscene. It sounds like they're grooming children to be dogfighters."

His shoulders rose in a shrug. "I think that's a fairly accurate observation."

"Coby wants to go to vet school. If he gets involved any deeper in this business, that won't ever happen."

"Agreed. I'll do what I can to put a stop to it."

"You? What are you going to do? Teach him new dogfighting tricks?" Carolyn's words were bitter, and she flung them at him like missiles.

"Look, I admit I have no business being here and no authority over what you do, but regardless of your opinion about me, you're wrong if you think I'd stand by while someone hurts a child."

If only she could believe him. Yet logic, her lifetime companion, pointed out the evidence her heart wanted to overlook. She lifted her chin. "I presume you've said everything you came here to say, although I can't imagine why you felt it necessary."

Silence crackled between them, uncomfortable as static from an old radio. She stood her ground stonily, with no intention of speaking first.

He sighed and shook his head. "Caro, you're more misguided than Coby if you don't understand the reason I'm here."

One side of his mouth rose in a half smile that disarmed her with the most infuriating effectiveness. Why was this man—wrong in every way for her—able to stir such a roller coaster of feelings? Maybe Teena could organize an intervention. No, wait a minute. Teena would probably throw a party. Rio's boot had a piece of dried mud on the toe, so Carolyn focused on it. If she looked at his face, he'd surely read her seesawing line of thought.

The boots came a few steps closer, and Rio grabbed her hand. "Listen to me, please. Swear you'll stay away from all this. No more ill-advised trips to the warehouse. A lot of things are happening, and they go way beyond Coby. Something's going to break loose very soon. You shouldn't be there when it does."

Drat it all, she couldn't help but raise her head to look at him. He waited for an answer, and the earnest sincerity she recognized bulldozed what remained of her defenses.

"I won't do anything foolish, but you need to start talking. There are pieces to this puzzle I'm missing, and for the sake of my own sanity, I've got to hear it. What's going on?"

A muscle in his jaw twitched. "I couldn't say anything even if I wanted to. Hell, I'm not even sure I know everything myself yet." He dropped her hand and scrubbed his fingers across the back of his neck. "But there's one thing I can say. There's a reason for what I'm doing. As soon as I can tell you, I will. Until then, I'm asking you to have a little faith. Trust me. Please."

Her mind blared an alert. Trust? She used to have no problem trusting people, but where had it ever gotten her? She kept her gaze locked on his and almost immediately found herself drowning in a pale blue sea—rescued by the crinkles at the edges of his eyes. Her head and her heart fought a swift battle. Disbelief widened her eyes when she heard herself say, "I do trust you. I don't understand why, but I do."

Face solemn, Rio swept her into his arms. The embrace turned her into a rag doll that molded neatly against him, a perfectly enticing fit. Her head rested against his chest, and she listened to the unhurried rhythm of his heart. Nothing seemed to bother Rio. Unruffled composure all but radiated from him in tangible waves.

She looked up at him, and her lips parted. She knew it was a blatant invitation, but who cared? His mouth tugged into a smile before he obliged and lowered his lips to hers in a kiss that quickly deepened. The scent of soap and musk enveloped her senses, and she knew she'd have dropped to the floor in a heap if her arms weren't wrapped around his neck. He broke the kiss, and she still held on to him like a lifeline. Who had ever kissed her until she felt lightheaded? No one, that's who. Not Clay and certainly not Jonathan.

Rio kept his gaze on hers. "Do you know your eyes are the color of grass in springtime? I've been carrying a picture of them in my mind since the last time we were together." He grinned. "And they get darker when you're mad."

Since when could a man make her feel so positively—swoony? She examined the strong planes of his face, his jaw bristled dark from a day's growth of whiskers. There was a lot she still didn't know about him, but somehow, any other questions didn't seem important. Her fingers skimmed his hair where it lay soft against the nape of his neck.

"I've been trying not to think about you at all, though it sure didn't stop me." She lifted her shoulders helplessly. "The night we—were together, I realized for once I'd done something major without a bit of advance planning. I'm sorry if it made you unhappy, but I'm not sorry it happened."

Rio rubbed his hands up and down her back, soft enough to make her shiver. "My fault. I shouldn't have let things go so far. It was something I swore I wouldn't allow. When I remember the look on your face..." This time his smile failed to reach his eyes. "Let's just agree it wasn't one of my finer moments."

He brushed a thumb against her cheek and lowered his head to hers again. A searing prickle of heat surged through her body that carried unnerving impulses to places she blushed to consider. Boldly, she took her arms from around Rio's neck and played with the top button of his denim shirt, fully aware he kept his eyes on her. She opened the first button and then the next and the next, until she could push the shirt's edges aside and pull it from his shoulders. The garment dropped to the floor.

Rio's skin looked swarthier than ever against his blindingly white T-shirt. Last time she hadn't the nerve to really look at him, so today she ran her hands over the thick muscle of his upper arms, fascinated at how pale her skin looked compared to his. A study of Rio's sculptured biceps and chest compelled her to send a quick prayer of thanks to whoever had created his workout program—a true genius. It amused her to see his normally self-assured expression become the slightest bit self-conscious, and she playfully said, "Is something wrong?"

"I've never been inspected quite like this. What's the verdict?"

"Oh, you definitely exceed my expectations." Did her remark sound brazen? A giggle escaped her. She sure hoped so. And just to make sure Rio hadn't misunderstood her intent, she stood on her tiptoes and pressed her mouth against his—a kiss as long and lingering and seductive as she could manage.

After that, it took quite a while before either one of them could say anything more.

Chapter Twenty-Four

Sun streamed through the bedroom window, cutting through her blinds to lie in bright narrow rows across the sheets. Carolyn blinked her eyes a few times and yawned. Stretching out her back like a cat, the images from the night before rumbaed through her mind in a tantalizing way, instantly setting her face on fire. Then she noticed Rio lying on his side watching her, his expression tender.

"Good morning." She caressed his stubbled cheek. "How long have you been awake?"

"Just long enough to notice how very innocent and sweet you look when you're sleeping. A person would never suspect what a stubborn woman you really are."

"M'mm." She stretched again. "I'm not stubborn. And not very innocent anymore either."

"Thanks to me," Rio said with a touch of self-mockery. "I could say I'm sorry for being such a bad influence on you, but it would be a lie of the highest order."

Carolyn moved an admiring hand to his chest, a feature she felt truly deserved a trophy—outstanding on any human evolutionary chart. "Believe me. Nothing happened that I didn't agree to—or want. Don't spoil it by apologizing."

"My lack of discipline lately is disturbing." He pushed a strand of damp hair off her forehead. "Unfortunately, when it comes to dealing with you, I don't seem to have much self-control. That can be a dangerous thing."

Carolyn turned her body to snuggle against him, and with one arm, he pulled her close. A swell of pure animal lust made her think hard about calling Teena to say she'd be late. The idea sounded delightful, so she asked, "Can you stay a while longer?"

He gave her an apologetic squeeze before rising from the bed to pull on his jeans. "Regretfully, no. I should have left hours ago. Maybe you're the one who's a bad influence on me." His mischievous tone caused something pleasant to swell in her chest.

I can only hope.

That's when the pesky voice of logic reappeared. "I guess you're off to go somewhere you won't share with me and do something we can't discuss. Isn't there anything you can tell me? This is all so baffling."

"Caro, please don't ask again. Just know I'm confident this will be over soon if it gives you any comfort at all."

"All right. I guess for now there's nothing I can do but wait." *If only he weren't such a sphynx!* "In the meantime, do you have any ideas on what I can do for Coby? I've been thinking I might have to let him go—stealing from the clinic. Jeanne will be furious."

"I wish you wouldn't. The best thing you can do for him is keep him busy. Extra hours. Anything you can think of so he won't have time left for the warehouse."

"It's been hard enough to get him to show up on a regular basis at all. How can I convince him to do extra hours?"

"You're shrewd enough to come up with something. I have confidence in your ability." He fastened the first button on his shirt. "To be honest, some things I've heard him say lately make me think he's beginning to come around, but remember, it won't be easy. He earns money at the fights. As much as he and his mom clash with each other, he does what he can to help out."

"But he's only fifteen. He's too young to have responsibilities like that."

"Sometimes boys have to become men a lot sooner than you'd think." A shadow passed over his face.

She remembered another boy doing what he could for his mother, and she wet her dry lips before speaking. "I do understand, but I can't help thinking how different Coby is when he's at the clinic. He's so eager to learn. I hope he doesn't think he's more skilled than he is. I really think he believes he's helping those dogs. But if one of them is badly injured, what can he do to save them?"

Rio stopped buttoning his shirt to look at her. "Think about it for a minute, Carolyn. Don't you know why he brought Stella to you?"

Carolyn's face angled upward, and her voice broke. "It's true then. Poor sweet Stella was hurt in those awful dogfights."

"Of course she was. Coby rescued her."

"Rescued her? How did he do that?"

Rio sat on the bed and put his hand over hers. "Stella wasn't a good fighter, and any dog who isn't game, dies."

Carolyn's hand went to her throat. The thought made her sick. "Somebody kills them?"

Rio nodded, his eyes hard. "They're used for training exercises, or sometimes an owner will find another way to get rid of them."

"That's horrible."

"One of the men let another dog attack Stella. Coby intervened and told the owner he'd take care of having her put down. When Coby asked me where to go for help, I suggested you."

"Oh, my God." Carolyn thought about Stella, happily chasing tennis balls and wagging her silly tail. "I knew he wasn't telling me everything, but I had no idea the situation was as dire as that."

"Both Coby and I were glad when you took Stella in. She needed a safe place to live and somebody to care about her."

"Rio." She chewed her lip. "There've been a couple of other people who've brought in dogs with bite injuries. Did you send them too?"

At once, his eyes lasered into hers. "Other than Coby, I haven't sent any dogfighters to you. It seemed safer to keep them away from the clinic's door."

"One of them mentioned a friend referred him. I assumed it was you."

"Not guilty on that count, but I have a suspicion of who may have done it. Thanks for letting me know." He let go of her hand and stood.

"So, you're leaving now?" *Oh, please let him say no. Pretty please?*

"I'm afraid so. I've got work, and I imagine you do too. Have you seen the time?"

She glanced at the digital clock on her bedside table and bolted upright, eyes wide. "Seven o'clock! Holy Shih Tzu, I forgot about a meeting with my boss this morning." She leaped from the bed, shivered, and grabbed for her robe.

"Young lady, the way you look without your clothes makes me very sorry I have to go."

Strange that she didn't feel a bit shy basking in the warmth of his appreciative review. "I'm sorry too, but I've barely enough time to shower and dress as it is. I'll need to have Teena cover for me until I can get to the office."

As she rushed past him, Rio grabbed her around the waist and pulled her against him. The heat of his body warmed her, as did the feel of his chin resting lightly on the top of her head.

"I think Coby will agree to pretty much anything you ask, so use it to your advantage. Whatever you can come up with, do it."

"I'll try, but how long can I keep him from something he's determined to do?"

He laughed and her insides melted like April snow.

"Simple. By being the relentlessly determined woman you are."

Not exactly a sonnet, but his velvety tone made the remark sound like a compliment. "Well, whatever it is you're off to do, be careful."

He nodded and bestowed a lingering kiss that curled her toes, before leaning over to rub Stella's ears.

As soon as she heard the door close, the captivating haze of happiness lifted, prodding her wide-awake and into the shower. Hot water pounded on her as she attempted to analyze what Rio said. Would the dogfights really disappear soon? She hadn't a clue why he seemed so certain but prayed he was right. Then her mind meandered to when she'd see him again, and her chest fluttered with anticipation.

Entertaining, but not very productive.

She applied a liberal blob of vanilla-scented shampoo and tried to scrub away her R-rated thoughts. The effort paid off in ideas, and she titled them.

Ways to Keep Teenage Boys Busy

First, she'd tell Coby the clinic had desperate need of his help (not exactly a lie) and request he work extra hours. Teena could send him on errands. The clinic could use a good deep cleaning, and what dog didn't want extra walks? She hoped such diversionary tactics worked better than some of her other Coby-interventions had done. And why wouldn't they? In more ways than one, things had changed since she left Kansas City—even kissing two men in one evening, thank you very much. If the new Carolyn could juggle two men, she could do anything.

Stella looked up, eyes filled with hope, and effectively stopped any further towel-drying. The horrors Rio had described stampeded back, making her lips wobble, which earned Stella three extra treats plus a hug, poor girl. The dog gobbled her treasures and responded with a rapturous slurp of thanks.

Rio's prediction couldn't come soon enough. When the dogfights ended, all her troubles would be over. Except for:

Coby's issues at home and at school

Getting the numbers she needed for the clinic

Figuring out Rio's secrets

Deciding how to get that sexy man back into her bed—STAT

How Jonathan might react if she canceled tonight's dinner

Yikes. Okay, maybe the new Carolyn did still have a few things left to figure out.

Chapter Twenty-Five

Carolyn rushed through the door with Stella galloping behind her. "Good morning, Teena," she said, puffing her words as she tried to catch her breath. "I'm sorry I'm late."

"I guess I won't fire you since you're usually early. Besides, your first appointment is a no-show, and Jeanne's not here yet. No harm done." Teena's gaze dropped to Carolyn's feet. "Did you look in a mirror today?"

"What?" Carolyn tilted her head.

"Look at yourself. You have on two different colored shoes."

Carolyn glanced at her sensible flats—navy-blue shoe on one foot and a black one on the other. When she'd found the shoes a few weeks ago at the store, they were so comfortable, three pairs in different colors went home with her. Apparently, she'd grabbed the wrong two from the jumble at the bottom of her closet. Maybe this shopping decision, which had seemed brilliant at the time, hadn't been the smartest thing she'd ever done.

"Oh, great. This would happen on the day I have a meeting with Jeanne. Well, thanks for letting me know. Maybe she'll just think I'm a trendsetter."

Even Stella looked up in canine disbelief. Carolyn turned away, thankful she didn't have a surgery scheduled. She really shouldn't have a scalpel in her hand on a morning like this.

"Um-hmm. It seems to me your head is occupied with something—or somebody else. Anything interesting going on at your place?"

"Oh, nothing really. Just a little bit of this and a lot of that."

Teena shook her head and then gave Carolyn a skeptical look. "I think you better check out your slacks while you're at it, Dr. Becker. Something's not right there either."

Carolyn looked down. She'd forgotten to zip up her slacks. "Whoops. Well, this is what I get for waking up late." She headed toward the bathroom. "I'd better check myself out to see what else I've forgotten."

With spots of color burning on her face, Carolyn closed the bathroom door. She really needed to get herself together. Scatterbrained had never been one of her traits before.

She zipped her pants and straightened her blouse, then tucked a strand of hair behind her ear and hoped today's clients all kept their eyes up. The worst part of the whole fiasco wasn't how she looked. It would be the interrogation she'd soon get from Teena, who no doubt would chip away at Carolyn until every detail emerged. Why her assistant hadn't gone into law enforcement instead of veterinary medicine bewildered her. The CIA would love to hire someone with her tenacity.

A tap sounded at the bathroom door. "Jeanne is here," Teena announced. "She's waiting in your office. Oh, and I'm buying lunch today. We haven't had a good talk in a long time."

Wonderful. "Okay. Thanks, Teena. I'll be right out."

After a final look in the mirror to smooth her hair, she took a deep breath and opened the door, walking past Teena who pecked at the reception area computer, earbuds attached. Halfway across the room, Carolyn could hear the music blaring. With decibels at that level, Teena would need hearing aids before she turned thirty.

She found Jeanne sitting in the office with a folder on her lap and a somber expression on her face.

"Good morning, Jeanne," Carolyn said with cheer she didn't feel.

"Good morning. I brought along the reports you sent me."

"I see." Carolyn sat behind her desk, and her knee started an anxious bob. "I know we're twenty-five percent under projections, but we are moving in the right direction."

"Yes, but unfortunately, not fast enough. I won't sugarcoat this. The mayor called me last week, and he said the board is inclined to close the clinic so they can use this building as a rental. They don't think the numbers justify anything else."

"Oh, no." Carolyn pressed her knee down to stop it. "Can't they give us more time?"

"We have the mayor and a couple of board members on our side. The rest, not so much."

"Don't they understand it takes a while to make progress?"

"When it comes to money, patience runs thin in government. We've got two months left on the initial agreement. Then we're through."

Carolyn's heart dropped to her toes. "I don't know what to say. This is awful. May I tell Teena? I imagine she'll want to start looking for a new job right away."

"No." Jeanne stood. "You're not authorized to say anything yet. The mayor prefers to wait before the news gets out. Right now, this is only between you and me. I'm truly sorry. It was a chance that just didn't work out."

Jeanne nodded and left Carolyn to blink in disbelief. Her eyes felt like they'd been rubbed with sandpaper.

Teena rushed into the office, earbuds dangling around her neck, eyes flared wide. "Her face looked like a prisoner waiting for the firing squad. What did she say?"

"Oh, we talked about the usual things. You know, like how numbers need to come up. Routine stuff." Carolyn cleared her throat and did her best to behave as though she hadn't received a gut punch. Teena's puzzled expression indicated she sensed something else was afoot.

They worked without their usual banter, and when lunch time came, Carolyn closed the office so they could walk to the sandwich shop. Teena chattered artlessly about her love life while Carolyn answered in monosyllables. After they ordered their food, she sank into a booth and looked at her veggie sub, feeling like a traitor.

Teena opened her bag of potato chips. "Let's see. You've got no appetite. Late to work. Acting like a zombie. Crazy clothing mistakes—by the way, it's a miracle the fashion police didn't arrest you. Something's up, and I'm thinking it has to do with you racing out of the clinic yesterday. Tell me."

At least the line of questioning didn't extend to the doomsday news Jeanne had delivered—not yet, anyway. "I'm fine. I just, uh, didn't get much rest last night is all. Granted, I'm not as alert as I should be, but I only realize how tired I am when I sit down."

"Isn't that funny? You're not sick, and yet you didn't get much sleep. Hmm. Did Stella keep you awake? No, wait a minute. She seems to be her normal happy self. Come on now, fess up to your Aunt Teena. Something more is going on. What's up?"

Distraction. It worked wonders on many levels. "All right. I know you'll keep hounding me until you find out what you want to know. I had sort of a date last night. It went later than it should."

The expression on Teena's face reminded Carolyn of a border collie's upon spying a wandering sheep. "I knew it! You've had dates before, but they never left you in a condition like this. I'm almost afraid to ask—who is it?"

Carolyn toyed with saying she'd met someone new, but she decided against it. Teena had her ways, and she'd rather not be caught in an outright fib to someone who wasn't merely a coworker anymore. Besides, for some peculiar reason, she wanted to talk about it. "Jonathan helped me find Coby, but after he took me home, Rio came over."

"What? You left the clinic with Jonathan and hooked up with Rio later? You go, girl!" Teena said, and leaped from the booth as though she'd been catapulted to do a little shimmy-shake dance. The other customers looked up from their food to stare. "So you finally came to your senses. For a minute, I thought you were going to tell me you'd gone google-eyed over you-know-who."

Carolyn eyed her assistant. "You don't like Jonathan, do you?"

Teena sat down and popped a chip into her mouth, which didn't stop her from talking. "There's something about him that sets my teeth on edge. Maybe it's the weird way he smiles and nods like he's pretending to listen to what you say. Maybe it's how he oozes over with fake charm. He's sure not the one I'd pick in a horse race."

Curiosity piqued Carolyn's question. "And Rio *is* the horse you'd choose?"

"You bet he is." Teena fanned herself with a paper napkin. "Tall, dark, and handsome, that man shivers my timbers with a single look."

With difficulty, Carolyn kept herself from nodding in agreement. She didn't want to disclose the private details, so she kept it simple. "We had a…really nice time. I'll see where things go from here."

"I need details. You've been fire-spittin' mad at Rio, but last night the two of you had sort-of-a-date. Come on, Carolyn. Spill it."

Carolyn obliged by grabbing her own napkin, rolling her eyes toward the ceiling, and fanning her face.

Teena snickered. "Well, well, well. It must have been quite a night. No wonder you're tired today. Don't you think for even a minute I'm going to forget about this. I'll let you get caught up on sleep tonight, but girl, we're going to talk tomorrow. And I do mean talk—about everything."

Teena's approval buoyed Carolyn's mood. "As they say, tomorrow's another day. Let's go. I need to get ready for our next appointment."

The rest of the afternoon, Teena looked smug with the information she'd gleaned. She strutted around the office, pulling files for the remainder of the day's appointments wearing a satisfied grin. Obviously, Rio presented a captivating subject. Thinking about him certainly made Carolyn feel giddy. She forced herself to settle down and look at a report, which immediately caused her knee to bounce again. How selfish must she be to spend time considering her love life? She and Teena were both near to losing their jobs, and the clinic she'd grown to love would be gone for good.

Yet it served no purpose to worry now, when she felt bleary-eyed and overwhelmed. Perhaps after she'd assimilated the true meaning of her night with Rio, along with the disheartening news from Jeanne, she'd have strength enough to face the clinic's pending demise. She might even come up with some amazing last-ditch solution.

But such a miracle wasn't going to happen today.

Following two wellness exams, the schedule of a spay surgery, and treating a dog with canine flu, Carolyn finished writing her notes on the last appointment of the day. She glanced at the clock and then at Fred, who offered no insight. Coby hadn't arrived yet. Fear nibbled the perimeter of her brain like a school of piranha. Surely, he wasn't heading back to that horrible warehouse—especially with the discussion they'd had.

She could call his mom, but why bother? Mrs. Jefferson never had a clue about her son's activities. Contacting her would only fan flames against him. Jonathan? Probably not the best choice since Coby didn't seem fond of him. Neither did Teena.

Yet she'd promised Jonathan dinner—tonight. She ought to touch base with him about the evening. As much as she'd like to cancel, he'd been nothing but decent and good to her. She at least owed him a nice meal. Carolyn entered his cell number, but he didn't pick up, so she left a message for him to call her.

Then a thought calmed her anxiety like oil over water. Rio. She started to call him but plunked the phone down in frustration. Why hadn't she asked him for his phone number this morning? This is what happened when she had her head in the clouds.

After more than an hour passed without a word from Coby, Carolyn told Teena, "I specifically told him to be here today so we could discuss his behavior. I guess he's not going to show up."

Teena puffed with conviction. "That boy needs a man to give him a good ass-whupping. That's what my daddy did to my brothers when they were too full of themselves to think they had to do the right thing. It worked too. They're both police officers now, and who'd ever have thought that would happen?"

The day became a dead weight settling like a herd of elephants on Carolyn's chest. "Well, it's almost time to lock up. If you want to run along, go ahead and I'll take care of it."

"I think I will go 'cause I've got a date tonight. Hope I get as lucky as you did. And don't forget tomorrow is Tell Teena Everything Day."

"It works both ways, my friend." Carolyn waved a hand as Teena grinned and headed for the door.

With her assistant gone and no overnight patients, silence surrounded her. Too much silence. She stared at a report on her computer screen until the numbers ran together. At once, the enormity of another loss sent her hands to cover her face. How excited she'd been when the clinic opened, and now it would all come to an end. And why?

Because of her. She hadn't been good enough for Clay. She couldn't make a success of the clinic. She didn't even have what it took to help one struggling teenage boy. She'd failed everyone. And as for Rio, who knew? The way he avoided serious relationships, perhaps what happened last night didn't at all mean the same thing to him as it did to her.

Time to let it go. Carolyn shut down her computer and picked up her jacket and purse. She checked the back door, then gathered some reports to take home. Stella followed behind her, whimpering a little, and Carolyn bent to pet the dog's head. Maybe she should just give up on everything and turn in her resignation. By tomorrow morning, she could be on her way back to Kansas City and leave all these problems behind. Her parents would be over the moon if she took up residence in her old bedroom again. Yet somehow the idea of escape didn't make her feel much better.

But it did light a tiny flame.

"Stella, I just know something terrible is going to happen at the warehouse, and Coby will be caught in the middle of it. I might not be able to do anything else right, but I can't ignore him." She walked to the door and looked outside. The sun had dipped lower in the sky, and a brisk wind whipped people's jackets. As hard as she squinted to see a boy racing toward the clinic, there was no sign of him.

Where else could he be but the warehouse? Rio had warned her away from it, but...

Resolve stiffened her jaw. "I'm going after him. I'll be back to get you just as soon as I have Coby with me." The agreeable Stella lifted her ears and wagged her tail as though in approval. Carolyn smiled grimly.

Well, at least that's one vote in my favor.

Chapter Twenty-Six

Carolyn climbed into a yellow cab, its color dulled by more than a few layers of grimy gunk. She gave the driver a location on the east side, and his eyes rounded. "Hey, lady, it'll be dark soon. Are you sure you wanta go there?"

"Yes, please. Is there a problem?"

The cabby shook his head and pulled away from the curb, merging into traffic while Carolyn considered various scenarios in between shivers vibrating her spine.

Possibility #1: She'd find Coby. He'd flash a charming grin and leave the warehouse without a question.

Possibility #2: Rio would be there doing whatever it was he so aggravatingly refused to explain, but he'd have no trouble making Coby do the right thing.

Possibility #3: One of the men who paid Coby would suddenly recognize the error of his ways and send the boy home.

Possibility #4: Nope. She didn't want to consider possibility #4.

The cab swerved to miss another car, and Carolyn banged her shoulder hard against the door. "Sorry," the driver muttered as she rubbed her arm.

The planning skills she'd found essential in veterinary school weren't always so helpful in real life. It all came down to one thing—winging it based on whatever she found. Notions flitted around like sparrows, her shoulder hurt like the dickens, and a tension headache started to ping at the back of her head. She fished through her bag for a couple of ibuprofen tablets and put them in her mouth. The taste almost made her gag, but under the circumstances, she needed as clear a head as she could muster.

When the cab rolled to a stop in front of the apartment building near the warehouse, she looked out the window to plan her next move. More men than before walked toward the ramshackle building, but she didn't see anything of either Coby or Rio. This time, the parking lot swelled with so many vehicles, it was hard to pick out one she might recognize—like a dusty black Jeep with a dent in the side, for instance.

The cabby's voice ground from patient indulgence to I've-had-just-about-enough irritation. "Do you expect me to just sit here? You're still on the clock, and I've got another fare to pick up."

"Yes, I know. Give me a minute, please." There wasn't any help for it. She had no other choice but to go to the warehouse. Surely, she could blend into this crowd of people, at least for a few minutes. And if Coby wasn't there, she'd simply turn around and leave. She didn't want to think about what might happen if she ran into Rio. He wasn't likely to be pleased discovering she'd ignored his instructions again.

"Sir," she said to the driver, "if I go in the building, could you please hold the cab here for me until I come out?"

"Why should I do that? We're not allowed to just sit around. I told you I've got another fare to pick up."

"I'll pay you well for your time, I promise."

"I don't know," he waffled.

Carolyn pulled out her money. For once a lucky break. She'd just cashed her paycheck. "Here. This is for my fare. After I come back, I'll pay you for the ride home plus a sixty-dollar tip. Now can I depend on you to wait for me?"

She saw the change in his eyes. "Well, I guess I can wait for a little while, but I ain't waitin' forever."

"Fine. I won't be long." Carolyn handed him the money she owed and gave him another twenty, hoping it would convince him of her good faith. "I'll give you the rest when you get us home."

"Us?" His eyes became slits.

"Yes. I'll have a young boy with me. You'll be driving both of us."

The cabby popped a piece of gum in his mouth and crossed his arms. "Okay, but don't make this too complicated, and no funny business. I ain't takin' any chances with losing my job."

Carolyn shoved her keys and a twenty in her pocket, in case she needed either cash or a weapon to tuck between her fingers. Her bag stayed on the seat. Carrying a purse into a crowd of strangers didn't seem at all wise. She opened the door and stepped from the cab.

A group had gathered outside the warehouse door. She tried to ignore them and tramped her way across the dusty gravel lot, eyes forward and chin up, despite the distress prickling her neck.

Several men cast a look her way that seemed as welcoming as a farm dog who saw a fox in the henhouse. There wasn't another woman in sight, which certainly didn't render her unnoticeable, but she still took a moment to peek around the perimeter of the warehouse. No Coby.

At the door, a burly man wearing a black T-shirt with a ball cap pulled low over his eyes, leaned against the wall. She decided a polite question might be better than grabbing for the doorknob. "Excuse me, sir. I'm looking for a boy. His name's Coby. Is he here?"

"I don't know any kid named Coby." He stared at her in a way that made her measure how distant the cabby had parked. "Who invited you here anyway?"

"The boy I'm looking for comes here sometimes. He works for me, and I need to talk to him."

"Since when does the boss run around looking for a worker? What'd he do? Steal your payroll or something?"

"Oh no, nothing like that. Look, would you let me check inside for him? If he's not there, I'll be on my way."

"Why should I? This is an exclusive club, you know. There are requirements for people to get in."

"Please. I promise I'll only be a minute." Carolyn thought about bribing him with the twenty but feared a flash of money might become an invitation to a bigger problem.

"The only people allowed inside are the ones who've been invited."

She hadn't counted on admission being by invitation. Winging it meant she didn't have a plan B. Carolyn thought for a moment and finally smiled. "Um, actually I was invited."

"Is that so?" The man's voice dripped sarcasm. "And who invited you?"

She played the only card she had. "A friend of mine. His name is Rio."

Suspicion kept the man's face dark. He looked the type to enjoy throttling someone, but his thumb gestured toward the door. "Fine. You can go in. If Rio sent you, who am I to say no?"

She nodded and crept past him, hoping she looked braver than she felt.

Inside, the place smelled of cigarette smoke, dogs, and urgency. A large group of people kept their eyes on a makeshift ring in the center of the room. Three-foot-high planks surrounded the area where two dogs, eyes alert and tails wagging in a not-so-pleasant way, strained forward, held in place by men who presumed to be the dogs' handlers. She didn't want to look at what happened next and focused her attention on a sweep through the crowd for Coby. A cacophony of voices mixed together in a way that made it nearly impossible for her to understand what anyone said. Dogs in crates outside the ring barked, and the mixture of sounds echoed through the warehouse so

loud it made her want to put her hands over her ears. She
stayed near the wall, hoping to look unobtrusive. Was such
a thing even possible? A few men turned to leer at her,
although no one so much as said hello.

Drat it all. She didn't see Coby. Or Rio either.

Ready to give up and head back to the cab, a familiar
voice from behind stopped her dead in her tracks.

"This one's a loser. He's had plenty of chances. Nothing
I've tried has made him any better. He isn't even good
enough for stud."

Carolyn turned and sucked in a breath. Her eyes
widened when she caught the gaze of the man who'd
spoken, in a moment that obviously startled them both.
Jonathan Locke handed the leash of a black-and-white dog
to a man standing next to him before he moved quickly to
Carolyn's side.

"Well," he said. "Of all the places to visit, this is where
you come? That's not a very good idea."

She discovered enough of her voice to squeak out a
question. "What are you doing here?"

"Darlin', a much better question is, what are *you* doing
here?"

Carolyn looked around and noticed that even though a
few men had watched her earlier, they'd all turned their
attention to the growling dogs. Jonathan took her arm. He
seemed unsteady on his feet and the stench of whiskey
nearly bowled her over. "Come with me. We need to have
a talk."

Never had his grip been so completely unfeeling. This
wasn't the Jonathan she'd been with before, who'd always

tried to charm her. Now he seemed stiff and abrupt, exuding an ominous vibration that sent a tremor through her. She'd seen plenty of people in college under the influence of drink, but none had ever behaved quite like this.

"I came looking for Coby. Since he isn't here, I'll be on my way back to the clinic. I've got a cab waiting."

He gripped her arm hard enough to make her wince.

"True. Your young man didn't show up today. Pity, because it's a busy night and we could have used his help. I must agree with what you told me. The kid does seem to have a knack with animals."

She took advantage of the moment to yank her arm from Jonathan's grip. The places where his fingers held her were probably already turning color. "You're involved in this? I can't believe it. Why?"

"Not everyone has things handed to them tied up with a pretty ribbon like you did. Some of us need to work hard to have cash in the bank and nice things. At the fights, I can have a good time and make a bundle of money too. It isn't so terrible if you stop to think about it. I'm giving people the chance to participate in a sport they enjoy. What's wrong with that?"

Carolyn wasn't sure if she should keep her voice low or scream. Noticing there weren't any sympathetic faces in the crowd helped make up her mind. "If for no other reason, you have to admit this is illegal. You can go to jail, and what good will money do then?"

He nodded. "You bring up a dilemma for me. It wouldn't be good to let this get out."

His behavior confounded her. He'd turned into someone else. Someone extraordinarily spooky. A memory clicked. A question on one of her exams. *How do you handle a frightened, aggressive animal?* In a low and calm voice, she spoke. "What you do is on your own conscience. My only concern is Coby. I'm going to leave now, and we'll call it a day. Please don't come by the clinic again."

She forced herself to saunter as though she had all the time in the world, away from the shouts and cheers. A few furtive glances thrown her direction from people standing nearby gave all the evidence needed to know she couldn't expect anyone here to be on her side. Her hand went to the doorknob.

Jonathan grabbed her wrist. "Not so fast. As I told you, we have things to talk about."

She faced him, her voice firm. "My cab is waiting. Let me go, or I'm going to scream for help. Someone's bound to call the police."

"You think so? Nobody wants the cops here. Do you think anyone cares what happens to you? You might be the divine Dr. Becker at the clinic, but to them, you're only the enemy."

The men filling the room kept their eyes averted from her obvious plight—busy with dogs, exchanging money, and laughing. Jonathan had a point.

"If I don't get back to the cab in two minutes, the driver will make a call." Carolyn threw out her remark in hopes it would convince Jonathan. She had no clue if it was true or not, but it sounded good.

"You're right. I suppose we ought to send your cabby on his way. His services aren't needed."

He walked Carolyn out the door, still holding her arm. When she saw the cab's headlights at the back of the parking lot, she almost smiled. "See, he's right over there." She pointed and stopped herself from sighing with relief. "I'm leaving now. Because we were friends, I won't say anything about what I've seen."

Yet he didn't let her go. "I've never been good enough for you, have I, Carolyn? You made it clear from the start. Seems you prefer trash. Like Rio Medina, for instance. What do you see in that lowlife? It might interest you to know he's here at the fights all the time, but I guess that doesn't bother you. And he's no stranger to your bedroom either, is he?"

She twisted to look at him. "How dare you say such things to me?" Her voice quivered, partly from anger, partly because Jonathan had begun to scare her witless.

"I've seen how you behave whenever his name comes up. And you don't seem to have any trouble inviting *him* up to your place."

"You have no idea what goes on in my personal life."

"But I do. Since I hoped we had a future together, on days you wouldn't see me, I kept an eye on your place. Wanted to make sure no one was interfering. Last night Medina showed up and he stayed until morning. I spent most of today nursing a bottle of whiskey and thinking about the two of you together. He's the reason you never took me upstairs, isn't he?"

Alarm bells clanged in her head at the new information. This was more than rambling from a man who'd had too much to drink. She searched for a way to distract him. "Wait a minute. Don't you remember? I did invite you to dinner. Tonight."

She hoped the comment would derail him, but he continued to speak in the most weirdly detached way, as though what she said hadn't sunk in.

"I've been focusing my time on dogs—and brokering bets. It's brought in a lot more money than I'd ever make in the electronics business. With the debts my father left behind, I had to do something." He gave a mirthless chuckle. "I plan to have the best fighters in the country, and I need a good vet like you to take care of any problem my dogs have without asking a lot of questions."

"You're not making any sense, Jonathan. You know how I feel about this."

"The minute I laid eyes on you; I knew it. You and I could have been a great team. I did everything I could to prove it. I thought you'd learn to want me as much as I wanted you." His left eye twitched.

What now? She couldn't outwrestle him, but maybe she could outsmart him. "Jonathan." She spoke in the most serene voice she could summon. "We both need time to think about this. I owe you dinner. We can figure things out then."

"Dinner? What did you say about dinner?" It felt like he wasn't holding her quite as tightly.

"Yes, remember? Let's forget what's happened, and I'll fix dinner at my apartment for you like we planned. You can have anything you like." She gave him a theatrical smile followed by a wink.

"Well," he said, as though considering the matter. "We might still be able to make it to your place later tonight, but not before we set a few things straight. It's time you stop treating me as second best."

This wasn't going quite the way she'd hoped. Carolyn took a moment to wonder again whether it would be safer to deal with him or the crowd in the warehouse. Then she batted her lashes at him in a way she'd noticed had never failed her former friend, Lisa. "You know I've always liked you, Jonathan."

With dimples bracketing his mouth, he took her hand and rubbed his thumb across her knuckles. "Then prove it."

"How can I prove anything like that?"

"My car's over there. We'll go someplace nice and private where you can show me exactly how much you care."

Chapter Twenty-Seven

He herded her forward. Dusk made it more difficult to see as they walked toward the Mustang parked in the second row of cars. Carolyn stumbled on a rock, but Jonathan's fierce grip kept her from falling. She glanced toward the safety of her ride parked behind what looked like a million other cars—much too far away.

"My taxi's still waiting for me."

"I'm not worried, darlin'. Drivers are only allowed to stick around for a little while. Company rules you know." As though in confirmation, the vehicle moved into a slow U-turn and then zoomed away with her cell phone, her purse, and her money. The cabby hadn't exactly been her friend, but having him nearby made Carolyn feel a little less alone.

Now what? With no other inspiration, a muddy-the-water approach occurred to her. "I told the driver I'd be back within a few minutes. He'll probably say something to his dispatcher. What if they make a police report on passengers who've gone missing? It could be a problem for you, Jonathan."

He cut a look her way. "Cabbies don't want trouble either, so they don't go looking for it. All he knows is you didn't come back. I'll bet that sort of thing happens all the time." Jonathan reached for the door handle of his Mustang. "Get in."

Plan C? Would it be best to refuse getting in a car where she'd have less control over what happened, or do as he said and hope the ride would get her closer to home? At the moment, neither option sounded appealing.

She touched his cheek. "You're right, Jonathan. Why don't we go to my place? I'll open a bottle of wine, and we can clear up this little—misunderstanding." She gazed up at him through drooping eyelids with what she hoped resembled a smoldering look.

The deep lines on Jonathan's forehead smoothed, and his finger touched the tip of her nose. "All you need to do is give me a chance. I guarantee you won't be sorry."

She leaned against the cool metal of the car and Jonathan pressed his body against hers. In a nanosecond, she felt something under his jacket. Something hard and gun-shaped. Every hideous news story her mother had ever reported rushed back. It occurred to her getting into a car with a man under the influence of alcohol operating somewhere to the left of normal while carrying a gun would be an exceptionally bad idea. "Jonathan." She filled her voice with smoke. "I'd love to give you a chance."

He grinned and stroked her arm. "We don't have a lot of time, so hop in…darlin'."

She took a step, then deliberately let her foot slide. "Oh," she said, staring toward the ground. He loosened his hold on her arm to look at the same place she did. In that moment, Carolyn pulled away and shoved his chest with all her might.

Off-balance, he fell with a grunt. She sprinted away fast as she could go, dodging between vehicles with her head down and heart pounding. A large pickup truck provided cover, so she ducked behind it, hoping the settling darkness would make it impossible for Jonathan to find her.

"You bitch." His cold-blooded tone unnerved her more than his erratic behavior had. She huddled against the truck tire, not daring to move, and listened as his shoes crunched across gravel. He stopped for a few seconds and then continued to work his way between the cars.

Her mouth went dry as dust. This had gone far beyond simple jealousy or a difference of opinion. It wasn't even the alcohol. Jonathan had a gun and acted as though he'd have no problem using it. Any second now she could become a headline on the evening news.

"Do you think you've outsmarted me?" His words slurred together. "Well, think again. There's no place for you to go, Carolyn, and I promise there's no one here to help you."

He was getting closer. Her skin tingled with apprehension.

"Hiding is a stupid thing to do. Why don't you wise up and come on out? It'll make things easier for both of us in the long run."

The sound moved a little farther away. If he found her, she was sunk. Carolyn remembered the apartment building nearby with its deserted stairs and dozens of places to hide. She crawled forward to peer around the truck wheel. Jonathan had wandered to the other side of the lot, working his way methodically down rows. She gauged the distance to the apartment. There might not be a better chance than now. Slinking forward along the side of the truck bed, she reached the fender and then bolted as though the hounds of hell were chasing her.

Over the blood throbbing in her ears, she heard Jonathan cry out and the pound of his feet on the gravel as he gave chase. A terror-fueled rush of adrenalin pushed her to move even faster. *If only I can outdistance him!* It would buy her enough time to consider her next move.

Not daring to look back, she spied the apartments only a short distance away. No longer a decrepit building, it became her oasis—a sanctuary that was as necessary as a life preserver to a floundering swimmer.

With the apartment only yards away, she felt a flash of hope. She might make it! But the toe of her shoe caught against a rock hidden in the weeds. She stumbled and fell. Her ankle twisted to the side, her palms scraped across gravel, and her lungs burned so badly she could barely breathe. *Get up! Get up!*

Seconds later, Jonathan reached her side, wheezing with exertion. He leaned over to grab Carolyn's arm and pulled her to her feet. Breathless and hands stinging, she tried to stand, but her ankle roared with pain. The urge to escape had all but vanished in a fog of misery. Even if she had a strategy, she wasn't in any shape to offer resistance now.

Jonathan jerked her around so she faced him. "That wasn't smart, but at least now I know where things stand. You're not only a threat to my business, you're a threat to me."

"Please, don't make this any worse than it already is. You don't want to be arrested for kidnapping or"—she considered the alternative—"anything worse, do you?"

"I don't plan on being arrested for anything, and I won't if I can keep your mouth shut."

Several new vehicles pulled into the parking lot, and Jonathan dragged Carolyn toward the building, away from the view of anyone in the cars. She had no choice but to limp along with him. The apartment's exterior had a few boards nailed over windows, and graffiti colored the walls. The grounds smelled of urine and stale beer. It didn't matter that she had no place left to go. Her ankle felt twice its normal size, crossing off the possibility of running anyway. A crisp breeze gusted, and she shivered.

A brilliant full moon on the rise provided just enough light to see. Her gaze darted from Jonathan to the building to the ground, in a desperate search for some other means to save herself. Dozens of old bricks scattered not far from where she stood, caught her eye. If she got her hands on one of them, it might work as a weapon. But would she have the nerve to use it on a human being?

"Why'd you do this, Carolyn?" Jonathan snarled his words and slammed her against the brick wall, hard enough to make her see stars. Something warm trickled down the side of her face.

Any doubt in her mind disappeared. Oh, she'd use it all right. Even if she only stunned him, it might give her enough time to get help or hobble away. She visually measured the distance between herself and the bricks and a frantic thought occurred to her. Like one of the dogs in the warehouse, this was a fight for her life.

"Too bad. As much trouble as you've given me tonight, you're still one of the prettiest women I've ever met. Things could have been different if you weren't such a fool." The words were horror-movie disturbing. Except this wasn't make-believe. She prayed some tiny core of decency remained in him.

"It isn't too late, Jonathan. If you just let me leave, I'll do what I can to help you. I'll tell the police you didn't mean to hurt me, that you're sick and need medical care. I have no problem saying this because I know it's the truth."

He shoved her against the wall again. "That's another thing you're wrong about. I don't need medical help. I need money. What I make here is my ticket to freedom. I won't jeopardize it for anyone—not even you."

Keep him talking. "What do you plan to do with me?"

"I'm afraid I can't let you go, but I can't keep you prisoner either." He shook his head. "That only leaves one option."

Her blood froze. "Don't even hint at things like that. If I disappear, my father will have detectives combing every inch of St. Louis. Teena knows where I went tonight too." She didn't care if she deceived him or not. "It's foolish to think no one will discover what happened. You'll lose everything you have and get sent to prison for God knows how many years." She knew she'd begun to babble, but right now words were the only ammunition she had.

"Nobody can connect me to the disappearance of Dr. Becker. You don't think I'd be dumb enough to leave behind evidence, do you?"

"What do you mean?"

"There are two sure ways to dispose of a body. The muddy Mississippi, with currents and undertows to carry away whatever falls in. Or a crematorium. I'm sure you're familiar with how a crematorium works."

"Are you saying you own one?"

"Not me. A friend does. It's his business, and a good one too. You know how much people shell out to have a loved one reduced to ash."

She swallowed past the mountain in her throat. "I can't believe you'd actually do such a thing."

"I'm finished wasting my time. Let's get this over with so I can go back where I'm useful. We have a lot of important people coming in, and the fights go smoother when I supervise. Tonight will probably bring in the most money I've earned yet." His grip on her arm hurt.

"Don't make matters worse for yourself. If you ever cared about me at all, let me go."

"We could have been good together." He inclined his head sadly. "And I did care, but you kept pushing me away."

His eyes were glazed and cold. He held her against the wall with one hand and moved the other to her neck. He squeezed.

Nowhere to go. No one to help. A peculiar calm brought clarity and an odd question. Was this how it felt to die?

Die? Wait a minute...

Before she left for college, her mother coerced her into self-defense classes. The lessons she'd learned came back bright as sunshine, like a reflex. She let her knees go soft and began to slide down the wall. Jonathan leaned forward to grab her arms, and in a move so perfect she couldn't believe her luck, she brought up the knee of her injured leg as hard as she could, straight into his groin and screamed, "No!" at the top of her lungs. She didn't feel a bit of pain, but Jonathan sure did.

He dropped to the ground like a felled tree and lay in a fetal position, whimpering.

Carolyn went to her knees and scrambled away from him toward the bricks, clawing through the dust. Even though Jonathan still lay prone on the ground, he wouldn't be incapacitated for long. She found a hefty brick and rose to stand on her good foot, trembling with effort. Both her hands lifted the brick high over Jonathan's head. She looked down at him and gulped.

In the few seconds she paused, Jonathan's arm snaked out to grab her injured ankle. Pain shot up her leg. She winced and doubled over. Almost immediately, a loud *pop* sounded, like someone had slammed a car door. Yet they weren't close to any cars.

Jonathan's grip on her ankle loosened. He yowled and grabbed his lower leg where blood streamed from between his fingers. A few wet spatters hit her foot.

She looked up to see the shape of a large man running toward her. Straining her eyes in the moonlight, she tried to figure out who it was, her heart revving up faster than a rabbit's. The man slowed as he got closer and she recognized the black leather jacket and dark jeans he wore.

It was Rio with a gun fisted in his hand.

Chapter Twenty-Eight

Rio kept the pistol leveled at Jonathan. A shorter burly-looking fellow followed behind Rio. He had a weapon in his hand too. The sight reminded her of something important, and she pointed at Jonathan. Through a spasm in her throat, she croaked, "He's got a gun."

Never once taking his eyes off Jonathan, Rio nodded. When he moved closer, Carolyn finally got a good look at his face and shivered. She kept herself pressed against the building.

"I was only trying to scare her," Jonathan whined. "I'll sue you for this, Medina."

"Have at it." Rio's words were deadly. "I can't wait to see you in court. And by the way, Jonathan, you're under arrest." Rio nodded at the other man. "Walt, take him away. I'll handle things here."

His partner grabbed Jonathan's arm, and none too gently hauled him to his feet. "With pleasure. Jonathan Locke, you have the right to remain silent…"

Jonathan's eyes widened as Walt half-walked, half-dragged him away.

Carolyn caught a glimpse of a shoulder holster when Rio tucked the gun away under his jacket. He turned toward Carolyn, all emotion shuttered from his face, his words careful. "Are you all right?"

"I'm—fine. But, Rio, you shot Jonathan. You could have killed him."

"Believe me, if I'd intended to kill him, he'd still be on the ground. And while we're on the subject, exactly what," he said dryly, "were you planning to do with this?" Rio took the chunk of brick she still clutched in her hands and threw it back with the others.

Her body began to tremble. She couldn't make herself stop.

Rio opened his arms. He looked so solid, safe, and *sane*, she hurtled against him. He held her and murmured comforting sounds she couldn't quite understand because they were muffled against her hair. Another shiver and his arms tightened, patient as though he had all the time in the world. When the worst of the tremors stopped, he stepped back, holding her at arm's length. His gaze ran from her head to her feet and then back to her face as though in assessment.

Wait. Had someone anesthetized her brain? Clouds of mist made it hard to think. She kept her eyes on Rio's, looking for anything that made sense. After a few minutes, she heard a dog bark, and the sound unknotted her tongue. "Jonathan is sick. Not drunk-sick, but really sick. I could see it in his eyes. He said he'd kill me and make sure no one ever found my body."

"I'd have sold my soul to keep you out of this, Caro. Didn't I tell you to stay away?"

"Yes, you did, but I was trying to find Coby." Then the mist cleared, and the night's horrors pounded her like a sledgehammer. Tears sliced down her face, which turned into a bout of involuntary sobbing gasps, making her stammer. "I'm sorry"—*hiccup*—"I've never been through anything like this"—*hiccup*—"before."

"It's reaction, Caro." He took off his jacket and put it around her, keeping her steady in a one-armed embrace. "I'm here now, and you're safe." His body anchored hers until, after a few more shuddering hiccups, she dashed a hand across her eyes. First, she wished for a handkerchief. Second, she hoped he'd never let her go. "I'm not usually so emotional. It's just that all this is so—shocking."

"It's not the kind of experience anyone expects to have. All things considered, you've handled yourself pretty well."

"When I went into the warehouse to find Coby, I looked for you."

"You went inside?" A muscle in his arm flexed. "We only got here a few minutes ago. I'd just left my car when I heard you scream."

"But you had a gun in your hand."

"I always carry a gun when I'm working."

The knife-sharp edge of her terrors had begun to soften. "You carry a gun when you work?"

"Carolyn, I'm with the State Highway Patrol. For the past year, I've been working undercover in an operation with the FBI."

Her hand went to her mouth. "An undercover officer?"

"That's right. My job was to infiltrate the dogfighting circuit. We finally gathered enough information to move. There were several major fights scheduled for tonight, involving the biggest players. By now, I imagine most of them have been arrested. We're ready to take what we've found to the courts."

"So when you warned me about Jonathan…" She knew her eyes had to be large as the moon shining overhead. "And when I kept seeing you on the street…"

"Doing my job, although I admit looking out for you wasn't part of the assignment." He shook his head. "I never knew a woman so determined to get herself into trouble."

"You're in law enforcement?" She still couldn't quite believe it. "But Rio, you shot Jonathan. What if he does sue you, or files a complaint, or whatever he decides to do? I know how people in law enforcement are treated. You could be put on suspension or arrested or something. You'll need the best lawyer you can get. I'm going to call my father—if I ever get my phone back."

"Slow down, Caro. Do you think wounding an armed criminal doing his best to murder you will cause me problems? Not in this lifetime."

"I know how it is. In anything to do with medicine or law, people are litigation-happy." A moment later, she brightened. "Do you have liability insurance?"

He laughed, and a huge chunk of her heart melted at the sound. "Thanks for looking out for me, but let's deal with first things first. Now, are you sure you're okay?"

She nodded.

"That's my girl. Come on then. Let's see how it's going." Rio took her hand and closed strong fingers around it.

She dipped her head. "I am so sorry. For the longest time, I thought you were involved in what happened here, and it colored the way I treated you. I should have known better."

The corners of his eyes crinkled. "If you thought I was a dogfighter, then I played my part well." He cupped her cheek, fingers surprisingly gentle. "I should have stayed away from you while all this went down, but the fact is, I couldn't. And I admit to lifting more novenas on this case than any I've ever had before, especially ten minutes ago. My aim is good, but a little heavenly intervention never hurts."

Heavenly just about described the way she felt. Forgetting her ankle, she took a step, bit back a cry, and stopped in her tracks.

His brows furrowed together. "Let me carry you."

"No," she said, "I can make it if we go slow. And I don't want to look any more conspicuous than I already do." The corner of his mouth flicked up, and she took his arm.

When they finally made their way back to the warehouse, men with official-looking jackets and badges swarmed the place. Flashlights made white circles of light on the ground as people walked in and out of the building.

Periodic flashes from a camera cut a blinding light through the dark, clearly outlining the group of men seated on the ground with handcuffs on their wrists.

Rio helped Carolyn to a folding chair near the warehouse with a gruff "stay put" before he left to assist with processing the scene. Still keyed up and a little astonished at what was going on—it reminded her of an episode from *Law and Order: SVU*—Carolyn noticed a few men and women in a different type of uniform. Animal control. The officers had placed—she'd counted them— twenty dogs in crates lined up side by side. The animals stood with their ears forward, watching the activity.

She ignored the pain in her ankle to hobble toward them. A female officer with a clipboard in her hand said politely, "What can I do for you, ma'am?"

"I'm a veterinarian," Carolyn told her. "Can I help with anything?"

"We only have a few minor injuries." She swept a hand toward the crates. "These dogs are lucky. Temporary custody will go to the humane society. They'll hold them until the court can be petitioned for permanent custody."

Carolyn felt certain no judge would hesitate an instant to remove the dogs from their current owners. She leaned over the crate nearest her. It held a tan dog with a splotch of white on his chest. He panted lightly, putting his mouth in a shape that looked exactly as if he were smiling. She spoke softly to him. "It's going to be okay now, boy." She placed her knuckles against the crate, and the dog licked her fingers.

Exactly like Stella.

Carolyn straightened, grimacing a little over the tight ache low in her back. After evaluation and retraining, most of these dogs—if not all of them—would be suitable for adoption. It would take time. Erasing the scars of a traumatic experience didn't happen overnight.

She ought to know.

Officers opened the doors of the transport van to start the process of moving crates inside it. Carolyn watched for a while, hollow with weariness. Then she shuffled back to the chair and sank into it.

With a deep sigh, she pulled the leather jacket tighter around herself and waited for Rio.

Chapter Twenty-Nine

Someone touched her arm. Carolyn's eyes flew open, and she muffled a squeaky gasp.

"I'm sorry, Dr. Becker." A man with salt-and-pepper hair, who looked like he might be close to her father's age, stood beside her. "I didn't mean to startle you."

"That's all right," she said, rubbing at her eyes. "I must have fallen asleep."

"My name's Frank. Rio's wrapping things up, but he asked me to check your ankle and look at the cut on your head."

"Okay." Obligingly, she let him dab the wound and examine her eyes with a pen-sized flashlight. "My head hurts where it hit the wall, but I'm not seeing double and I'm pretty sure my ankle's not broken either. I took some ibuprofen earlier, but it doesn't seem to be helping much."

"Let's take a look." Frank went to one knee and gently moved her foot to the right and left, then up and down. "You have a lot of swelling." He moved her foot again, and she pressed her lips together hard. "A little tender too, huh?"

She nodded with a tight smile.

"Looks like you've sprained it, but not too badly. A compression bandage ought to do the trick. It'll help with the swelling. I imagine you know the drill: rest, ice, and elevate. If it's not better soon, have your doctor do an X-ray, and monitor your headache. Get to the ER right away if anything seems out of the ordinary."

He pulled an ACE bandage from the bag sitting next to her and then wrapped it snugly around her ankle.

Carolyn wrinkled her forehead. "I didn't know medics assisted when the police swoop in to make a lot of arrests." She waved her hand toward the officers.

Frank secured the bandage and stood. "Actually, I'm doing double duty today. Since a bust can go any number of ways, we needed to be prepared."

"Jonathan—the man who was shot—is he okay?"

"He's on his way to the hospital for evaluation. They'll take care of him."

"Thanks for your help. I appreciate it."

"All in a day's work. Here." He handed her a pill and a bottled water. "With that headache and the wrenched ankle, this pain pill will help you sleep. Be prepared though. You're going to hurt even more tomorrow." He watched her down the pill and then patted her shoulder before walking away.

Carolyn leaned back in the chair. There wasn't a muscle left in her body not screaming for attention. Out of habit, she looked down for her purse. Oh, yes. By now, her bag and her phone must be miles away on the back seat of a yellow cab. Along with her money. Not much she could do about it now, especially when her eyes felt so heavy. She'd notify the cab company and file a police report in the morning. Surely she'd feel better by then. Her eyelids drifted together.

When a warm hand rested on her back, she roused herself again, blinking a few times to clear her vision.

"Come on, Caro," Rio said. "I'm taking you home."

She yawned. "Are you finished?"

"We've done all we can for now. Give me your hand." He helped her rise from the chair, and with his arm around her, they crept to his Jeep. He sat Carolyn in the passenger seat and buckled the seat belt for her as though she were a toddler. Good thing. Her limbs felt so weak and achy— rule-follower though she was—she would probably have taken a chance on riding without one.

Rio slipped behind the wheel. "We're going to your place, and I'm staying with you tonight. With that bump on your head, you shouldn't be alone."

Logic pointed out it really wasn't necessary for him to stay, but then and there she decided to boot logic right out the door.

"That sounds wonderful," she replied dreamily. "My purse and my phone are both gone. I wouldn't be able to call anyone even if I needed to."

Rio kept his attention on the road as his tires clunked hard over rocks and potholes. Even that wasn't enough to keep her eyes open. Weariness and the pill she'd swallowed had her head nodding along with the rhythm of the Jeep.

She'd nearly drifted off when an intruding thought entered her consciousness and bolted her upright. "Wait a minute, Rio. We need to go to the clinic first. Poor Stella's been there for hours!"

"I'm on it." He turned the wheel.

With her eyes open again, she felt in the mood to talk. "Do you know anything about Coby? He didn't show up or call today."

"Believe it or not, he's at home doing schoolwork. I stopped by his apartment late this afternoon to check on him because his mom's phone was turned off again."

Relief swept over her. "That must be why I didn't hear from him. I was so sure he'd gone back to the dogfights."

"Which is what led you to the east side." He speared her with a narrow-eyed look.

"Well, I thought about calling you, but I don't have your number."

"We'll take care of that issue as soon as we get to your place. Then you won't have an excuse to go off half-cocked again."

She didn't answer him, relishing the feeling that turned her insides to a gooey melted marshmallow.

"Are you asleep again? I'm not hearing any argument."

"What's there to argue about? This time, I think you're absolutely right."

"That's one for the books." He shook his head. "I'm not sure about this new Carolyn."

"Actually…" The edges of her mouth turned up. "I've been turning over an idea, and I think I've come up with a perfect plan."

"I'm not sure you're in the best shape to be coming up with any plans."

"No, listen to me. I'm always worrying about Coby—where he is and what he's doing. Maybe I've been going about this all wrong. Instead of centering my attention on him, I should be thinking of a way to help his mom. I know they're struggling. One minute they have a phone, and the next minute they don't. We could bring in Mrs. Jefferson as a volunteer, if she's willing, and train her to answer phones. She could learn to do some of our paperwork too. Any time she's at the clinic, she'd have some support, plus we'd have a reliable way to communicate."

Rio nodded thoughtfully. "I know she's desperate for work. Learning some marketable skills would help. Jobs are scarce when you don't have much to offer an employer. Hell, they're scarce even when you do."

"I'll talk to Teena tomorrow and see what we can work out."

"Still saving the world? Maybe you should have become a social worker instead of a veterinarian."

She mulled over his comment for a moment. "I love to work with animals, but I'm not jaded enough to mind helping people either. Is there something wrong with that?"

He stopped the Jeep in front of the clinic. "Not a thing. I find stubborn, annoying, soft-hearted women rather appealing."

The smile in his voice felt so right, it entered her heart, put on a pair of fuzzy slippers, and made itself right at home.

She leaned over to kiss his cheek. "Here's the key. Will you get Stella?"

Her digital clock read eleven fifty-eight. Given the sunshine streaming through the window, Carolyn figured it wasn't nighttime anymore. Threads of a sweet dream lingered, and she stretched. *Ouch*. Apparently, her body had been trampled by a herd of wild horses. Swinging her legs out of bed, she tested her ankle. Still sore, but a little better. She pulled on a robe and heard the television, its volume turned down so low she couldn't make out the words.

Carolyn shuffle-limped to the living room. Stella lay next to Rio, who had a laptop open and a cell phone to his ear, forehead grooved in concentration. He looked preoccupied and capable and heart-stoppingly handsome. When he noticed her standing there, he winked, and her knees went wobbly as a colt's.

"She's awake now," he said into the phone. "Call me after you get those statements." He turned his attention toward her. "How do you feel?"

"Better than I did. How long have I been asleep?"

"A day and a half."

"What?" Her mouth gaped open like a fish. "I was supposed to work!"

"Don't worry about it. I called Teena and she got a sub from the Humane Society. You have the rest of the week off." At the look on her face, he said, "Even if you went in, Caro, you couldn't do anything with a bunged-up ankle. Give yourself a few days to mend."

"I guess you're right." She leaned down to nudge Stella. "Scootch over, girl."

Stella reluctantly gave up her spot next to Rio, and Carolyn took the pup's place. The dog made a circle on the sofa and then curled up, resting her muzzle on Carolyn's lap. A canine huff of satisfaction followed.

Rio draped his arm across Carolyn's shoulders, his eyes on the television screen. "Here it comes. Take a look." He turned up the volume.

A young dark-haired anchorman spoke in the somber tone of unpleasant news. "A spokesperson for the highway patrol and Federal Bureau of Investigation announced warrants were executed to break up a dogfighting ring operating on the east side. Thirty-one people were arrested. Officers seized twenty dogs, and one hundred more were impounded from various locations throughout the metro area. The animals were turned over to the Humane Society. Officials say most of them will soon be available for adoption."

"Wow! There were more dogs?"

"It was a large sweep. We had other officers who raided the properties that breed and sell dogs without a license."

"Like Jonathan?"

"Exactly, although he'll be facing assault charges as well. When you're up to it, you'll be asked to write a statement about what happened."

She shuddered. "I don't want to think about it."

He pulled her closer. "I know, Caro. For the time being, Jonathan's still in the hospital. His leg's okay, but they're keeping him in the psych unit."

"This is all so unbelievable."

"Well, here's other news to distract you." Rio stood and went toward the kitchen. He picked up her purse from a chair and carried it to her, dangling from his fingertips.

She squealed with delight. "Where did you find it?"

"The cabby turned your bag in. His dispatcher called the clinic, and Teena brought it here. She wanted to see you, but you were still sound asleep."

Carolyn rummaged around to check. "Everything's here. My cell phone—even my money. I'll be sending a huge tip to that driver."

"I thought that might bring a smile. Now behave yourself and elevate your ankle like Frank told you to do. I'll fix you something to eat before I go."

At the thought of food, her belly rumbled. "I guess I am hungry."

"Teena brought a few groceries along with the purse." He grinned. "You don't keep much food on hand, do you?"

"Cooking isn't my thing." A thought sank in. "Wait a minute. Have you been here all the while I was sleeping?"

"Yes, ma'am. And I came in to wake you up every few hours as Frank recommended, though I doubt you remember it."

Carolyn's insides tingled. "I thought I was dreaming." She propped her leg on the coffee table so he wouldn't see her expression, then leaned back. *Pampering? Yes, please.*

Throughout her one and only relationship, Clay had never done anything that rose to the level of caretaker status. It had always been up to her to assist him in the lab, mother him when he didn't feel well, or flatter him by saying what a terrific veterinarian he'd be whenever he got discouraged.

She watched Rio move efficiently from pantry to the counter, chopping an onion with the speed of a practiced chef. A man with a generous heart who also knew his way around a kitchen. And—bonus!—he could melt her with a single look. Could Rio be…the one? He had so neatly removed any doubt about her own feelings. She could practically envision the cute little home with white picket fence they'd share. Except for one single teeny question. He'd voiced his opinion about relationships more than once. Casual. That's the way he preferred things.

Exactly where did that leave her?

Chapter Thirty

Carolyn wasn't certain if she'd heard Teena's news correctly. "Are you positive?" She notched her voice higher.

From her perch on Carolyn's sofa, Teena sipped from a mega-sized QT cup and then nodded like a newly elected politician.

"Absolutely. I talked to Jeanne this morning. The story made national news. People are donating money like crazy from all over the country to support the humane society's work. She's done four interviews so far. In every single one, she talked about how important it is to neuter pets and described the work we're doing at the clinic. Our phones went crazy. There are so many surgeries scheduled, she might have to bring in another vet to help."

"I can't believe it. Who'd have figured a story on the news would change anybody's mind?"

"Easy. It's like the Home Shopping Network. You hear people talk about how much cubic zirconia sparkles and suddenly everyone wants to buy it. But that isn't all." Teena grinned. "With the publicity, *everybody* knows we exist. The board backed off. They'd look like a bunch of unfeeling jerks if they tried to close the clinic now. Public opinion counts at election time, you know."

Carolyn felt heat rise to her face. "Jeanne told you the city planned to shut us down?"

"I flat out asked her what was going on. She said you were ordered not to say anything, so you're off the hook this time. That's when I told her we had to have more help. Get this…she's going to let us hire a receptionist to handle the office work—appointments, phones, files, billing. Maybe even someone to clean too. Pretty cool, right?"

Carolyn would have danced a jig if her ankle didn't still hurt. "Fantastic! And you know what? I have the perfect person in mind to hire. Mrs. Jefferson needs a job, and I know you can train her to do it well. Everything will go much smoother with Coby if we're all on the same page." She beamed. "They say good can come from anything. I guess this is proof."

"Humph. Looks like I'm going to have my hands full. By the way…" Teena glanced around the room curiously. "Where's your hunky guy?"

"He's back on the job. There are lots of loose ends to tie up." She hadn't heard a word from him in two days. Thinking about it gave her a case of the fidgets. "Anyway, it sure is hard to believe how far this story traveled." She'd heard from her mother and father right away—and had to all but order them not to drop everything and race to St. Louis. She only shared the private details with her sister, who had immediately texted Carolyn two thumbs up.

"You're one lucky woman. Rio Medina is hot as the Fourth of July. The day I brought your purse along with the groceries he asked for, I said I wanted to see you. He just gave me his slow sexy smile and said he'd have you call when you felt better. I almost spontaneously combusted." Teena kept her eyes on Carolyn and simpered with satisfaction. "Uh-huh. There it is, written all over your face. Why don't you go ahead and own it? You're in lo-ove."

"Well." Carolyn brushed Stella hair off her jeans. "There's one thing for sure. I've never felt this way before. But even if I am in love with him, I don't know how he feels." Teena opened her mouth to speak, but Carolyn held up a hand to silence her. "Yes, I know he cares, but it doesn't mean he loves me. Maybe we're just—what's it called?—friends with benefits."

Teena rolled her eyes. "Well, don't be a twit. Why don't you ask him?"

Carolyn's face flushed, but a firm knock on the door stopped her from saying more. Teena went to answer it with Stella following close behind. The dog's tail wagged with hyper-canine enthusiasm.

The door swung open, and Teena boomed a greeting. "Hello, Rio. Your timing is perfect. I'm on my way home."

Rio bent to pet the prancing dog and smiled at Teena. "Thank you. You've been more helpful than you know."

"Not a problem." Teena turned toward Carolyn. "See you later. I've got another date. Fifth time with Sketch. I think we'll be doing some talking tonight." She narrowed her eyes at Carolyn. "You better do some talking too." Teena didn't bother to lower her voice, and Carolyn imagined by now Mrs. Manafee had her head pressed against the door of her apartment, with ears perked higher than Mother's little poodle.

Rio's laugh bounced off the walls, and Carolyn's stomach responded with a summersault. She could listen to that sound forever. He came to sit beside her, and Stella snuggled against his leg. "Teena's a pistol. I like her."

"She likes you too. So how did it go?"

"We've pretty much wrapped up the details. This whole thing has taken a year of my life, but it's worth it. The prosecutor says we've got a strong case. Between my statements and the information we've gathered from snitches, it looks good. In fact, there's a lot of people in the dogfighting world running scared right now."

"What do you think will happen to them?"

"The people we arrested will lawyer-up and try to plea-bargain. Who knows how it will all shake out in the end?"

"And Jonathan?" It made her shiver a bit, even now, to say his name.

Two lines appeared on Rio's forehead, and his words were tight. "Much as I'd love to nail him to the wall, he may not be competent to stand trial. You're right. Apparently, it wasn't just the alcohol fueling his behavior. We'll see what the doctors say. Unless he accepts a deal, you'll have to testify."

"That would make me seriously not happy. I never want to see him again, even in a courtroom."

Rio squeezed her hand. "Whatever happens, I'll be there to help you through it."

He leaned over to place a light kiss on her forehead, and even though she could tell he had a lot on his mind, she still felt a glow of contentment. It would be awfully easy to get used to this. She cleared her throat. "I've got news for you too. Teena told me publicity from the raid brought attention to what the clinic's doing, and a ton of people have responded. We're overscheduled with new clients, and donations are pouring in to support the dogs and the clinic's work. It looks like we're going to be so busy, we can hire a receptionist, and I'm going to recommend Coby's mom for the job."

"Nice work, Dr. Becker." He looked genuinely happy. "That reminds me, I stopped by to see our young man. This whole situation has him so shaken up, he hasn't missed a minute of school and hightails it straight home afterward." Rio's mouth twitched. "He even volunteered for extra hours to help Teena at the clinic since you haven't been able to come in."

"Tomorrow it's back to work for me. I've missed the clinic, and I can't wait to see Coby." She snuggled into the curve of his arm and considered whether or not to follow Teena's suggestion. *Might as well come right out and say it.* Her voice went husky. "Rio, I have a simple, straight-up question for you." Heart knocking, she wet her lips. "Will you tell me your opinion on falling in love?"

"Sure. It's a definite recipe for trouble," he replied without a second of hesitation.

"Oh." *Regroup, Carolyn.* "Trouble? That's how you feel?"

"I do. But on the other hand…"

"On the other hand, what?"

"Nobody can dwell on demons from the past forever. And if you're with the right person, trouble keeps life interesting."

There it was. His ridiculously seductive smile sent tingles zinging everywhere. She jabbed his side with her elbow—but not too hard. "Care to explain?"

"Trouble is healthy in small doses." His brow lifted. "But why don't you and I start working harder on the non-trouble side of things?"

"A sensible observation, sir. How long do you suppose it'll take for us to get the right balance?"

Rio's hand tangled into her hair, and he grinned. "Most likely the better part of a lifetime."

A pleasant assortment of emotions expanded her chest with—dare she admit it?—love. "As my favorite professor always said, good planning brings close to perfect results. I hope you've got as much time to invest in this project as I do."

His blue eyes gleamed with mischief. "Maybe we ought to discuss the possibilities, and—"

She couldn't wait another second. Carolyn grabbed Rio's shirt collar to pull him closer and planted her lips against his.

At a moment like this, who needed to talk?

If you enjoyed Carolyn and Rio's story, stay tuned. Don't miss the next book in the Becker family series featuring Kat Becker, Carolyn's irrepressible younger sister.
Along the Road
Coming soon!

Acknowledgments

Writing a book is a solitary pursuit. But the art of polishing and publishing one most certainly is not.

The inspiration for *On a City Street* came a number of years ago after I read several newspaper accounts of Highway Patrol officers who worked in conjunction with the Federal Bureau of Investigation and other agencies to infiltrate a large organized dog fighting ring. To gather evidence against the perpetrators, a few officers volunteered to immerse themselves in the dog fighting world by posing as participants. What incredible bravery it must have taken to do such a thing! I couldn't resist the temptation to fashion a hero based on this concept as an homage to what they accomplished. These men were true heroes—along with so many others in law enforcement who risk their lives every day to protect the community. Thank you, many times over, to all those who serve.

I'm quite fortunate to have a strong and supportive writing community. Coffee and Critique, the most eagle-eyed and encouraging critique group on earth, will forever have my gratitude. You make everything better in hundreds of ways. A special thanks to Alice Muschany, beta reader extraordinaire. You don't miss a thing! And a heartfelt shout-out to Jeanne Felfe, for reading the manuscript early on and writing a lovely endorsement for it. A village filled with writing friends makes the journey much more fun.

To Angie Wade at Joy Editing, thank you more than I can say for the thorough and insightful edits. Your guidance helped me better shape my story.

To Jenny Quinlan at Historical Editorial, you create the most gorgeous covers. This one may be my favorite of them all. Thank you!

To my family, words aren't enough to express how much I appreciate your love and support. You are my everything, always.

And last, but never least, to you readers. With all the millions of options available, you chose my book. I'm honored and humbled by your support.

A Note to Readers,

I am deeply grateful you chose to read *On a City Street*. I hope you'll be watching for Kat's story in *Along the Road*—coming soon!

Connecting with readers is a treat, and I'd love to hear your feedback. You can find me on the following social media platforms:

PatWahler.com
Facebook: Pat Wahler, Author
Twitter: @PatWahlerAuthor
Instagram: patwahler
I am also on Pinterest, Goodreads, and Bookbub.

If you're like me, you often discover a new book when someone recommends it, or because you've read a short (or longer) review about the story. Reviews and recommendations *do* make a difference.

If you enjoy my books, please take a moment to leave a review on Amazon, Goodreads, Barnes and Noble, Bookbub, or other social media outlets. A reader who shares what he or she likes with family and friends is the number one way of spreading the word. I humbly thank you for your support.

With warmest regards,

Pat

ABOUT THE AUTHOR

 Pat Wahler is a Missouri native and avid reader with a love for a story well told. She is also an award-winning author who writes in multiple genres including historical fiction, essays, short stories, poetry, children's fiction, and romance. Pat's work has appeared in sixteen *Chicken Soup for the Soul* books as well as *Sasee Magazine, Storyteller Magazine, Reader's Digest*, and many other publications.

Her literary memberships include the Missouri Writers Guild, Saturday Writers, the St. Louis Writers Guild, the Historical Novel Society, and Coffee and Critique. She's grown accustomed to scheduling her life around the demands of one feisty rescue pup and a rescued tabby who rules the homestead with an iron paw. Pat is currently at work on her next novel.

CPSIA information can be obtained
at www.ICGtesting.com
Printed in the USA
BVHW011529240619
551793BV00016B/46/P

9 781732 387621